STATE OF DENIAL

IAIN KELLY

By the Same Author

The State Trilogy

A Justified State

State Of Denial

State Of War

State Of Denial

© Iain Kelly, 2019

First Published 2019

Independently Published.

www.iainkellywriting.com

ISBN – 9781070692005

PART ONE:

CAPITAL CITY

JUNE 21st

1

The heat was stifling. There was no air conditioning in the press briefing room, another victim of the continuing energy restrictions. There were no windows – the room was situated in the basement of The Palace – just four dull, grey walls. A single bulb in the middle of the panelled ceiling was the only source of light, its weak glow failing to reach the darkened corners of the room. One woman sat alone in the back row, allowing her a full view of the podium and the empty seats in front of her. She was in her early thirties, slim, with keen sky-blue eyes and sharp facial features dusted with plain make-up. She was dressed casually and simply in a grey blouse and fitted trousers with a high waist. Her light brown hair was tied up in a functional ponytail. On the stage at the opposite end of the room stood the familiar podium with the official State crest on the front: a white dove of peace flying over the black bull representing magnanimity, strength and valour. A remote camera situated behind the rows of seats clicked. The sole occupant of the room turned her head and saw the red light on the side of the black machine blink on, a sign that the conference would begin in the next few minutes. The woman waved her notepad in front of her face creating a welcome zephyr that failed to disperse the suffocating air. She could feel beads of sweat beginning to form under her arms and on the back of her neck and regretted her choice of light-grey blouse thrown on that morning. She checked under her arms to see if any sweat patches were visible.

Maxine Aubert had felt daunted as she walked along the wide avenue towards The Palace that morning, even though she had visited many times before. Her earliest memories included trips taken through the Capital City with her parents, travelling from their home on the coast into the centre of the great megalopolis. While many of the old, ornate buildings from those childhood days had been demolished to make way for modern housing, the imposing seat of government had been preserved. There had been a museum built nearby charting the story of The Palace from seat of Royal power and ancestral home to modern day seat of State power and home of the State Chancellor. When the Central Alliance Party had come to power and implemented their manifesto of political change the monarchy was dissolved and the new position of elected Chancellor replaced them, combining their ceremonial role with far wider political power wrested away from the Senate parliament. The Royal family had been shuttled off to new accommodation, with a considerable settlement fee to tide them over and the Chancellor took up residence in The Palace. The top floors comprised of her personal living quarters and office, the lower floors the offices of government and staff. And in the basement a car park and the press room.

When Max had visited as a child the streets and park around The Palace were crowded and bustling, filled with cars, buses and tourists, even though the First Strike War and the subsequent restrictions on public gatherings had been in place for a number of years. Families took photographs and videos, smiling in front of the famous building steeped in history. On sunny days the parks were full of citizens strolling, playing, eating ice-cream and lazing on the lush green grass.

Now the area around The Palace was shrouded in an eerie silence. The occasional bus swept along the road. The travel ban that had spread through the State had finally reached the Capital City and only essential journeys could now be undertaken by motor vehicles. The parks had disappeared under housing developments and The Palace now sat encircled on three sides by the uniform white cubes of accommodation. The citizens' homes and The Palace were separated by a large security wall that towered over the surrounding buildings. Tourism had dwindled away, partly due to the closed border security policy of the State, partly because citizens were discouraged from gathering in groups no matter how informally. The drones that criss-crossed the Capital City sky continuously creating a background hum to everyday life were not permitted within two hundred metres of The Palace walls, leaving a disconcerting hole in both the empty blue azure above and the soundscape around the building. However, the front of The Palace was still open to public view, unchanged for centuries behind a tall black railing, and it was that familiar and imposing edifice that Max approached.

Passing the roundabout dominated by the large statue of 'The Working Man,' Max fell under the shadow of the building, blocking out the blistering heat from the sun and giving her a chill as the temperature dropped. It was another day of searing warmth in the city, part of another tropical summer. One of the few benefits of the climate change that had not been reversed was the longer, hotter summers in the northern hemisphere. Max had shown her press credentials at the side entrance and gone through the thorough security searches and scans given to all visitors, even those colleagues from the press who covered The Palace on a daily basis. Few citizens were allowed inside the walls of The Palace anymore, the press were one of the few remaining groups who could gain access, and even then it was a short list of approved journalists who were allowed into the press room and nowhere else.

The door at the back of the room opened. Horace Frinks entered the room, his loud boisterous laugh announcing his arrival before Max could see him. She turned now and gave him a welcoming smile, which he returned with a recalcitrant glance. Behind him followed his usual acolytes, Timothy Pigeon and Kelvin Mothersby. The three men formed the core of the press team situated at The Palace. This was their turf and they didn't warm to newcomers. They swaggered past Max and took their seats in the front row – they had assigned seats to reflect their favoured and regular status. As they sat down the main lights flickered on, then off, then on again. A spotlight hit the podium on the stage and ceiling lights around the side of the room cast away the shadows. Max closed her eyes for a moment to allow her pupils to adjust to the incoming flood of artificial illumination. She wondered if anyone else would turn up to hear the Chancellor's speech. The elections were only a fortnight away and no one seriously expected anything other than the Central Alliance Party returning to the Senate with a vast majority, and the Chancellor continuing unopposed in her role for another decade. The Central Alliance Party was the only organised political party contesting the election.

The door at the back of the room opened once more and an elderly gentleman peered into the room. Max watched as John Curran scanned the empty seats. At first glance his weary eyes missed her perched in the back corner. When he finally spotted her a smile broke over his creased face and he strode along the back row of chairs to join her.

'Maxine Aubert,' he beamed, pronouncing the silent 't' with a harsh tut as he had always done. 'I heard you might be gracing us with your presence today.'

'You heard right,' Max smiled fondly at her senior colleague. John Curran had been at The Star Tribune longer than anyone cared to remember. When she had been starting out as a fresh-faced graduate he had taken her under his wing and become her mentor. That was over ten years ago now and they still kept in touch, although Max had long since carved out her own reputation in the media world.

'I could have sent you my notes from the press conference and saved you the trip,' Curran offered. 'Would've made an old man feel useful one last time.' Max recognised the familiar refrain from her friend. Now in his late eighties, Curran had spent his entire career as The Star Tribune's top reporter, covering all the big stories for the last half century, from the start of the First Strike War and the terror that followed to the emerging energy and population crises of more recent decades. Three years ago he had been given the choice of retirement or a move to cover the day-in, day-out business of The Palace. It was a token gesture to a much-loved servant, but Max knew Curran only took the assignment because he had given his whole life to news reporting and without it he would have nothing. Curran was as professional as ever, duly logging his copy each day and seeing his reports crop up occasionally on The Star Tribune's site, far down the page and in small type.

After years of top page headlines it must have been degrading to him, but he never complained publicly. When he made an infrequent visit to the Tribune office it was always with a fond smile and a familiar wave to old colleagues. Only in private conversation did Max hear any animosity, disguised with self-deprecation. The fact that Max had replaced him as the Tribune's go-to reporter had put an unacknowledged stress on their friendship.

'Only a couple of weeks until polling day, the Election Special Correspondent has to show face at The Palace at some point,' she answered with a smile.

'You think the Chancellor is going to say something interesting for a change?' Curran raised his grey eyebrows in mocking conjecture. It was a well-established formality that very little of any interest ever happened at State press conferences.

Very little of any interest had happened so far in the entire election campaign, if Max was being honest with herself. She had hoped something juicy would have occurred at some point, the elections were, after all, only held every decade and for the first time in living memory rumblings of discontent were reaching the Capital City, the Senate and the Chancellor's Palace. She had tried to write about some of that discontent in a few of her pieces: she had travelled north to the MidLands City, where the disaffection was more keenly felt; where the ongoing power shortages were unalleviated; where resistance to the First Strike War was becoming quietly vocal. She heard stories of ever–increasing numbers who were illegally abandoning the megalopolis cities and living in the wilderness, the areas outwith the city boundaries cleared decades ago in order to let the natural ecology recover. Her editor had filleted the meat of her stories, leaving just the bare bones. She had convinced some of the dissenting voices to speak to her off the record, to tell her how they planned to use the election as the start of a burgeoning opposition to the Central Alliance Party that had ruled the State unimpeded for so long. Her editor had refused to publish unverified sources and circumstantial speculation. But it was there, it was real. She could sense something bubbling under the surface. Any decent journalist who worked around the seat of power in the Capital City could feel it, but it would be a brave media outlet that published something that criticised the Party.

There were four national media outlets licensed by the Senate to operate within the State. Three of them were State-owned and State-subsidised. Frinks from The Senate Star, Pigeon from Capital News and Mothersby from the State television broadcaster represented them at the front of the conference room. They specialised in harmless celebrity gossip, endless weather speculation and puff pieces lionising the State's efforts in the First Strike War overseas. Their political coverage amounted to reproducing press releases issued by the Chancellor and the Senate, with editorial comment wholly in line with their paymaster's views. The Star Tribune stood alone as the only independent media outlet in the State, funded by wealthy individuals and companies who still valued the idea of a free press, even in principle only. The ability of the Tribune to operate in the State was dependent on the Senate granting it a licence, so the idea that they could be critical of State policy was fanciful at best. When Max tried to press her editor to even hint at unrest among the citizens, she was given short shrift - which was why she had come to the Chancellor's briefing this morning.

'Probably not,' she answered Curran, 'but I thought I might ask a couple of questions of our Chancellor just to liven up my coverage.'

Curran caught the twinkle in her eye. 'What are you up to?' He had heard from Buzz Mayfield, editor of The Star Tribune and old friend, about Max's stories of spreading unhappiness among the citizens of the major cities in the State. He had nodded as Buzz had grumped and moaned that Max was pushing her luck. He had privately wished he was thirty years younger and had the energy to sniff around the story himself.

Max only smiled at him in reply and before he could caution her against doing anything foolish, a door at the side of the room opened and clerks, assistants and various hangers-on filed into the room. They took their seats in front of the podium, filling the rows to give the impression there was a healthy attendance for the Chancellor's routine briefing. At the door, the Chancellor's Press Secretary waited until everyone was settled before striding onto the small raised platform and taking her place behind the lectern. Max watched Curran turn on his TouchScreen and click record. He had been one of the few remaining journalists who, like her, had used an old-fashioned paper and pencil and shorthand in order to record speeches or interviews. 'Never trust a machine to tell you the truth,' he had told her years ago, 'a good reporter trusts their own eyes, ears and instincts. A machine can tell you word for word what was said, but it can't record the tone or the look of the speaker.' This wasn't entirely true, Max had thought at the time. The ubiquitous cameras picked up the smallest drop of sweat, the tiniest wrinkle of strain, the merest hint of vocal stress from any politician, but gradually she began to see what the veteran reporter had meant. If you relied on recorded footage and sound to cover an event you did miss out on something. You missed out on the atmosphere of the room, the taste in the air, the demeanour of those surrounding the speaker. She had gone to the State library and, thanks to her profession, had been allowed access to the old books that taught shorthand writing. Now she was perhaps the only person left in the State who could use the old art form. She flipped open her notepad and slid the pencil free from the spiral binding. It was not easy to come by these traditional materials anymore. Max had a deal with a specialist who provided her with them at a discounted rate for being a loyal customer. There were many people of her own generation who would not recognise the tools she used for her trade. Curran glanced at the notebook as it rested on her knee and gave her a resigned smile which simultaneously managed to chide her for living in the past and be proud of her for carrying on with the old ways. Max scribbled down a few descriptive words as she always did, little crumbs that would trigger memories of the scene in which the Chancellor was about to enter from the wings.

The Press Secretary, a woman in her seventies who had held the same role and carried out the same ritual since the Chancellor had been elected leader, finished her preparations by adjusting the microphone and clearing her throat. As well as the main camera at the rear of the room there were now several TouchScreens and SmartCameras trained on the podium, including those that were wearing SmartLenses over their eyes, who would be beaming the speech live to followers across the State.

'Citizens,' the Press Secretary announced from the podium, 'the Chancellor of the State, Ms. Lucinda Románes.' The introduction never changed, despite the fact that there wasn't a single person in the State who wasn't aware of the Chancellor, or her name. Lucinda Románes had been in control of the State, the Senate and the Central Alliance Party for three decades. When she had first been elected leader of the Party she had been a forty year old woman in her prime. Now seventy, her appearance had barely altered and she strode across the stage with her usual vigour and energy. Max made a note of her good health, the smooth skin, the trademark long, dark hair, the perfectly applied, tasteful make-up and the piercing grey eyes. No doubt she had benefited from modern medicines and anti-aging procedures in the past, but there was no denying that her toned looks and supple movement were also the result of daily exercise and a healthy lifestyle. She smiled to the Press Secretary as she took her place on the podium, hands gripping either side of the lectern. She graced the room with a quick smile before she looked straight down the lens of the main camera. Her address, as always, was to the camera which projected her image and words around the State. It was to the citizens that she spoke, not the press or staff gathered in front of her.

'Good morning, my fellow citizens. I have a short speech to make before I will take questions from the gathered press here and, if time, from the official forums that you, the citizens of the State, are encouraged to use to get in touch with your government.' She paused for effect, looked down at the lectern, looked up again and then began her speech proper. Her voice was strong, full and authoritative. 'I speak to you today from the press room of the Chancellor's Palace. It has been my privilege to live and work in this building for the last thirty years serving you, the citizens of our fine State. In just two weeks' time you will be asked to go to the polls across our great land and take part in our decennial elections. In the ongoing spirit of democracy, every ten years we ask you to pass judgement on your senators and your government with open, free and fair elections.'

It was the lack of irony that had always troubled Max when she heard any of the elected officials speak in this way. The Chancellor really believed what she was saying. In a society with only one all-powerful political party and system, with tightly controlled and restricted media networks, where the right to protest and demonstrate was severely limited, and where the citizens were only given the chance every ten years to express an opinion through a rigged ballot, Lucinda Románes really believed that she was ruling over a free and fair democracy. And that belief seemed to be shared by the vast majority of the citizens. Max may have heard faint echoes of discontent, but she had to dig deep to find them. Among a population of a hundred million people, only a tiny, insignificant minority had the courage to express a dissenting view of the Party.

'Three times you have voted to elect me as your leader, and I do not take that trust for granted. In this election you will be asked to put your trust in me once more. I recognise there will be some who feel it is time for a change of leadership. I recognise I am not getting any younger. As I have said before, and I reiterate today, I pledge to dedicate another ten years to the honour of serving as your Chancellor, after which I will step aside to facilitate the transition to a new, younger Party leader.'

Max scribbled a quick note and looked round. She was the only one who had a sardonic smile on her lips. Románes had made the same promise ten years ago, insisting that it would be her last decade in office before changing her policy halfway through the ten year term. No one else in the room seemed to have noticed the repetition of this empty vow. In reality, there was no one in the Central Alliance Party who could challenge Románes's authority. Her likely heir, Vice-Chancellor Patrick Donovan had been killed in a terrorist attack three years earlier. Without him there was a vacuum at the top of the party, reflected in the weakness of the upcoming election. In the Chancellor Ballot it was a straight run-off between the incumbent, Lucinda Románes, and the challenger, Johnathan Sadiq. Sadiq was also a member of the Central Alliance Party. He served as a Junior Senator in the Department for Climate Sustainability. He was young, in his thirties, and had only been elected to the Senate for the first time at the previous elections. He was a lightweight, a patsy, put forward by the Party to give the impression that there was an alternative to re-electing Románes as Chancellor. The pay-off for Sadiq would no doubt be a promotion within the Party. Max wondered what Sadiq had been offered. It depended how ambitious he was: Defence Secretary? Head of the War Committee? Vice-Chancellor even? If Románes was being genuine perhaps Sadiq was being lined up as an eventual replacement for her in ten years' time - he agrees to take the humiliating defeat this time round with the guarantee of the Chancellorship coming his way in the future.

Max tuned back in as the Chancellor continued her monologue. 'As well as the election of the Chancellor, there will of course be the Senate elections. The Central Alliance Party will be putting forward candidates in every Senate seat. In more seats than ever before there will be independent candidates standing against the official Party representatives. We welcome this, it is healthy for our democracy. But I would urge you all,' her piercing stare hardened, daring the faceless citizens behind the camera lens to defy her, 'to think very carefully before choosing not to back a member of the Central Alliance Party. I do not deny there are challenges ahead for our glorious State: the First Strike War goes on without an end in sight; the energy crisis, I know, has brought hardship and sacrifice upon many of us; the population crisis still looms over our packed cities. But I ask you this: who do you trust to deal with these problems? Who do you trust to continue to look after the best interests of our country? Remember, citizens, what the Central Alliance Party has done for you. Look back in history and see where we were before the Central Alliance Party saved this State from certain ruin. Look at our achievements: poverty eradicated thanks to the Universal State Income; homelessness a thing of the past; climate change halted and reversed; secure borders; life expectancy for all increased thanks to our advances in science, technology and healthcare. Together we have achieved so much, together we can deal with any new threats to our way of life. We have taken positive steps in our battle to combat the energy crisis – trust us to ensure we can continue to resolve this problem once and for all. We have taken steps to ensure we will never back down in the ongoing war. We will stand with our Allies who suffered so greatly during the First Strike and never surrender until we have victory. Trust us to continue to build the housing we need while controlling the population of our cities and minimising the impact on the environment, so that the disaster of climate change will never again rear its head around the globe and within our State.'

Max's pencil stopped. The words continued to flow from the podium, words of strength, determination and positivity. There was an archaic term for what Max was hearing now: spin. Max took no more notes because she heard nothing new, just the same old refrain of the Central Alliance Party, the saviours and protectors of the State and her people. Long ago, when the Party had first risen to power and brought in a wave of positive steps that greatly enhanced the lives of the citizens, perhaps some of what Lucinda Romànes said would have rung true. There was no denying that the Party had averted disaster – along with their global friends – in combating climate change, reversing centuries of human negligence, and at the last moment saving most (though not all) of the planet from catastrophe. The mega cities formed around the country had been a success: the Capital in the South; MidLands; the Central and HighLand cities further north. The rest of the land in the State was given back to nature, while the cities provided modern, uniform housing for all. The State Income for all had provided people with a sustainable life despite the lack of work as more and more jobs were given over to machines. The initial response to the First Strike, when the Civil American States had suffered the horror of nuclear attack, had been lauded by all, from Allied partners to citizens on the street. No one argued when the borders were tightened and then closed. No one demurred when the foreigners were extradited guaranteeing the State's security and relieving the expanding population crisis.

17

Hard decisions, tough times and through it all the State, her government and her citizens had survived and prospered.

But most of those decisions and actions happened forty years ago. The citizens were told the borders would be reopened one day. The families of the extradited foreigners were told they would be allowed back to visit and eventually to relocate. The First Strike War had continued and showed no sign of end. The energy crisis was the latest sign that the Central Alliance Party had run out of ideas to solve the many ills of State society.

The atmosphere in the room changed and brought Max back from her own thoughts. The speech had ended with a ripple of applause and the Chancellor had thrown open the platform for questions. As always the first three questions were from the Palace correspondents of the State-owned media. Horace Frinks raised his hand, needlessly, and with a nod from Lucinda Románes began his pre-approved question. 'Can you confirm reports that the Universal State Income is set to rise by five percent if you are re-elected as Chancellor on July the fifth?'

'I'm glad you raised that point, Horace,' the Chancellor smiled benignly upon him, then turned to face the camera once more. 'I can confirm that part of my pledge, and the Central Alliance Party manifesto is a commitment to raise the basic Universal State Income for all.' There followed a further three minutes of continued promises and platitudes that could have been easily accommodated in the original speech. The fact that it was given as an answer to a planted question was merely to give legitimacy to a policy that appeared better than it actually was. Within government, and whispered quietly to trusted press, it was known that placed against the rising cost of energy a five percent rise would be nowhere near enough for the average citizen to live on. Max had heard this from several sources within the Senate and Party and from citizens out in the cities, but not a single one would allow themselves to be quoted.

Pidgeon's question followed, more hot air answered. Then Mothersby took his turn. While Románes was performing, Max whispered to Curran next to her, 'Think you can let me have our question today?' The Tribune was allowed one question at the end of every press conference.

'It's already been vetted,' Curran whispered back out of the corner of his mouth. Max could hear the panic in his hushed voice.

'Come on, give me this one.'

'What are you going to ask?'

The Chancellor's raised voice interrupted the murmured argument. 'Are there any further questions for today?' Before Curran could gather himself, Max had raised her hand. The Chancellor craned her neck to see who the unfamiliar hand belonged to. Just possibly there was a hint of uncertainty behind those steel grey eyes.

'Max Aubert, from The Star Tribune,' Max called out before Curran could pull her arm down.

There was a barely imperceptible pause from behind the podium at the change of script before the Chancellor gathered herself. 'I trust everything is well with Mr. Curran. An unexpected pleasure to have you join us, Ms. Aubert,' Románes lied. As soon as Max had entered The Palace that morning her presence would have been noted. No doubt the Chancellor would have been briefed before entering the room that there was an additional member of the press present today. 'You have a question?'

'You mentioned the unprecedented number of independents gaining enough support to be put forward as Senate candidates at these elections. I have seen internal Party polling that suggests these independents may win up to ten percent of the seats in the Senate.' Max paused to see if there was any reaction.

The cool grey eyes looked steadily at her, the welcoming smile fixed unwaveringly in place, 'Is there a question to follow such a wildly inaccurate statement?' One or two heads in the forward rows now swivelled round to look at her. She felt Curran next to her put a hand over his eyes. The room had fallen quiet; only the hum of the electricity feeding the lights and cameras was audible.

Max took a deep breath, there was no turning back now, 'If that was the case, would you consider resigning your position as Chancellor?'

2

'Do you realise the damage you have done?' Byron 'Buzz' Mayfield slammed a TouchScreen down on his desk in front of Max. She sat unmoving, allowing his rage to pass before responding. His tirade had lasted for ten minutes and only now showed signs of abating. He was an imposing figure, strong and tall with a sharp jawline and a military crewcut. It was three days after the press conference. After being politely escorted from The Palace, Max had been told to stay at home and not venture into work while those at the top of The Star Tribune decided how to deal with her and the fallout from her unscripted question.

In a brief pause, while the editor of the Tribune stood, balled fists on hips, looking out of the plate-glass wall of his room to the open plan office beyond, Max spoke her first words since entering the room. 'It was a valid question, Buzz.'

Buzz turned and glared at her. The eruption of initial wrath had passed but pent-up anger still seethed in his eyes. Through gritted teeth he spoke, 'I know it was a valid question, Maxine, that isn't really the point though, is it?' He unclenched his fists and slumped back into his chair across the desk from her. 'You realise how difficult my job is here?' It was a rhetorical question. 'Every day before we publish I have to send everything we have written to the State Media Compliance Department. They scrutinise everything. They remove words, sentences, they kill entire stories, and they have the final say on what

21

images we can use. If we step over the line too far, we lose our licence. Do you ever ask yourself why we go through with it? Why we don't just give up and let the State carry on with its own press organisations?'

Max thought he was being rhetorical again until the pause lasted long enough to imply Buzz was waiting for an answer, 'Out of principle?' she guessed.

'You're damn right out of principle,' Buzz erupted again, but this time calmed himself straightaway. 'It may only be a pretence of a free Press, but it's better than having none at all and if just once, just occasionally, we manage to sneak through a tiny editorial, a morsel of fact, that causes just one citizen out there to stop and think for themselves just for a moment, then the fight is worth carrying on.'

'I couldn't agree more, Buzz, that's why I wanted to ask a question that wasn't just pandering to exactly what the Chancellor and the Party want everyone to hear.'

'It's Mr Mayfield or Sir at the moment, Maxine, you can call me Buzz again when all this blows over. *If* all this blows over,' he corrected himself.

'What I'm trying to say is that this is the time to ask these questions, to push a little harder. The Party won't revoke our licence before an election and for the first time in my life, and yours, they are vulnerable. The energy crisis, the population crisis, the war – people are finally beginning to question what the Party and the Senate and the Chancellor are up to. Do they know what they are doing? The Star Tribune should be the leading light of that questioning, not lying down and toeing the party line.' Max had more to say, but Buzz stopped her with a weary shake of his head and wave of his hand.

'I know all that Maxine. You're young, you're keen, you're fresh, that's why you're good at your job, but don't pretend you're as experienced as John Curran or myself. You have to know when to squeeze and when to release, and you have to know when and who to pick your battles with. Rushing in for a pop at the Chancellor straight off the bat is not the way to go.' Max took her admonishment without reply. 'By the way, this polling information you've seen, where did you get it from?'

Max hesitated. Buzz was right - he and John Curran had been around a lot longer than she had. He had a lot of contacts within the government and the Party, he had to have them to do his job, and no doubt to keep them on side he had to give them something now and then. Alarms rang in her head, was she being paranoid? Was he looking for a source to feed back to someone in State Security perhaps, or in The Palace itself? Something to smooth over the ripples Max had caused. Her instinct told her not to reveal anything to him. 'You know I won't tell you my source.'

He peered at her across the desk for a moment, his eyes trying to judge her in some way, 'I'm your editor and more than that I'm your friend, Maxine, I'm trying to look out for you. You don't trust me?'

She only looked at him in reply. She couldn't lie to his face but she didn't want to tell him that she no longer trusted him. She knew a veteran like Byron Mayfield would be crushed if one of his reporters were to doubt him, his entire career was built on trust. 'Lecture over,' Buzz put his hands on the table and looked at her with paternal empathy. 'I have been instructed to relieve you of your position as Special Election Correspondent. Your access to The Palace and all State, Senate and Party buildings has been revoked. You will take paid leave for the next month until well after the elections are finished, after which you may be allowed to return to work in a less prominent role. The Media Compliance Department have suggested you may be more suited to covering celebrity news or entertainment reviews. You understand that this is not my choice. I argued in your favour, tried to get them to give you another chance, but my hands are tied. These instructions I suspect came from the Chancellor's office directly. It's only thanks to John that The Star Tribune still has access at The Palace. He and I have had to smooth over a lot of ill feeling and call in a lot of favours to repair the damage you caused.'

Max had not flinched as her punishment was delivered but inside her mind was in turmoil as she heard her career, such as it had been, evaporating. Through her stoic, clenched mouth she repeated her only defence, 'It was a valid question, Sir,' she spat out the last word while managing to hold back welling tears from her eyes.

'That's not the issue, Maxine, I'm sorry.' Buzz Mayfield's tone softened. 'Take a couple of weeks, until the elections are over. Who knows? Maybe this polling you've seen is accurate and we will get a new Chancellor. Just lie low, take a few days down at the coast with your parents, they would love to see you. We can talk again when you come back.'

Max picked up her bicycle from the parking station outside the offices of The Star Tribune. It was a non-descript white cube like all the other buildings packed into the city, and until this moment she had never given any thought to how she felt about it. Now, as she cycled away from it, she realised how fondly she thought of that building and the people inside it. Buzz's words came back to her - there was a principle worth fighting for and the people behind those white, square walls were the only ones fighting for it. In doing so they made sacrifices. It was an open secret that employees of the Tribune were subject to surveillance from State Security. On more than one occasion employees had found themselves being visited by the State Police concerning minor infractions that other citizens would never be cited for. By working for the only 'free' media organisation in the State, the journalists and staff were inviting unwanted attention on themselves. If they raised their head too far above the parapet, they could and would be shot down without reservation, and Max had willingly vaulted over the parapet.

Whether it was worth it or not remained to be seen but the fallout from her ill-fated question to the Chancellor had told her something. It had confirmed to her that the information she had seen, the internal Central Alliance Party polling that suggested they were set to lose between five and ten percent of the Senate seats to independent candidates, was true. If it had been falsified or fabricated it would have been dismissed with a laugh and a slap on the wrists. They were nervous. Cycling along the quiet city streets between avenues of square white buildings, she recalled the look on the Chancellor's face as her question hung in the air. The silence had seemed to go on for an eternity. In reality it had been momentary. For the first time Max had seen Lucinda Románes stumble. She had looked down at non-existent notes on the lectern, she had looked back up with a smile. She had glanced at Max and Max saw through her bravado, behind the grey steel eyes of power, for the first time. Those eyes showed just a trace of doubt. Then the Chancellor had collected herself, turned to the camera and dismissed her question with a flurry of equivocation. The whirring of the camera ceased as Lucinda Romànes wrapped up her comments quickly and descended from the platform, swiftly exiting the room. As always the promise of answering questions from citizens was broken. All eyes left in the room focussed on Max as she flipped her notebook closed. Security personnel were already approaching her. They looked in puzzlement at her paper. If she had had a TouchScreen or SmartLenses they would have been seized instantly. As it was they let her hold onto her scrawled unintelligible notes. A journalist's indecipherable shorthand account of the incident didn't threaten the legitimacy of any recorded footage of the press conference. Sure enough, when Max had returned home and found the news coverage of the morning's events, the press conference had been edited so that Max's question had been removed. They had done a good job, Max couldn't even see the edit where her presence had been deleted. Only those citizens who had been watching the live event would have seen her question and she couldn't be sure how much of that had been broadcast before communications had been cut. Certainly the only outrage expressed so far had come from inside The Palace and the Party, and now from her own editor. Outwith those controlled spaces it was as though the incident had never occurred.

Max turned into her own street and reached her apartment building. One or two people were walking along the road in the sweltering sunshine. She didn't recognise them but that in itself wasn't unusual. Max spent little time in her apartment, returning late in the evenings to sleep before getting up and leaving early the following morning. A rare car swooped along the road from the opposite end of the street. That was unusual. Max dismounted her bicycle and stood watching the car as it passed, her head following the blacked out windows until it reached the junction and turned away. She locked her bicycle in her numbered bay and headed inside. When she had first moved into the apartment the lifts around the Capital City were still in use. Had she known they would be switched off in all buildings as part of the State energy saving drive, she would never have taken a home on the twenty-first floor. It took her ten minutes to climb the twisting, square staircase. The heat seemed to seep through the walls and by the time she was at the top she could feel the sticky sweat dripping down her back. Perhaps it was the tiredness from the ascent or perhaps it was the accumulated stress of the last few days that caused her to miss the brown envelope that lay on the doormat as she entered her home, dropped her backpack, walked straight into the bathroom, stripped off and ran herself a refreshing cool shower. She contemplated Buzz Mayfield's suggestion of spending a few days at her parents' house and began to be seduced by the idea. It was a chance to get out of the centre of the City, find a bit more open space and enjoy the warm weather rather than be smothered by it. The idea of lying on the beach for the next two weeks, taking daily walks along the clifftops and catching up with her mother and father didn't seem such a bad proposition. She hadn't seen them in three months now and she was lax at keeping in touch with them.

Refreshed and robed, Max was running a towel over her damp hair when she stepped back into the hallway

27

and froze. The innocuous envelope lay on the doormat at the end of her hallway. It was incongruous because it was rare for any citizen to communicate in such an old-fashioned way and because it was the second time in less than a week that Max had found such an envelope waiting for her. The first had included no message, it had simply contained strictly confidential Central Party Alliance polling figures for the Senate races in the upcoming elections. Her source, whoever they may be, had decided to get in touch with her again.

Barefoot, leaving ghostly footprints on the grey enamel floor, she walked along the narrow corridor, the towel now hanging limply round her neck. The envelope looked identical to the previous one: manila-brown, plain, with no writing or printing on the outside. She knelt down and picked it up. Unlike the previous delivery this one was thin, perhaps only containing a single sheet of paper. The polling data had been bulky, fifty pages worth of sampling numbers, percentages and extrapolated outcomes. That envelope had been sealed with tape, this one had only the flap glued down.

Max took it through to her kitchen, holding it with her fingertips along the edges. She placed it on the clean worktop and retrieved her bag from the hallway. She took out her old SmartLenses and placed them on her face. They took a minute to boot up after she had turned them on. Unlike most citizens, Max loathed wearing SmartLenses and only kept this decade-old pair for rare occasions like this. Once the start-up cycle was finished she selected the PrintScanner programme and focussed the lenses on the envelope. Even before the application had given her an answer she could see through the ultraviolet lenses that it would be negative. She flipped the envelope over and got the same result on the reverse – no viable fingerprints could be recorded. Now she reached for the small cooking knife hanging on the wall among other infrequently used cooking utensils. She carefully slipped the knife underneath the glued down flap and drew it across the width of the envelope. She tipped the contents out. One single sheet of paper fluttered facedown onto the worktop. Max focussed the SmartLenses across the white surface, first one side, then the other. Again the PrintScanner gave a negative reading. She took the glasses off and returned them to her backpack. It had taken her only a moment to read the message, printed in black capital letters on the paper. Now she picked it up and contemplated them again:

TIME TO PICK A SIDE…
MIDNIGHT TONIGHT
CAR PARK BASEMENT; F STREET NORTH

A drip of water ran from the end of her dank brown hair and landed on the paper, forming a circular splash that expanded outwards, smearing the letters of the word 'NORTH' as it did so. Max shivered and realised her cold hair was freezing and she was standing with her robe hanging open.

3

She waited until nine in the evening before setting off. By then the streets of the Capital City had cooled to a bearable temperature for light exertion and she emerged in her exercise clothing – black leggings and a black sweatshirt over a vest top – like any other citizen setting out for a run. She left behind her TouchScreen, SmartLenses and any other device that could be used to trace her movements.

F Street North was situated seven kilometres away from her apartment. The 'F' area spanned the central river through the city, with south and north designations for each side of the waterway. It had a reputation, as far as anywhere in the Capital City could have, of being a downtrodden area, with many of the old warehouses, piers and accommodation abandoned to disintegrate into the rising river decades ago. Work had only recently begun, through necessity as the city ran out of space, to reclaim the land and regenerate the river banks for housing accommodation. It was not the sort of landscape through which any citizen would choose to run, especially at night and alone. While the other cyclists, runners, and strollers veered west towards the centre of the city or north towards the perimeter walls where the streets where marginally wider, Max headed south towards the river. She was in reasonable shape and ran every other morning. She calculated it would take her under an hour to arrive at F Street North. That would give her two hours before the scheduled meeting, and an hour of fading daylight to reconnoitre the area. She felt tense as she ran, she knew she was taking a risk, a big risk. She should have told someone where she was going, but who? Her older colleagues like Curran and Mayfield would advise her against it, or worse, would betray her confidence. She shook her head at the paranoia that now affected her every decision. She had no friends outside the world of her work. She was on nodding terms with her neighbour, old Mr Lau across the landing, but Max wasn't inclined to start sharing secret information with him. She could have called her parents but telling them about her night time rendezvous with a stranger in an empty car park would only cause them to worry. Besides, they were too far away to do anything and there was always the chance the call would be monitored, as the State Security Service was legally allowed to do with any communication.

Her trainers pounded the hard surface of the pavements. There was a clammy moistness in the air, a sense of an oncoming downpour gathering in the skies above. Her hair, tied up in a ponytail, irritated her as it bounced along with her running motion. She stopped and took off her sweatshirt, tying it round her waist, letting some air get to her arms. Her clothes soon became damp with sweat. Down the side of her thigh, nestled into the tight pocket of her leggings, the blade of the kitchen knife chafed against her skin despite being wrapped in a cloth to stop it from cutting into her. She had almost left without the knife but halfway down the stairs from her apartment she decided to return and collect it. It was the only available weapon she possessed. If she was caught with it she would be jailed – only State Police were allowed to carry anything deemed to be a weapon on the streets of the Capital – but it gave her some sort of defence if she was walking into a trap. She felt foolish knowing it was unlikely she would have the guts to use it except in the most extreme circumstances. She wouldn't make it back to her apartment before the 1 a.m. curfew imposed on all citizens, so she was already destined to end up on the wrong side of the law. Her black clothing gave her the prospect of making it back to her apartment undetected under the cover of darkness. The cutbacks to street lighting and police night patrols also gave her a fighting chance. She would worry about getting home when the time came, for now she concentrated on the encounter that lay ahead.

Max crossed over Billings Bridge, named after the city destroyed in the initial attacks of the First Strike War, and took the steps down to F Street North, which ran for three kilometres along the river, from one end of the 'F' zone to the other. Although Max didn't know the area well, she knew the huge multi-storey car park about a kilometre from the bridge which towered over every other building in the zone. She slowed her pace to a comfortable jog. Traffic was sparse. Max spent most of her time on the road as the pavement disappeared behind hoardings which barricaded building sites behind them. Stack after stack of apartment buildings loomed upwards in various stages of construction. Up ahead the sun hit the top of the huge car park reflecting against the glass panes, glinting upon cracks and fractures and disappearing through holes where the glass had completely shattered. Max crossed to the opposite side of the road as she approached. Despite the ill-repair of the exterior the flickering coloured sign above the entrance read 'OPEN'. There was no one else around and no sign of any cars coming or going. The only sounds were the lapping of the river against the inadequate flood defence wall behind her, and the ever-present hum of delivery drones overhead.

It was now just after ten and the sun was beginning to dip behind the city skyline, creating blocks of heavy shadow cast by the encroaching building sites surrounding her. On the far side of the car park Max saw some scaffolding with a platform three floors up. From there she would have a good vantage point of the car park entrance and would be hidden in shadow. Checking she remained unobserved she walked past the entrance and crossed the road. As the light waned, the air cooled and Max untied her sweatshirt and threw it back on over her head. It took her five minutes to walk round the complete circumference of the building. Apart from the main entrance there was a door at the rear. It had no handle but beside it on the wall was an identity PalmReader with loose wires dangling from it and no power. Max gave the door a gentle shove, aware that it may be alarmed even if the PalmReader was disconnected. It didn't budge. She gave it another, stronger, push to be sure then carried on walking. She saw no sign of any State Surveillance Cameras around the perimeter, although she knew that didn't mean they weren't there, concealed from view.

She arrived back at F Street North satisfied that the main entrance was the only way in or out of the multi-storey garage. There was still no sign of anyone else on the street. Max approached the scaffolding she had seen earlier. She jumped up and grasped the metal bar above her head with both hands. She was light enough and strong enough to pull herself up. Balancing on the first bar she repeated the manoeuvre twice more until she reached the metal platform three floors up. She crouched down, leaning back from the edge so she was obscured from the ground below. The car park entrance was in full view across from her. She sat, waited and watched.

An hour and a half later Max uncurled her stiff legs and rubbed them to increase the blood flow through her aching joints and muscles. It was almost midnight. While she had kept vigil over the entrance only two cars had left, probably the last of the construction supervisors from adjacent building sites, and no one had entered. No one had approached the building by foot or on bicycle. Sitting still did not come naturally to Max. Her mind, given time to ponder, had contemplated the various scenarios that could be about to unfold. Was this a setup? After her public display of insubordination had the State decided to entrap her in a further act of sedition? Was it simpler than that – some lone citizen luring her to a remote spot to do with her what they wished? She knew nothing about the person who had left the envelope at her apartment, whereas they knew who she was, where she lived, what she did for a living and presumably a lot more. If this person wanted to provide her with genuine information, it seemed likely it would lead her into further confrontation with the State and the Party. What would she do with such information? She was already in enough trouble and effectively suspended by The Star Tribune.

She descended from her perch on the scaffolding. If her mystery visitor was genuine they were already inside the building or knew of some other concealed entrance she had been unable to discover. The air had cooled considerably and the first few spots of rain were beginning to fall as the threatened downpour finally arrived. At the foot of the scaffolding Max took the knife from her pocket and removed the cloth. She carefully concealed it in the waistband of her leggings, pressed against her back, with her sweatshirt hanging down to cover the exposed handle. Then she walked up the ramp that led into the parking garage.

Inside was murky and dark. Max cursed herself for not bringing a torch with her; it would have been more useful than the knife she could feel pressing against her coccyx. The further she moved away from the entrance the darker the gloom grew. She ducked under a barrier and in the distance saw a small light against the wall. It illuminated a number '1', a door and a sign for a stairway. There were no cars in any of the parking bays. Across the middle of the empty floor there were two rows of pillars, spaced evenly every ten metres. Max kept to the edges of the space, keeping the solid glass wall at her back. She was grateful that her soft-soled running trainers meant her footsteps were silent. Walking around the side she reached the door, which opened automatically as she neared. She ducked through it and paused on a staircase landing. There was low-level lighting here creating a flickering pale silver atmosphere. Looking up she could see the stairs rising into the distance, the light seemed brighter and more welcoming the further one ascended. She turned her head downwards, looking over the railing to see the stairs descending to the basement. Evidently the light on the basement level was broken, or had been deliberately turned off. All she saw was a black void. For a moment Max considered abandoning the meeting, the ominous surroundings telling her what she already knew:

trouble lurked in the darkness of that basement. She silenced her own doubts. If she was going to make any impact as a journalist this was what it would take, this was what she had been waiting for. It was worth the risk. She began to descend.

At the bottom of the stairwell she could see a patch of square light. It was a small window in another door that led to the basement level. The door swung open automatically accompanied by a grating screech as metal abraded against rusting hinges. The layout of the basement was identical to the floor above as far as Max could see. A dull light next to a 'B' sign was the illumination she had seen through the door. The empty grey floor was divided by old-fashioned painted lines into parking bays. She had no further instructions. There was no sense that anyone else was there. Moving quietly, she walked across the floor to a pillar that was roughly in the middle of the cavernous space. The ground was covered in a thick layer of dust, interrupted by occasional debris: broken bricks and pieces of shattered glass from the damaged panels on the building's exterior. She stood next to the pillar and waited.

Outside she heard a rumble of thunder as the storm finally broke in anger. Any lightning strikes failed to penetrate the gloom of the basement but soon there was the constant drumming of heavy rain. Ten minutes passed. Max began pacing round the pillar, re-evaluating the space as her eyes grew accustomed to the darkness. How much longer should she wait before giving up and returning home? Had it been a hoax after all? A plan to lure her out into the open? For what? The drumming rain eased but then grew heavier again. She had no wish to get soaked and decided to wait until the worst of the storm had passed. Then she would have to get home as quickly as she could – it was already too late to make it before the official curfew began. She looked at her watch once more. Quarter past. Then she froze, the hairs on her neck stood on end and she caught her breath. The screech of the basement door opening echoed around the derelict expanse.

Max turned and strained her eyes through the dark. She could hear the footsteps approaching and distinguished a shadow appearing through the murk. He was tall with short dark hair and a confident stride. Beyond that she couldn't ascertain anything else about his appearance and when she thought back on the meeting in the hours and days that followed she struggled to remember what he had looked like. He stopped two metres from her, his face partially hidden in the shadows.

'You've chosen a side then.' His accent was educated, from the Capital, but like his appearance, deliberately unmemorable.

'I haven't chosen anything,' Max answered. She kept her hands by her side, one hitched under the hem of her sweatshirt in case the knife was required.

'You're here though.' Was there a hint of a smile on his obscured features?

'Call it curiosity. Who are you?' she asked.

'You can call me Phillips.'

'Is that your real name?'

'It's a name people know me by.'

'Was it you who left the envelopes at my house?'

'Guilty.'

'Why me?'

Phillips avoided answering her directly. 'Tell me, Ms. Aubert, do you believe in the impartiality of the media?'

Max couldn't help releasing a nervous laugh, 'Are you joking?'

'But you think it should be impartial, that it should be a tool to hold those in power to account - a check and balance against those with the unlimited authority to control the lives of the citizens over whom they rule.'

'In an ideal world, yes.'

'We do not live in an ideal world, Ms. Aubert, far from it, as you have recently discovered.'

'Is that why you wanted to meet me here,' she gestured to their eerie surroundings. 'To tell me the obvious truth about the State media?'

Another smile, like an adult tolerating a petulant child, 'Your attempts to deliver some honest reporting ahead of the upcoming elections haven't gone unnoticed, even if your editor doesn't approve.'

'You should have read them before the best bits were cut out.'

'I have, and so have others that I work with. Your visit to the MidLands and the disquiet you found there was very illuminating, before it was edited.'

'How could you have read it? My editor killed the story.'

'You must not be too hard on Byron Mayfield, he has to walk a very narrow path.'

'That was why you decided to share the polling information with me?'

Phillips nodded, 'It was a test to see what you would do with the information.'

'And I passed?'

'With flying colours,' Phillips smiled. 'In fact, you went a lot further than I thought you would have. I had expected a story in The Star Tribune, heavily edited of course, rather than a confrontation with the Chancellor herself. It seems I underestimated you.' He moved towards her, his footsteps echoing around them. 'Come on, we should walk while we talk.' He stepped away and Max fell into stride beside him. She assumed it was a security measure in case someone was listening in, footsteps and movement would make it harder to trace their conversation. Or perhaps it was just to ward off the chill that had descended on the dark basement. Phillips kept his hands in his pockets, managing to keep his face hidden in the shadows. Max let her arms swing by her side. The knife pressed against her lower back. They reached the far wall before following its path, walking in a circuit around the rectangular perimeter.

'What you saw in the MidLands was just the tip of the iceberg, further north things have developed beyond whispers of disquiet with the State. Citizens are actively campaigning against the Central Party candidates.'

'Independent candidates?' Max asked. There was nothing new in that.

'More than that. Organised opposition.'

It was illegal for any group of citizens to form a new political party without first gaining permission from the Senate – and if such an application had been made to the Senate, then there would have been a record of it. 'That's impossible, we would have heard about it.'

'Would you? What makes you think that the State would allow you to hear about it?'

'They would have to apply in the Senate to form a political party.'

'Only if they were going through official channels. This is more of an underground movement.'

'A revolution?'

'In a way, although the aim is to win Senate seats rather than riot in the street. For now at least.' Phillips added the caveat with a shrug. 'They've defied the State Police and held small rallies in the streets, they're co-ordinating candidates to make sure every Senate seat is contested, volunteers are going door-to-door to spread the word, posters and graffiti with anti-Party slogans are appearing round the City.'

'It all sounds very low-tech.'

'They have no choice. The State controls all the high-tech.'

'And you want me to go to the northern cities and report on what's happening? Bad news I'm afraid, I've been put on enforced leave from the Tribune until the election is over.'

'I'm aware of your current employment problem. I want you to go and have a look, yes, and write about it as a journalist – an honest account of what you see, nothing more, nothing less. Once you've written something I have ways to distribute it.'

'You want me to get the word out, influence the election against the Party, spread the revolution to the south?'

'If citizens read the truth about what is happening then there may be consequences. I can't control what they may be.'

'Of course not, you're just an innocent facilitator standing for truth and freedom,' Max's voice was laced with sarcasm.

'If you like.'

'Tell me,' Max's confidence was growing, she was beginning to think like a journalist again instead of being fearful about the clandestine meeting, 'what makes you so

40

sure the Party and the State are so bad? Why do you want to see this revolution succeed?'

It took Phillips a moment to ponder his reply. He stopped walking and looked at her. 'I used to work for the State, in the military and then the Security Service. I have seen things.' He left it at that.

Max wondered exactly what these things could be, 'Then why don't you share these things with the citizens? Why do you need me?'

'I was forced to leave The State for a while. Only now have the conditions arisen that allow me to return, but I am still forced to live in the shadows, Maxine. If I was to become exposed in such a public way I would be eliminated.'

'Eliminated? How? You mean assassinated?' Max couldn't believe what she was saying, it sounded ridiculous. 'You're saying the State go around killing anyone that disagrees with them?'

He only nodded. 'I used to facilitate similar incidents on behalf of the State.'

Max suddenly felt fear creep over her skin, 'You killed people? Citizens?'

Phillips moved on without reply, his silence spoke volumes.

Max shook her head, her mind was spinning. She took a few hurried steps to catch up with Phillips. 'I hope you have something more than some circumspect polls and wild stories of assassinations if you want to take on the Party.' Max could feel the man looking at her carefully, making a decision about her before he spoke again.

Phillips nodded, 'You understand I am telling you this in the strictest confidence.'

41

It was Max's final chance to walk away, but how could she now if what he was telling her was true? Her instinct told her to stay despite the difficulty she had in believing what she was hearing. It was too late to turn away, he had her hooked. 'It's one thing to disagree with the State and Party policy, it's another to accuse them of murder.' She sensed the man was tired, that he was looking for a chance to unburden himself of something. 'Okay, tell me.'

'Three years ago the Vice-Chancellor Patrick Donovan and Defence Secretary Ishmael Nelson were assassinated on the same night not far from where we stand now. No one was ever convicted for the killings, no motive was ever determined beyond the official State report that terrorists were involved.'

'Yes, I remember,' Max continued her show of bravado but the mention of the assassinations made her nervous. She had been around the edges of the story, writing about the political fallout, the tightening of security and background pieces on the terrorist groups believed to be responsible.

'Donovan and Nelson were involved in the systematic murder of defenceless newborn children under the guise of finding a solution to the overpopulation problem within the State.' Phillips spoke in a flat, matter-of-fact voice, completely at odds with the horror of what he was revealing to Max. 'The Party had decided, correctly, that the expanding population was at the root of all the problems that have continued to plague the State: the energy crisis; housing; food shortages; climate control. They instigated a trial in one of the northern cities to control birth rates and had decided to expand that trial to citizens across the whole country.'

'They would never have been able to get away with it,' Max interjected, struggling to take in what was being revealed to her.

'They did, almost. They were recorded, unwittingly, discussing their plans for widening the process and someone decided to intervene. You may recall the killing of another politician, a local City Consul named Donald Parkinson?'

The name rang vague bells in the back of Max's mind, 'That was part of the same thing?'

'Parkinson instigated the trial in the City with the help of a paediatric doctor.' They had reached the doorway having walked a full circuit of the floor. He stopped walking and turned to face her. In the light cast from the dull bulb Max could finally see the dark pupils of the man's eyes. Max thought she saw a hint of weary sadness pass across his face.

She shook her head in disbelief at his story. 'Okay, say I believe all you're telling me. It's ten days until the elections. You're almost out of time. Why now? Why didn't you do something a month ago?'

'Events have coalesced. All the evidence of what Parkinson, Donovan and Nelson were up to was destroyed. Others who could have exposed the scandal were eliminated or induced to keep quiet.'

'Blackmailed?'

'Or given certain benefits and favours.'

'So no one will back up your story. Even you must know that a journalist can't publish something so outrageous without any source or evidence to back it up.'

'There is one person who could help you, a witness to some of the events. The State Police officer who investigated Parkinson's murder.'

43

'I doubt a State Police officer is going to talk to a journalist.'

'Ex-officer. He left the force shortly afterwards. He fled the City and has been living in the northern wilderness ever since. The State have made the odd attempt to hunt him down but he has managed to evade them.'

'And you expect me to be able to find him?'

'No need. As I said, things have coalesced. This ex-officer, Daniel Samson, is currently in a jail cell in the custody of the State Police.'

'They caught up with him then.'

'It appears he returned to the city of his own free will.'

'Why would he do that?'

'I haven't been able to find out why as yet. I have a contact in the City force, high up, someone who can keep Samson safe for now, but he is in danger. The Party and the State have powerful resources and reach.'

'If what you say is true and if the police know who he is, they won't let Samson talk, especially to me. What exactly do you want me to do?'

'Take your time off work, head north, report on what you see and hear about the elections and the rise of the opposition candidates.'

'And in return, what do I get?'

'You get the chance to be a proper journalist, to do what you've always wanted to do.'

'You understand I will write about whatever happens, good or bad, whether I agree with you and your friends or not. If I think what you are doing is wrong, I report it that way. If what you've told me turns out to be speculation or falsehood, I won't report it at all.'

'I would expect nothing less.'

'And this Samson will go on the record about the Donovan, Nelson and Parkinson murders? You can get me inside a State Police prison to talk to him?'

Phillips stepped towards the door, pushing it open with one hand. 'You won't need to get inside a prison to see him. I have someone in place to extricate him from his current predicament.'

'You mean break him out of State jail?' Max called after him as Phillips slipped through the door. The only answer was the screech of the rusted hinges as the door closed behind him. She stood alone in the darkness. The rain had stopped outside.

PART TWO:

THE NORTHERN WILDERNESS

ONE WEEK EARLIER

17th JUNE

4

Danny stood up and stretched his aching back. He looked at the furrows in the small field around him. Behind him lay rows of unsettled earth where he had pulled out the crops of mixed vegetables, in front of him the rest of the field waited to be harvested. It was hard manual labour, the sort that he hadn't been used to for most of his life but which he had become accustomed to in the four months since he had settled in the small community. He didn't begrudge the hard work, in fact he enjoyed it. The crop had been a success this summer and the food would comfortably feed him over the coming months, with plenty left over to share with the other villagers. In return, he would be able to trade for other crops, dairy, eggs or perhaps meat to supplement his own pantry. Underneath his tattered t-shirt, which hung loosely from his frame, the middle-aged paunch that had been developing when he had lived in the city had disappeared thanks to the necessity of hard work, and the scarcity of food that had become routine in the last three years. His limbs were sleek and toned and muscles had developed that he had never noticed before. What remained of his receding hair was cropped short in uneven patches thanks to the rudimentary haircut he had given himself with a blunted knife. A thick shadow of stubble ran along his strong jawline. He scratched at the scar behind his left ear. Three years ago he had dug into his own scalp to remove the tracking implant and the scar tissue still formed a raised lump.

Further along the valley he could see the other buildings – cottages, barns and tents – that made up the small settlement of which he was now part. His own dwelling, a simple hut made from timber and topped with a thatched roof, lay two hundred metres away from the main community. It had been his preference when he first arrived to live at a distance from the others, he did not wish to intrude on their society. On hearing his story, particularly learning that he was an ex-State police officer, the villagers had been wary of accepting him. Now though, he had earned their silent respect, if not their full trust. It was the first time in three years that he had found anyone with whom he could form any relationship.

The sun reached its zenith in the clear blue sky. It was not a time to be outside, especially doing any sort of labour. Danny lay down his tools, ready to resume harvesting his crop later in the afternoon when the midday heat had subsided. He walked over to the small porch that he had built onto the front of his home, which was covered by a corrugated tin roof, providing shade from the sun. Even this far north the summers had become sweltering and lasted longer than Danny could ever recall. Some of the more ambitious villagers had expanded their crops to include fruits and vegetables normally only grown further south in the tropics – coconuts, bananas, cassava and cocoa. On the porch, Danny used a crude metal cup to scoop water from a wooden bucket and poured it over his head and shoulders, allowing it to dampen his dirt-covered clothes. He took another cupful and drank it down in one deep, grateful swallow. The water was warm after sitting out all morning. After a rest he would walk into the village to collect a fresh, cool bucketful from the water pump. The nearest body of fresh water was at the other end of the valley to the south. From it a channel of water ran underground right through the village and a simple water pump had been installed to provide enough clean water for everyone. Danny sat down on the wooden stool he had made and leaned back against the sturdy wall of his hut. He watched the calming, still landscape for a moment. The village was quiet as everyone had moved indoors, avoiding the midday heat by having a well-earned meal or rest. The sounds and smells that surrounded him were still novel to him after forty years of living in the city. Birds of various kinds sang in different voices, somewhere distant a stag bellowed and a welcome breeze rustled the leaves on the forest of trees that ran along each side of the valley slopes.

It was hard for Danny to accept that, after everything that had happened to him, he would feel this at ease once again. With a sense of guilt he admitted to himself that he was at peace now more than he had ever been when he had lived in the city, happier even than during those few contented years when he had first met Rosalind, before it had all gone so horribly wrong. The only thing that could have made his current situation a complete idyll was if Rosa and the twins could be here with him. He shut the door on that memory, knowing that every time it surfaced it led to a period of melancholy and regret. Only in his unconscious mind were they allowed to appear, when he had no control over the images that his brain decided to show him. Danny's eyelids drooped now as the combination of the heat and morning exertion led to the inevitable daily siesta.

In the wild meadow in front of his hut, Isla and Hanlen ran through the grass and the yellow and white flowers that grew up to their heads. They were older now, growing into playful, exuberant children. Their skin was olive and tanned, like their mother's, bronzed by a lifetime spent outdoors with the wilderness as their playground. Their laughter floated over the meadow to the hut where Danny stood watching them, leaning against the wooden post that supported the porch roof. As he stood there, arms circled his waist. He looked round into the wide hazel eyes of Rosa, who smiled up at him. He kissed the top of her head, breathing in her comforting scent.

'Elysium,' he said to her.

'Hmm?' she replied.

'Nothing,' he held her closer. 'This is the place I've always wanted to be, right here, like this.'

They stood holding each other, watching their children chasing butterflies through the sunlit haze, motes of dust dancing around them.

'Elysium.' He shouted it this time, louder and harsher. 'Elysium. Elysium.'

Danny jerked awake, half-toppling from the stool.

'I see them. I see them.' The shouts came from the rough path that ran past his hut down to the village. 'Come on, they're here, they're back.' It was Anderson, one of the men from the village who had been on lookout duties further up the valley. He ran on, shouting at Danny as he headed towards the settlement where faces could be seen emerging from doorways, anxious to see what the commotion was about. As they began to realise the alarm had been raised, not for something sinister, but because some of their own were returning, people emerged from their dwellings and by the time

Anderson had sprinted the final few metres to reach them, a small crowd had gathered.

Danny roused himself, picked up the bucket and emptied the lukewarm water onto his unpicked crops as he walked past, heading to join the others in the space that loosely formed the central square of the village. He nodded to one or two as he arrived. Everyone had now appeared. About a hundred people made up the community and everyone knew each other. There was an excited buzz of voices and anxious, keen faces looked down the valley from where Anderson had appeared. The elders of the village, those who had been here the longest had assumed leadership of the commune, stood at the front of the group. Danny stood to the rear. He saw the back of Eilidh's head towards the front, her tousled sandy-brown hair tied up in a familiar functional bun, her face stiller than the others who chatted around her. She strained to catch a glimpse of the returning party. She was on her own, her young boy was too weak to venture out in the heat.

In a short time, figures approached along the path. They emerged through the heat haze as though a mirage, one or two at first then others joined them, appearing from the flanks of the path. They would have travelled in a spaced out formation, using as much natural camouflage as they could through the wilderness. Only now, as they neared home, could they relax and converge into a group. Danny, like the others, tried to count how many individuals made up the group as they neared. Six had formed the raiding party that had left over a fortnight ago. All were wearing faded green and beige military clothing, merging into each other, but as far as Danny could tell, six people were returning along the path towards them. Their approach now was languid following days of forced marching. Each was weighed down by a heavy, fully-packed rucksack and additional bulging holdalls. That was a good sign: it appeared that they were returning with a good haul of supplies. The village elders stepped forward to meet them, and others joined them to relieve the party of their heavy luggage. Of the six, four had partners in the village and they were soon embracing one another. Hassan, the commander of the returning party, a large man with dark features, was greeted by Rona, the acknowledged leader of the commune. They hugged, Rona's small frame almost disappearing beneath Hassan's broad encircling arms. Accompanied by shouts and smiles of familiar greeting, the homecoming group now reached the village.

Rona addressed the waiting crowd. There were no rules or statutes that determined her position as leader, but she had assumed this mantle naturally as the strongest and most forthright of the original settlers. Her voice was listened to with reverence. Her appearance suited her position: though small and thin, her face, bordered by fiery red, tangled hair, spoke of determination and knowledge; her natural firm demeanour spoke of survival and persistence. She had lived in the wilderness longer than any of them, having left the HighLand City when she was only twelve years of age, leaving behind her family and surviving on her own for several years before meeting fellow refugees.

'I know we are all anxious to hear from our returning brothers and sisters, and I am sure they have much to tell us,' she told the villagers. 'Let us give them one hour to feed, wash and rest themselves before all meeting in the large barn.'

The crowd turned away in small groups, happy to abide by Rona's command. Only Eilidh moved forward, approaching Hassan. 'Did you get some?' she pleaded.

Hassan's grim face looked at her. He opened the chest pocket of his shirt and removed a small container, handing it to Eilidh. 'This was all we could find. Three vials.' Eilidh grabbed the box. As she did so she crumpled to the ground. Danny stepped towards the fallen figure. He looked up at Hassan and nodded to him in gratitude. Hassan moved on, his head hung low.

'Come on, Eilidh,' Danny whispered to her, picking her up under her arms and leading her in the direction of the small lean-to that was her home. Others who had watched the exchange with a look of pity on their faces moved away sullenly, the joy of the return tainted by the desperation of their fellow comrade.

The lean-to was shaded, with thin shafts of light penetrating the gloom through gaps in the sticks, twigs and moss that constituted the outer wall. The narrow space was divided into a living area at the front and a sleeping area at the rear. Furniture was sparse: there was a small wood stove in one corner next to the entrance and a basic table with two rickety chairs next to it. Some clothes were bundled in a wooden chest and a shelf on the wall held a mixture of basic cooking utensils. The floor was hard slabs of stone covered with threadbare rugs. The sleeping area had an old double mattress on the floor, covered with a thin sheet. Under the sheet Danny could make out the form of Eilidh's son, Lucas, lying prone on his side. The bedsheet rose slightly every few seconds, accompanied by a shallow, weak wheeze. The atmosphere was stale, a sickness pervaded the air. Danny pulled out one of the chairs and sat Eilidh on it. She lay her head on the table and looked at the small container in her hand. 'Three vials is not enough.'

Danny stepped round and took the box from her hand. 'It's better than nothing. Come on, help me give him an injection.'

'It won't last long enough. He needs more.'

'We have this right now. We can think about what to do next once we have given him this.' He opened the box. Inside, kept cool by a refrigerant gel in the outer layers, were three glass vials containing a clear liquid. Carefully, Danny removed one vial and sealed the other two inside. On the side of the vial, printed in black, was the symbol for the State Medical Supply Company and next to that the simple description of the liquid inside: INSULIN DETEMIR (LONG-ACTING). From the shelf, Danny took the syringe with a small needle needed to inject the solution into Lucas. 'Come on,' he encouraged Eilidh again, 'you need to help me do this.' Although he had seen Eilidh administer the medication to Lucas before, Danny had little knowledge of how it was done and the injection provided a reason to focus Eilidh's mind on helping her son.

She lifted her head and wiped the tears from her face with her sleeve. 'Give it here.' She took the vial from Danny and pierced the cap with the needle, drawing clear liquid into the syringe as she pulled back the plunger. 'I'll give him five units to start with. I have nothing to measure the exact amount he needs anymore.' She handed Danny the syringe while she resealed the vial and placed it carefully in a shaded cubby hole in the wall. She took the needle back from Danny and walked towards the bed. Danny followed her and stood behind her as she kneeled down next to Lucas and rolled him over onto his back.

'Lucas, we've finally got some insulin again. I'm going to give you an injection, okay?' The pale heap of skin and bones mumbled a drowsy reply. Danny was startled at the appearance of the child. He had visited only a few days ago and although Lucas had looked underweight he had been bright and alert. Now he looked like a skeleton, his ribs and spine showed up through clammy pellucid skin, his cheekbones had sunken into hollows, pulling his face in tightly around the skull. His eyes were ringed with dark shadows. Eilidh felt around his narrow waist and stick-like arms. 'There's not enough fat to inject into.' She pulled the covers off the bed and exposed thin white legs. Around the upper thigh she managed to pinch a small roll of fat. 'This will have to do. You have to inject the insulin into the layer of subcutaneous fat under the skin. Go in too far and you inject into the muscle, that's no good.' She was explaining it to Danny as though teaching him what to do. He watched as she pricked the skin with the needle and pushed in the clear liquid. She held the needle in place for ten seconds before withdrawing it. Lucas didn't stir.

'Will we notice a difference?' Danny asked.

'Hopefully he will brighten up if the insulin starts working on the blood glucose. I dread to think what levels they have reached now. He will have ketoacidosis for sure, hopefully the insulin will bring down the acid levels in his blood.' She pulled the sheet back over her child and they retreated to the living quarters of the lean-to.

'Three vials won't last us a week,' Eilidh said as she rinsed the syringe in warm water, 'and he needs more than that anyway. The diabetes will already have started to affect his kidney function.'

Danny stared at the immobile, wheezing human form on the shaded bed. 'We'll think of something, Eilidh, I promise,' he tried to reassure her, but in his heart he knew it seemed hopeless. They had been relying on the raiding party returning with a good supply of insulin that would have lasted three or four months. Now time would run out for Lucas within days, and there was little that could be done to save him.

5

Eilidh stayed with Lucas while Danny went to the barn an hour later. The rest of the village had gathered to welcome the returning party and hear about their adventures.

Hassan began by making a short speech detailing some of what they had seen in the City. 'There was a real change in atmosphere. We saw it with our own eyes: a march of citizens right in front of the City Parliament building, at least a hundred people all gathered together. I had to stop Matthias and Tyrell from joining them,' Hassan laughed at the two members of his team who stood next to him. 'There were posters on the walls of buildings, telling people to vote for independent candidates. There was graffiti, anti-Party slogans, sprayed on white walls everywhere.' A murmur spread around the barn as the significance of the news filtered through the commune members.

Tia stepped in front of her commander and unfolded a piece of paper, which she held up to the crowd. 'I picked this up from the street.' Eyes and necks craned over heads to read the flyer she held:

STOP THE WAR.
SAVE THE STATE.
VOTE INDEPENDENT ON ELECTION DAY.

'And another,' Tia said, pulling a second poster from her utility belt and unfolding it:

NO MORE LIES.
SHARE THE ENERGY EQUALLY.
END THE PARTY RULE!

The physical proof created an audible gasp among the people. For those who had never known life in the cities of the State, who had been born and raised in the wilderness, it represented only an abstract idea, a foreign notion of protest against an enemy they had only heard about in stories and encountered only infrequently. For those who had spent time living under the State rule of the Central Alliance Party, it represented concrete evidence of something they could never have believed possible. For Danny, the person present with the most recent experience of living in a city, it seemed scarcely real, despite what his own eyes saw.

The questions began:

'Is it a rebellion?'

'What chance have they to succeed against the Party?'

'It is foolish for them to even try, they will be crushed.'

'Surely, the State Police would have stopped any gathering?'

Rona raised her hands and called for quiet. There was a hush as the last shout faded. Several heads turned to face Danny, who stood to the side of the group. He had told the village elders of his past life when he had arrived, it was only right that they knew he was an ex-State police officer and that his presence among them may bring risk. He had no idea if State Security were still looking for him. It had been more than two years since he had found any evidence that they were still tracking him, but he could not discount the possibility that one day a hit squad would arrive at the village looking for him. Although the elders had made no announcement, the rumours about the mysterious new member of their society soon filtered around the village. Danny was used to the suspicious nature with which he was viewed and the guarded interaction most of the villagers had with him. It never materialised into words or actions, but when he walked through the village he sensed the occasional wary glance directed towards him. When it was time to share crops or trade goods, he was accepted in the same way as anyone else.

At the previous gatherings Danny had attended he had never spoken a word but now he felt a contribution was expected. 'The law prohibits any gathering, never mind one of protest,' he stated.

Hassan spoke up. 'The State Police were at the gathering. They stood round the citizens, forming a cordon to prevent them getting into the City Parliament but they did not interfere with them at all beyond this.'

'The elections are in three weeks. Do you think the Central Alliance Party will be defeated?' Rona asked.

'It is unlikely. Perhaps they will lose a few Senate seats, but there was no sign of another organised party that could defeat them totally.' The kindling of hope that had briefly flickered across the gathered faces was extinguished. Hassan continued, 'We also heard that more and more people are leaving the cities and heading into the wilderness. We should be alert and ready to receive new arrivals.'

'We barely have enough to sustain us as it is,' cried out Palmer, a tall elderly man who had recently lost his wife to illness.

'Let us not panic about what may never happen,' Rona placated. 'We will deal with any refugees as and when they find us. Perhaps we should think on our own experience and those of our forebears. If we dismiss people who need our help then we behave no better than the Party.' Danny watched Palmer retreat as Rona's words were absorbed by nodding heads of general agreement. 'Let us deal with the here and now for the moment. Hassan, what have you managed to bring back with you?'

The heavy bags and holdalls that the raiding party had returned with now lay empty on the ground and the contents were piled on a table. Hassan stood in front of them. 'Our usual contacts have looked after us well, although all warned us that it was becoming more difficult to spare resources for us. We have plenty of clothing, materials and some food supplements. We were less successful with medical supplies again, they just aren't being made in big quantities anymore.'

'What about power supplies?' a tall woman named Jeanne called out. A consistent source of electricity was one of the main problems for the commune. They could grow crops, make clothing, burn wood and had a supply of clean water, but they could not manufacture a sustainable supply of electricity. Some had learned to live without it, others, particularly the younger inhabitants of the wilderness, still clung to it. There were some bits of machinery around the village that relied on it: the refrigeration and freezer units that allowed them to preserve food for longer; torches and basic communication devices that allowed those that went hunting or were on lookout duty around the valley to remain in touch with the village.

'We could only get two power cells. We took a risk to steal them. Our contacts had none to spare. The energy shortages are getting worse. There are hardly any cars on the roads now and little lighting at night.'

'The power cells will be kept for the refrigeration and freezer units. Apart from that we will just have to make do as best we can.' Rona stood next to Hassan at the front of the group again. 'Thank you Hassan, Tia and the others for what you have brought us and we are so grateful for your safe return. All are welcome to return to the barn tonight for a welcome home meal.' With mixed feelings the group began to disperse. From the snippets of conversations that Danny could hear as people passed him, there was much excitement about the news of an active resistance to the Party growing in the City. Danny wondered if they should be glad of such news within the commune. If the status quo remained in place then the way of life they had carved out for themselves in the wilderness was not threatened. The State had largely given up on hunting down those citizens that had refused to be moved into the cities during the clearances. The occasional surveillance drone passing overhead was about as much interference as the State had with them now. He knew there were other, larger settlements to the south that perhaps drew more attention than their own humble community, but by and large the State was happy to leave them be – they had enough things to worry about inside the walls of their cities to be too concerned with those who chose to live outwith them. If the state system were to collapse somehow, if the Central Alliance Party was to lose its grip on control, then the future would become uncertain. Who would fill that vacuum of power? Would the cities retain their hold on their citizens, or would they flock back to the wilderness lands, not only causing the regression of the restored natural world and harming the fight against climate change, but also invading the space that the commune had become so used to having to themselves? The reaction to Hassan's warning of potential newcomers had already revealed a leaning towards isolationism in some of the inhabitants of the village.

'Daniel,' Rona beckoned him to approach her. 'How is the child?' she asked as he came to stand next to her.

'Not well. The insulin will help, but it will not last long.'

'Bring Eilidh to my house. The elders and I will discuss what can be done.' Danny nodded his agreement and left the barn.

They sat round Rona's kitchen table. Danny shifted uncomfortably on the hard wooden chair. He had returned to the lean-to and woken Eilidh, who had curled up next to Lucas on the mattress. When he had delivered her to Rona's house he had expected to depart and leave the elders to discuss with Eilidh what could be done for her son. He had not expected an invitation to be present for the discussion. He sat at one end of the table, with Eilidh on the corner next to him. Rona sat opposite them. Hansel and Bruce sat on either side of the table while the tall, elegant Jia Li stood to the side, leaning her back against the old ceramic sink. As well as Danny, Hassan had been invited to join them and sat on the floor in the corner of the room. The sun, heading west and starting to dip, indicated the passing of the afternoon through an open window in the wall. Rona's house was the only one in the village constructed from stone, rough grey uneven bricks held together by haphazard cement and roofed with black slate tiles. Inside, she had to make do with the sparse furnishings that the rest of the commune lived with, although she did have running water in her kitchen, fed from the village pump. Whenever someone used the water pump outside, the metal pipes that ran under the sink gave a grinding 'thunk'.

Rona spread her hands on the table and looked at Eilidh, 'How is Lucas?'

'Weak,' Eilidh answered, without elaborating.

'You have given him insulin?'

'Yes.'

There was a pause before Rona began speaking again, 'The time has come to discuss what can be done for Lucas. What may be in his best interests.'

Eilidh looked up now, staring wide-eyed at Rona. 'You can't mean…' Her voice trailed off, unable to utter the thought that Rona had implied. 'No.' Eilidh looked away again, her voice was not defiant or bold, but a defeated whisper.

'He is in a lot of distress, Eilidh. If there was a chance of him improving and surviving then of course we would do all we could.' Eilidh didn't respond. She didn't break down, there were no tears or shrieks of anger. She just sat, head bowed, eyes wide open staring at the top of the table, her hands on her lap.

Danny reached out and placed his hand on top of hers. He addressed Hassan who still sat in the corner behind the elders, his head also cast down. 'There is no chance of finding more insulin?'

Hassan looked up, pity in his dark eyes, and shrugged, 'There are no longer many, if any, citizens in the cities who suffer from Type-1 Diabetes. It has virtually been eradicated. Without the disease they have no need to make insulin anymore. It's not that we couldn't find it or couldn't get our hands on it, it just no longer exists to be found.'

Danny nodded in agreement. Lucas had developed Type-1 Diabetes when he was only two years old. Before that he had been a perfectly healthy baby. Of all the major diseases, Type-1 Diabetes had been one of the last to be eradicated by modern science and medicine. While gene-editing, stem cell research and DNA manipulation had conquered cancers, Parkinson's Disease, Alzheimer's, malaria, influenza and the common cold, the simple act of making the human pancreas function properly remained beyond the grasp of the best scientists and doctors in the State. Type-2 Diabetes, which was brought on by poor diet and lack of exercise, had gradually faded away as citizens had adapted to new healthy lifestyles and obesity had become a thing of the past. But those unfortunate few who contracted Type-1 Diabetes had no option but to continue with the centuries-old treatment of injecting insulin into their bodies to replace that which the pancreas no longer produced. Then came the breakthrough, almost sixty years ago now. Scientists were able to identify the genes that led to the development of Type-1 Diabetes in the embryos of unborn children. Once they had identified them, they could operate on the foetus, manipulate the cells and correct the error. The limitation of the treatment was that it had to be done before twenty-five weeks of gestation within the womb. Mandatory screening was introduced and within only a few years the number of new cases of Type-1 Diabetes in children had dropped to zero.

The ethics around genetic editing and altering DNA coding on medical grounds had been argued and resolved decades earlier and there was little resistance to witnessing the end of one of the major chronic diseases that still afflicted humankind. However, left behind were those children and adults who had already developed Type-1 Diabetes. Their fate was to carry on as they had before, controlling their blood glucose levels as best they could using manufactured insulin solution. The technology around the administration of insulin and the equipment available meant it did not hamper their lifestyles significantly, provided they carefully looked after carbohydrate intake and insulin administration. Life expectancy for those with the disease rose, although it was never as high as for those without diabetes.

Sixty years after the inception of the foetal treatment, those who remained with Type-1 Diabetes were few. The older generation had died away and, with no new cases arriving, the pharmaceutical companies had no need to produce insulin in the large quantities previously required to treat the disease. The State stepped in and funded the production of insulin for those who remained with the autoimmune illness. That was the situation in the cities. In the wilderness there was no screening system for Type-1 Diabetes and no procedure to alter faulty genes. There was no rhyme or reason why Lucas had developed the disease and there was no one with whom to lay the blame. It just happened.

For three years Lucas had survived and for much of the time he appeared a healthy child. Regular forays to HighLand City and Central City had returned ample supplies of insulin to adequately treat the disease. The natural diet that was the only option for those living in the commune was one low in carbohydrates – meat, vegetables, eggs and fish. Less carbohydrates required less insulin to help the body process them. Gradually though the supply of insulin became depleted. It became harder and harder for the raiding parties to lay their hands on any of the precious vials of liquid. Now, it was proving almost impossible.

'It seems obvious that there is nothing more we can do for Lucas, not if he is to remain among us.' Rona spoke softly. 'It is time to make a difficult choice, Eilidh.'

'What choice is there?' Eilidh whispered. 'Without the insulin he will die.'

It was Jia Li who spoke next, her soft, distinct accent floating around them. 'We see only one hope if he is to live, but it will be your decision to make.'

'I would do anything, of course I would.'

'It would mean giving Lucas away, taking him to Central City.'

Eilidh turned to face Jia Li, a mixture of anger and desperation etched on her face.

Hansel took over, his blond beard moving up and down along with the hidden mouth it concealed, 'The only place where Lucas can get the care and medicine he needs to survive is in the city. We can no longer provide it here.' Danny began to sense the orchestration of the meeting. The elders had already discussed among themselves how to break their news to Eilidh.

Bruce took up the explanation, his eyes downcast, his remaining hand on the table. The other sleeve of his shirt hung loosely by his side, the scar tissue on the left side of his face was mottled and warped. Danny had heard the story of Bruce's narrow escape from a pursuing State drone. His injuries had been severe but treatable with painkillers, sutures and bandages. He had adapted to compensate for the amputated limb, the scar tissue he wore as a badge of honour. There was no visible sign of Lucas's disability from his external appearance, yet his small body could not adapt in the same way that Bruce's had. 'He must be delivered to the city, to the doctors and medical supplies they have there. There he can survive, he can live a normal, full life with access to the insulin he will always need.'

There was silence for a while. Eilidh sighed, thinking about what had been said to her. She knew they were right. She had to accept the inevitable. Slowly, she looked round each of the faces of the elders and nodded her head. 'Very well, we shall leave at first light.'

'It is not as simple as that, Eilidh. You cannot go with him,' Rona said starkly.

Eilidh stared at her. 'I'm his mother, of course I must go with him.'

Again the calming softness of Jia Li stepped in. Danny knew this was her role in such discussions - her placid, kind natural appearance gave her the ability to defuse moments of conflict with subtle ease. 'The journey will be arduous. Lucas is weak, he will not be able to walk himself, he will need to be carried. Whoever takes him will have to deliver him into the city. They risk being captured and jailed, or worse. You will not get to be with Lucas if you are caught by the State authorities. You

67

would be tried and left to rot in jail as a traitor.' Jia Li let this thought hang in the air for a moment.

'I can look after my son,' Eilidh said, looking down at the table again, her jaw set firm.

Jia Li continued, 'You have never visited Central City before, Eilidh. You were born and raised in the wilderness. You do not know your way south and you do not know the City. Whoever takes Lucas must have this knowledge and the ability to evade capture. They must be able to move with stealth, with pace. They must be able to survive on their own in the wilderness if they are to make it back here. It is the work of a soldier.'

'That is why I have volunteered to take Lucas to Central City.' It was Hassan who spoke. Eilidh looked directly at him.

Rona continued, 'This decision has not been taken lightly. Hassan is our most able commander. Should he be caught it will be a great loss to our commune, but we accept that Lucas must be given the best chance we can give him. Hassan has a route that will take him four days to reach the City. The insulin he managed to recover from his last trip will keep Lucas alive that long.'

For the first time Eilidh let out a small sob as the realisation hit her. This was her choice as a mother. To stay with her child, keep him here, and watch him grow weak and die in front of her, or hand him over to the State so that he may live, with the knowledge that she may never see him again. Danny looked at her shoulders trembling as grief gradually took over her body. He looked at Rona, Jia Li and Hassan. The idea crept up on him and he knew what he had to do.

'I'll take him,' Danny said. Eilidh's quiet sobs stopped. She joined the elders and Hassan in staring at

Danny. 'Hassan is needed here more than I am. He needs to rest before the next raiding party is sent out. There are a hundred people here who depend on him. If he was not to return everyone would be worse off. I know my way through the wilderness and I know the City better than anyone here.' He turned to face Eilidh, 'I'll take him.' She looked into his eyes and he saw acceptance in them. Her hands clasped around his on her lap, gripping him tightly.

Rona looked from Danny to Bruce, Hansel and Jia Li in turn. Each nodded their assent. 'Very well. We accept your offer, Daniel. Hassan will brief you on the route and plan he had in mind. Eilidh will prepare all that Lucas will need for the journey. We will leave you to discuss the details.'

6

The elders departed the room, leaving Eilidh, Danny and Hassan alone. 'You're sure about this?' Hassan asked, pulling himself up from the floor and leaning over the table. Danny only shrugged in reply. How could he be sure of anything? But as soon as the idea had come into his head it had felt right. For the first time in years Danny sensed he had a purpose, a destination, a reason to carry on.

***

The weather had been cold that day. Snow had finally fallen over Central City for the first time that winter. Danny had awoken in his father's apartment, lying on the sofa in the living room. He smelled the loose blanket that covered him and took in the familiar scent of his father. He knew it would be the last time he would experience it. The previous night he had watched his father shuffle away for the last time. He tried not to think where his father's body would be now, lying somewhere in the chilled depths of the river that ran through the centre of the City. It had been a subdued farewell. Now, in a sense, Danny felt free. There was nothing to tie him to the City anymore, only memories of those he had loved and lost. He had made up his mind to leave a few days previously when his boss, Superintendent Janette Michaels had paid him a visit at his home. He was still officially on paid leave, being given time to recover after the events of the last few days. He had been offered his job back, with the enticement of a promotion if he wanted it.

But how could he return to the State Police after what he had discovered? The Police Commander Lars James was dead, having been implicated in the cover-up of a State Party policy to kill unborn children with detected disabilities or defects without the consent or knowledge of the parents. Consul Donald Parkinson, the politician who had overseen a State-sanctioned trial of the scheme had been assassinated. Danny and his partner Henrik James had been investigating the killing when they uncovered the truth. He had been killed by a woman called Gabriella Marino, who had been hired by an underground nightclub owner called Elisabeth Sand. It was Sand who had overheard a meeting at which Parkinson had been discussing the trial. Sand had been killed by a State hit team right in front of Danny's eyes. He had been lucky to escape with his own life. Henrik was still in the hospital recuperating after being shot; the State Security Agent Phillips, who had been assisting the inquiry, had disappeared and the assassin Gabriella had vanished from Police Headquarters where she was being held. On top of that, a few days ago in the Capital City there had been the double assassination of Vice-Chancellor Patrick Donovan and Defence Secretary Ishmael Nelson. State media was reporting it as terrorist attacks, but Danny knew they were the Party Senators who had authorised Parkinson to go ahead with his horrific trial. That was the problem: Danny Samson, a lowly State Police Detective, knew the truth and because of that he was a danger to the Party and the State, and Danny had seen first-hand how the Party dealt with threats. The choice for him was simple: return to work and spend his life looking over his shoulder, wondering if today would be the day that they decided it was time to get rid of him and everything that he knew; or run, get out of the City and try to survive on his own.

He decided against returning to his apartment that day. Instead he packed one of his father's old rucksacks with a few items of clothing, food supplements and a water bottle. He found a large knife in his father's kitchen drawer with a sharp point. He smiled - it was illegal to own a sharp knife of that size - Franklin Samson always had had a bit of a rebellious streak. In the bathroom he pierced the side of his scalp with the point of the knife. Blood poured down the side of his face into the sink as he carefully dug the point in deeper until he felt it wedge behind the tracking implant in his head. All State employees had such tracker implants. He gouged and sliced his skin until the implant loosened and he was able to prise it free. The small oval-shaped pellet fell into the sink. He pocketed it and stemmed the flow of blood from the wound. He added the knife to the rucksack and closed the door on his past life. He couldn't risk visiting the City Cemetery to say good bye to Rosa and the children. If a hit squad were looking for him they were sure to be watching the gravestones. Instead he walked to the arch bridge and stood in the spot where Rosa had thrown herself into the river that bleak winter night a year ago. He took the tracking implant from his pocket and threw it into the clear blue water below and whispered one last goodbye to his love.

Then he ran. By nightfall he had reached the huge wall that separated the city from the wilderness beyond. The only opening was the road that ran north upon which hardly any traffic flowed anymore. It was the one moment of real danger he knew he would face. Up until that moment it had been a surreal feeling to move through the streets of the City he knew so well in the process of escaping. There were moments of guilt as he looked at the families and children he was abandoning to their fate with the State while he fled. He made no promises or proclamations about returning one day to expose the truth, to avenge the victims, to free the people. What could he do? One man against the unhindered power of the State and the Central Alliance Party? He was sure no one had followed him. He had learned that wasn't how the State Security Service operated. There may be drones or satellites above him that were tracking his every move but there was nothing he could do about them.

He approached the gate that blocked the road out of the city. There was one guard on duty, sitting in a small shelter. Danny smiled at him, trying to look confident. He stood at the scanner on the wall and put his palm on the screen. He placed his pupil in front of the eye scanner. The guard watched as Danny waited for the inevitable rejection. Both scanners buzzed as they declined to open the gate for him. The guard stood and walked over to him.

'Don't get many people leaving at this time of night. Everything okay?' Danny noticed the guard's hand near his hip, poised to pull out his ShockBaton if required.

Danny flashed his State Police identification, 'Guess the authorisation hasn't come through in time. Typical of the office.'

The guard looked wary. He saw the small wound on the side of Danny's head. 'No problem. Mind if I scan that?' he motioned to the code on Danny's identification.

'Sure, no problem.' Danny handed it to the guard. The guard turned his back on him to scan the code with the TouchScreen in his shelter. It was now or never. Danny was not a violent man. He had experienced more violence in the last few weeks than he had in his entire previous career. A few days ago he would never have contemplated assaulting a member of the State Security Force. Now he lunged forward and ripped the ShockBaton from the guard's belt. Before the guard could react Danny smashed the metal stick across the back of his head. On impact the baton sparked with a jolt of electricity. The guard crumpled to the ground. Danny had no idea how long he had before more State Security officers would arrive. He grabbed the prone body and hefted it upright. He flopped the guard's palm on the reader and managed to hold his eye open in front of the scanner. The gate clicked and motors whirred as it slid open. He dropped the guard and ran. Only later did he remember he had left his identification lying next to the unconscious guard. He felt aimless, he had no destination, only survival, and for now that had to be enough.

***

'I'm sure,' he answered Hassan, 'you're needed here more than I am.'

'Okay, here's what I had planned to do.' Hassan unfolded a yellowed piece of paper and spread it out over the table. It was an old map, from the time when they were still printed on paper, of the northern half of the country, covering Central City to the south, the Lakes and the HighLands across a vast swathe of the land, and the

74

HighLand City to the north-east. Hassan pointed to a patch of green in the top north-west corner. 'This is where we are.' Danny had never seen exactly where he had travelled to. He was vaguely aware he had been heading north for most of his travels through the wilderness, but he was surprised at how close to the northern coast of the island he had come. Hassan drew a line diagonally south across the map, following a blue meandering river through areas of green and brown, which Danny assumed were forests and hills. 'Tomorrow we set off on foot and trek ten miles to here,' his finger stopped where the river widened and transformed into a large body of water. 'From here there is an old road that is still passable. We have a car hidden here. From there you're on your own. It should have enough power in the battery for you to drive to,' Hassan's finger followed a rough grey line that curled further south, winding between mountains and lakes, stopping roughly halfway down the map, 'here.'

'The Fort,' Danny read the printed name. He knew of the small outpost that belonged to the State Security Force. It was used as a military base to protect the western coastline, providing a port for naval vessels, an airstrip for military drones and aeroplanes and early warning radar against incoming attacks. It was also rumoured that the State housed some of its own offensive weapons there, including nuclear warheads. 'Surely we should avoid going anywhere near there?'

'It's the only place where you will be able to get more power for the car. Otherwise you'll be on foot for the rest of the way to the City, which will take four of five times longer and which Lucas is in no condition to attempt.'

'What if we get caught?'

'The Fort is mainly automated now. There are only a handful of soldiers posted there. Most likely they would send you to the City and hold you as prisoners and traitors.'

'Great,' Danny stared at the map. 'What about the HighLand City? It's closer.'

Hassan shook his head, 'There is only a small medical presence there, no hospital and probably no insulin treatment. It just isn't needed anymore. Anyone who does require medical help is sent to Central City, or in extreme cases the Capital City.'

'What if there is no way to get more power for the car?'

'Then you'll have to improvise. There may be military vehicles you could steal, but they would be tracked. There is the intercity transport shuttle but we have no idea what timetable it runs and it may be well guarded.'

Danny didn't like what he was hearing. 'This won't work with just one person,' he protested, 'we need a team of people.'

'The elders have decided. It was all I could do to convince them to sacrifice the car which we're unlikely to retrieve. Anything more is out of the question.'

'I want to go with you to the City,' Eilidh said.

Hassan stood up straight and looked between Eilidh and Danny, 'I'll start preparing some equipment.' He left them alone in the kitchen.

Since stumbling across the settlement four months ago, Danny had not made close friends within the community. He got on well enough with most of them, there was no unpleasantness, but he kept himself at a distance. He knew that one day he would have to move on, that either he would become restless or the State may come looking for him. He had never revealed to anyone the reason he had fled the City or why the State would be so eager to catch up with him. The only person he had gravitated towards was the quiet, demure woman who cared for her sick child. Eilidh had been born in the wilderness, though Danny had never learned what had become of her parents. Nor did he ever discover who Lucas's father was or what had become of him. Eilidh was about the same height as Danny, slightly below average, thin but with the sinewy arms and shoulders that were common among those who were accustomed to the daily manual labour required to survive in the wilderness. She wore her brown-blonde hair tied up in a loose bun and her eyes were constantly downcast. Something about her reserved nature drew Danny to her. He was well aware that Lucas was the main reason why he had become close to Eilidh. He was five, the same age that Hanlen and Isla would be now if they had survived. Danny's experience with his own children and his discovery of what the State had done to thousands more made him consciously aware of wanting to help Lucas in some way. It was all he could do by way of atonement for those lives lost.

He had started bringing Eilidh extra crops from his field, knowing they were good for Lucas to eat, despite Eilidh having nothing with which to trade for them apart from the eggs her few hens laid. A reserved friendship had grown. Occasionally he stayed at the lean-to, keeping a watchful eye on Lucas through the night and allowing Eilidh a night of uninterrupted sleep. In return, they would visit him at his hut when Lucas was well enough to sit on the porch and play. Danny crafted simple games out of wood for them to play: he taught the five-year old boy draughts and marble solitaire. He made the marbles from smoothed circles of wood and the board from a flat cross section of tree trunk into which he carved a border for the marbles to run round the outside and small divots arranged in a cross around the centre for the marbles to sit in. Lucas delighted in swirling the marbles around the edge of the circular board, never growing frustrated that he could not complete the game.

While they played and laughed, Eilidh would watch them, her eyes gleaming at the happiness Danny was able to elicit from her son. While Lucas gabbled away, pouring over the draught board trying to figure out his next move, Danny and Eilidh's eyes would meet over the boy's head. Both would smile at each other and both would see the sadness that lay hidden behind those smiles. Through conversations that went on into the night while they watched Lucas sleep, Eilidh learned about the family Danny had lost. Their company comforted each other. Danny could feel stirrings in his heart for her but the memory of Rosa held him back. It felt like a betrayal to be falling in love with another person. One morning Danny had woken in the lean-to to find Eilidh curled up next to him. They had spoken to one another late into the night and at some point fallen asleep in each other's arms. From then on they often spent the night together, sleeping on the same bed in her lean-to or at his hut, with Lucas beside them. It never progressed beyond that innocent physical contact. There was an invisible barrier between them that prevented anything more developing in their relationship; their pasts drew them back from committing to each other fully. They both knew they loved the other and both were content to express that love in companionship and in caring for Lucas.

They sat together in the lean-to, their faces lit by the flickering orange glow of a candle on the table between them. Lucas was asleep on the mattress. He had woken for an hour in the evening and managed to eat a meal of vegetables and poached egg. For the first time in a few days a smile had formed on his face and he had managed to speak a few words. Eilidh had given him another five units of insulin before putting him back to bed. As yet they had not told him what lay in store for him the following day.

'You cannot go with him to the City,' Danny said to Eilidh as they both watched the shape on the mattress. The wheezing that had accompanied each breath over the last few nights had subsided for now. 'If you are caught you will be thrown in jail for the rest of your life, or worse. You would never see him again. If he is caught with you they will treat him the same as you, as a traitor of the State.'

'How could they? He is only a child.'

'I have seen what the State is willing to do to a child, even one that is a legal citizen.' Danny didn't elaborate. He didn't want to worry her more by telling her all that he knew.

She looked at her son, his tiny frame tucked under the sheet. 'What will happen to him?'

'If I can get him to a hospital they will be able to take care of him. When he is better there are places that will take him in. They have orphanages; there are still people who will adopt children. So long as they do not know where he has come from he should be protected. The most important thing is he will have the medication he needs to live.'

'I cannot bear to think of him living with another family, being away from me.'

'This way there is hope, Eilidh,' Danny reached over and took her hand and wiped away a tear that rolled down her cheek. 'There is hope that one day you could be reunited with him. That is worth the risk and better than the alternative of watching him die.'

'He will forget me.'

'Never.'

'You have to promise me that you will make it to the City with him.'

'I promise you I will do everything I can,' Danny said, and Eilidh could see in his eyes that he meant it.

That night Danny sat on his ramshackle porch. He had packed a few essentials that Hassan had given him into his father's old rucksack. There wasn't much to take really, beyond as much food and water as he could carry to sustain himself and Lucas on the journey, and a few extra layers of clothing. The sun dipped behind the hills and the air cooled. A full moon in the clear night sky provided enough light for him to carry out his task. He selected a handful of the wooden marbles he had made for Lucas and with a knife he carved a letter into each. Then he placed them back inside their small cloth pouch. He slipped the pouch into his bag. The circular board was too heavy and awkward to carry with them, but he would leave the marbles with Lucas if they made it to the City safely, a small memento that one day might trigger a memory of a lost life in the wilderness, and the mother who waited for him there.

7

They set off early the next morning after breakfast. Lucas's condition had improved over the course of the night and he had received another insulin injection. The first vial would be finished by the evening, leaving only two more. Lucas insisted on walking as they left the village, his small paces forcing them to adapt to his gentle pace, but a few hundred yards along the track he accepted he had not got the stamina to carry on. Now he lay on the stretcher that they had brought with them, roughly fashioned from two long branches and a piece of sackcloth. Danny carried the rear of the stretcher, looking down into the wide open eyes of the child's face staring up at him, squinting into the blue sky. Hassan led the way at the front, with Eilidh walking alongside her son, carrying supplies on her back and holding onto Lucas's hand.

That morning around a small fire in the lean-to, Eilidh had told Lucas they were heading to the city to get help for him. They had agreed not to tell him his mother was not going with him until the last possible moment. It was important in managing his condition that Lucas was agitated or stressed as little as possible. 'It'll be an adventure,' she played with the fringe of his sandy-brown hair, brushing strands away from his eyes, 'seeing the big city for the first time, all those buildings and vehicles, lights and people.'

'It'll be an adventure for you too, Mum,' Lucas had replied innocently. Eilidh turned away before he could see the glistening tears around the edges of her eyes.

The path kept going through the base of the valley and curved round the head of the lake as the river flowed into it. 'From here the path becomes rougher,' Hassan said, as the flat land began to slope upwards and smooth gravel was replaced by broken rocks and protruding roots. They trooped on. The open meadow of the valley was replaced by forest along the side of the lake. Danny cast a glance over his shoulder at the small dwellings in the distance, wondering if he would ever return. They kept going for forty-five minutes before Danny called a halt and was allowed a rest. Hassan reckoned they had travelled two kilometres already but progress would be slower from this point onwards. As the sun rose further into the sky and the temperature once again began to climb, the towering trees provided welcome shade. Lucas drifted into a light sleep though his eyes kept opening with each jolt or bump along their route. Around them a varying symphony of nature accompanied their journey. A constant melody of bird calls echoed from the branches above them and occasionally the sound of a bigger mammal reverberated through the foliage. Deer had flourished in the wilderness along with bears, wildcats, wolves and foxes. Hassan reassured them that they would be safe from any predators unless they stumbled into their territory by mistake. As the day grew warmer Danny began to sweat, drops gathering on his eyebrows and trickling down his face and neck. With both hands on the stretcher he was unable to wipe his brow clear. Eilidh noticed and gently dabbed his head with her handkerchief. Soon his hands were wet with his own sweat causing the stretcher pole to slip from his grasp and requiring him to muster an even firmer grip.

Another hour later they stopped again, having reached the far end of the lake. Danny's shoulders and back ached. He found a boulder to sit on. Hassan remained on his feet, scanning the horizon around them through binoculars. What he was expecting to see, Danny couldn't imagine. Despite the constant buzz of nature around them, they had not seen anything other than the odd bird or insect flying around in the forest. There was a peaceful calm now that they had emerged from the forest again. There were no cities this far north so the sky remained clear of any drones, the intercity rail shuttle veered east at The Fort, never venturing this far north, and no roads had ever been built in this corner of the country. Water lapped against the shore gently in the background. Lucas stirred as the stretcher was put down and sat up. Eilidh fed him a selection of vegetables: carrots, tomatoes, lettuce and cucumber; a few pieces of apple and some cheese and pork – foods low in carbohydrates that wouldn't raise his blood sugar levels radically. Lucas asked Danny about the City: what was it like? Did they really have screens where you could watch people acting out stories? Could you buy things on a TouchScreen and minutes later a drone would deliver them to your door? What toys did children have there? Danny tried to answer the flurry of questions as best he could. He tried to emphasise the positive things about living in a city. He avoided mentioning what Lucas would be losing: the wildlife, nature and open spaces that the wilderness had in abundance. Eilidh sat watching them, staring at her son, letting their final moments together sink into her memory.

Hassan approached them after ten minutes. 'We should push on,' he said. 'We want to reach the car before the sun reaches its peak.'

'A car?' Lucas exclaimed, his eyes wide with wonder.

'Sure, we can't walk all the way to Central City,' Danny smiled at him.

'The path disappears now,' Hassan continued, 'it's rough terrain from here so watch your step.'

With the news that a car journey awaited him and revived by food, Lucas stayed awake and alert lying on the stretcher. He tried to sit up, but the imbalance it caused as they travelled made it too difficult for Hassan and Danny to keep the stretcher upright. They were walking through wild meadows now: long, thick grass and abundant wild flowers hampered their progress. Hassan took the brunt of the extra work as he cleared a path by trampling down the vegetation for the others to follow through. Eilidh dropped behind Danny, following in their footsteps. Danny's hands began to hurt. Although his skin was rough and calloused after his years living in the wilderness, the strain of gripping the rough wooden branches began to cause blistering. Hassan seemed immune to any such problems. Eventually, after Danny had requested another stop, Eilidh and he shared one pole each at the back of the stretcher, while Hassan continued on his own at the front.

Lucas's constant excited chatter sustained them: a game of 'I-Spy' dissolved into fits of laughter after the umpteenth spying of 'grass,' 'flowers,' and 'sky.' They sang songs and even Eilidh joined in, rousing herself to enjoy these last precious moments with her son. They ate sparingly from their food supplies, but they were able to drink abundantly to quench their thirst as there were

85

plenty of fresh water lakes along the way that could be used to top up their bottles. Eilidh dipped cloths in the cool water and placed them on the necks of Hassan, Danny and Lucas. The boy laughed as the cold water trickled down his back, Danny was grateful for the moment of chilled relief.

It was close to midday as the sun reached an apex in the sky above, beating directly down on them. Danny was exhausted. Eilidh had stumbled on a few occasions and even Hassan's relentless pace seemed to slow. Lucas had gradually slipped back into a peaceful doze, opening his eyes only fitfully when disturbed by pieces of long grass brushing along his side.

'One last ridge and we're there,' Hassan called over his shoulder. The ridge was a steep climb and the lush vegetation gave way to a crumbled, dry scree slope. They had no choice but to abandon the stretcher halfway up and Hassan took Lucas on his back, scrabbling up the incline at a snail's pace. Every few steps the rocky surface would give way and he would slide back a few metres before collecting himself and restarting the unremitting climb. Danny and Eilidh took Hassan's bag between them and managed to aid each other slowly upwards. After a brief pause on a narrow plateau, they descended down the far side of the ridge, this time with the opposite problem, trying to slow their hasty decline as their feet threatened to run, then slide away from beneath them. Kicking up a trail of rock dust, they reached the bottom and five minutes later Hassan stepped into a clearing in the forest where the lush green carpet was replaced by a hard, grey tarmac surface. The reason for the existence of the road had been lost to history. Why had it been built this far north, beyond any major settlements? Why did it abruptly stop? No one knew. Perhaps it had been intended to lead to a new town or city that was never built, or perhaps it was built to allow military access further north, just as the original roads had been used centuries before. Eilidh sat on the hard surface but was forced to move to the side – the flat, black road was burning hot in the sweltering sunlight. She tended to Lucas, giving him water and the final portion of home grown vegetables from her pack. Danny checked the insulin vials were intact and still cool in their pack. Neither of them spoke about the imminent parting.

After a moment to drink and douse himself with water, Hassan crossed over to the other side of the road and began walking, looking into the forest that lined the verge. He was three hundred metres further along when he called out and waved for them to join him. He began removing branches and leaves from an object next to the road, just hidden beyond the tree line. By the time the others had caught up to him, with Danny carrying Lucas on his back, Hassan had revealed the side of a rusted car.

Lucas was fascinated. He had only heard about these machines in stories spoken by those villagers that had come from the City. Hassan heaved the stiff door open and Lucas climbed inside, sitting behind the steering wheel, pretending to drive with a grin on his face, his short, thin legs dangling off the seat, unable to reach the pedals. Even Eilidh seemed curious. She had known about the car that the commune kept hidden but had never had occasion to need or use it. It was kept for occasional excursions that required urgency, usually medical. Once when a raiding party had been ambushed by a wild bear while resting in the forest, the car was retrieved and used to transport the badly injured as far as the road end before they were carried on stretchers the rest of the way home.

Danny helped Hassan remove the rest of the foliage that had been used to camouflage the vehicle. 'We have to push it out onto the road,' Hassan instructed. Eilidh sat in the driver seat and Hassan showed her how to release the brake and steer the car. Then he and Danny took up position at the rear of the car and began pushing. Incrementally the wheels began to inch round, resisting after months of idleness, until they reached a slight dip in the roadside. The car rolled down and then up onto the road before crawling to a halt. Lucas ran after it and Eilidh admonished him. 'Save your energy for the long journey ahead.' It was impossible to curb his excitement about the upcoming trip in the motor vehicle.

Danny had hardly seen a vehicle since he had left the City. He knew enough to see that this car had seen better days. 'How old is this thing?' he asked Hassan.

'No idea. The main thing is it still runs. Have you driven before?'

'A long time ago.' Manual driving had almost died out completely once self-driving cars controlled by intelligent computers had become widespread, however as part of his police work Danny had occasionally taken control of police vehicles.

'It should be straight forward, it's a basic model. Gears are automatic, one pedal to accelerate, one to brake,' Hassan pointed out each feature inside the car. 'Button to start and stop the engine. You shouldn't have to worry about anything else.' He reached inside and pulled a lever under the driver's seat. The bonnet at the front of the car popped open and rose automatically. They moved round to look inside. Where the battery for the electric motor should have been was an empty space. The problem with the commune having a car was sourcing the electricity to power it. Hassan walked to the back of the car and opened up the boot. 'Give me a hand,' he called. Danny joined him and saw an old power unit. 'We picked it up in the City during a raid last year. Took two of us to get it all the way back here. Not an exact fit for the power unit this car needs but it was the closest we could find. I should be able to hook it up.' They took an end each and heaved it round to the front of the car. The battery wedged into the gap for the power unit, but was too big to depress all the way down. Hassan was unperturbed, 'Just have to make a hole in the bonnet. You should be able to look over it to see where you're going. Will take me half an hour to get this fitted.' From his rucksack Hassan removed a selection of metal tools and set to work. The others sat on the edge of the road watching him.

With the clanging of metal in the background, Eilidh explained to Lucas what was about to happen. 'Danny is going to take you the rest of the way to the City, while I go back to the village with Hassan.'

'You're not coming with us?'

'No, Danny knows the City much better than I do. He'll get you safely to the doctors that can help you.'

'Then we will come back home?' The puzzled innocence on his face brought an ache to Eilidh's chest.

'It's not as simple as that, Lucas. Remember your diabetes is for life, there is no cure for it, only management of it.'

'So I will live in the City forever?'

'I think so, yes.'

'When will you come and visit me?'

89

'I can't,' Eilidh stuttered, unable to watch her son's face fall as realisation struck. 'It's too dangerous for me to go to the City. I would be put in jail.'

'But I don't want to live with Danny. I want to live with you.'

'It's too dangerous for Danny to stay in the City too. He is going to take you there and leave you with the doctors. When you're feeling better they will find a new home for you. Somewhere where you will always get all the insulin you need and you can live for a long time.'

'No,' Lucas was defiant but the tears began to form on his thin face, 'I don't want to leave you.'

'You have to. If you don't you will die.'

'Will I ever see you again?'

'Perhaps, one day. Who knows what will happen in the future? This way we still have hope.' Lucas threw his arms around his mother, the sobs uncontrolled now. Danny placed a supportive hand on his frail back. Lucas slapped it away. Danny left them alone.

Hassan had used a hammer and chisel to create a rough square hole in the bonnet. Now it closed with the top of the new battery sticking out this new opening. 'Will be fine,' he reassured Danny, 'so long as it doesn't rain. If water gets inside it then…' he shrugged. 'I've hooked it up, why don't you give it a go.'

Danny got into the driver's seat. 'Gear in neutral, then push the starter,' Hassan shouted from the front of the car. Danny gave the button a firm push. There was a weak whirring noise from the battery, then nothing. 'Try it again,' Hassan called. Danny pushed it again and got the same result. 'Okay, let me have a look.' Hassan opened the bonnet again and started testing each of the cables he had connected to the new battery unit, shaking them firmly, taking them off and reapplying them. Danny got the impression Hassan liked this sort of mechanical work. Perhaps he had been a mechanic or engineer in his past life. After ten more minutes he called out to Danny again, 'Okay, give it another go.' This time when he hit the starter button the whirring was louder and constant. The lights on the dashboard came to life, various dials and instruments flickered and then awakened. Hassan gave a satisfied smile and slapped the rusty grey metal. 'I knew you wouldn't let us down,' he said to the machine.

He stood looking in the driver side window at the dashboard readings and flicked a couple of switches on the steering wheel. The number '250' appeared on a small screen. 'That's how many kilometres you've got in the battery. Should be enough to get you to The Fort if you drive steadily. We've got no idea what condition the road is in further south, it may be overgrown. Try and stay out of the pot holes, the suspension is old and rusty. Other than that, good luck.' He offered his hand through the window to Danny, who took it. They shook and Danny felt he had achieved some kind of respect from the rugged commander. Eilidh picked Lucas up in her arms and brought him round to the passenger side door. Hassan opened it for her. As she tried to place Lucas into the seat he grabbed at the sides of the door frame, clinging to them, trying to stop himself being forced inside. His earlier enthusiasm for the ride in a motor vehicle had disappeared.

'I don't want to go,' he screamed, becoming louder and frantic.

'You have to Lucas, I'm sorry,' Eilidh eventually turned away and Hassan stepped in, pushing Lucas inside and holding him down while fastening his seat belt.

Wordlessly he closed the door and nodded to Danny who slowly pressed his foot down on the accelerator. There was a grinding squeal as metal parts started to revolve and they began rolling along the road. Lucas sat sobbing next to him, staring out of the side window, refusing to look at the man who was taking him away from his mother and his home. Danny looked in the rear view mirror. Eilidh stood in the middle of the road, hands at her side. Hassan, business-like as always, was picking up their bags and preparing to set off back to the village. They would have to leave now to be back before dark. The sun glinted off Eilidh's tear-stained face. A grey tongue of road lay ahead of them, cracked by pot holes and tree roots. Danny increased their speed and the next stage of their journey south began.

8

Progress was slow and bumpy. Often the road disappeared under encroaching vegetation or had crumbled away leaving large sink holes. Danny was forced to weave around boulders and roots and squeeze between overhanging tree branches that scraped the sides and roof of the metal car. Their passage became easier when the route rose above the tree line, following the contours of the hillsides and snaking along the slopes, looking down on the valleys below. Danny was able to increase their speed on these longer, clearer stretches and the aim of reaching The Fort by nightfall seemed achievable. Lucas stared at the landscape he had never seen before, but he refused to look at Danny and said nothing. Danny tried pressing the buttons on the entertainment unit, but the only sound they could pick up was static noise and the monitor remained blank. He switched it off and concentrated on the road ahead.

After an hour they came to a junction. Danny paused and consulted the map Hassan had given them, spreading it out over his knees. He was able to pinpoint their exact position. As expected this was where the narrow trunk road joined the wider highway that had once been a busy intercity route filled with self-driving cargo lorries transporting goods around the State. Drones and the intercity shuttle did much of that work now and the condition of the road had deteriorated. Using the scale of the map as a guide, Danny estimated another two hours of driving and they would reach the outskirts of The Fort.

He checked the dashboard reading. The battery range number had crept down to 120 kilometres. He reckoned they had about a hundred kilometres left to go.

'Should make it with a little power to spare,' he said, starting to fold the map up. After a minute spent bending the paper backwards and forwards along the creases, he threw the unfolded map onto the back seat in frustration. Out of the corner of his eye he saw a brief smile appear on Lucas's face, before the boy checked himself and resumed his sullen demeanour. Danny turned right, taking the road south.

Although uneven and irregular, the old highway was less overgrown and dilapidated than the trunk road had been and Danny was able to relax as they cruised along. The forest scenery around them continued without interruption, the deciduous vegetation sitting below them in the valleys while above them coniferous pines dominated the higher slopes. Passing open fields they could spot wild animals in the distance: herds of deer, elk, sheep and what appeared to be buffalo, although Danny wasn't sure they were indigenous to the State. When the road curved round a hillside to face west the bright sun shone straight into Danny's eyes. The adaptive windscreen shade on the car didn't work, so he had to resort to shielding his eyes with his hand. Once, as Danny was distracted taking a drink from his water bottle, the road took a sharp bend to face into the sun. Lucas cried out as a young deer suddenly sprang across the road in front of them and Danny slammed on the brakes, dropping his water bottle and gripping the steering wheel with two hands. They skidded to a stop in the middle of the road, the battery motor automatically shutting down as it was programmed to do in such a situation.

'Dammit,' Danny said, looking at the widening wet stain of spilt water running down his chest and gathering around his groin. This time Lucas couldn't hide his laughter.

The warmth of the day soon dried out his clothes as they carried on. It was late afternoon when they were forced to stop as their path was blocked. There had been a landslide on the road. Mud and dirt and several larger rocks had tumbled down the slope above and come to a rest on the tarmac, making it impossible for the car to get through.

'Seems like a good time to stop for something to eat,' Danny said to Lucas, reaching behind for his backpack. He split another packet of food between them. They sat in the car, the windows down to allow some fresh air inside. A breeze drifted over their elevated position on the hillside, making the trees around them rustle, breaking the stillness and the silence. High above them a few birds circled, Danny couldn't identify them but they looked big enough to be birds of prey, their long wingspans allowing them to glide on the air currents.

'You know your mum loves you,' Danny said, staring up at the birds through the windscreen. The five year-old carried on eating. 'If there was a way you could be together, she would do anything to make it happen.'

'I know,' Lucas replied. 'Sometimes I wish I was dead, it would make things much easier.'

Danny looked at him, 'You can't think like that. Imagine how sad your mum would be if she heard you say that.'

'What's the point of being alive if I can't stay with her?'

'Look, Lucas, you got a raw deal with your illness, but you can't let it beat you like this. You have to fight it and you have to survive. Once you get to the city you will be looked after, you can have a normal life like everyone else.' Danny felt inadequate trying to explain such big concepts of life to a child.

'Why do I need to survive? What's the point? I will always have this stupid diabetes. I hate it.'

'You have your whole life ahead of you. You might not feel like it now but you're going to grow up and you can be happy. You're going to make new friends, play, laugh,' Danny faltered. How to explain to a child all the things that make life worth living? 'You know, I once had a son, and a daughter. Twins. They would have been the same age as you are now.'

'What happened to them?'

'They died not long after they were born. They were just too weak to survive.'

'Do you miss them?'

'Every second of every day and, you know, I feel like you do right now a lot of the time. What's the point in carrying on, drifting along, when you can't be with the people you love? When you've lost all that you care about?'

'So why do you?'

Danny shrugged, 'I don't have an answer for you at the moment. You just have to keep going somehow and hope that one day things will get better. I guess that's what it comes down to - hope.'

'You think you will get better?'

'I think I'm starting to. I'll always miss them and remember them. But you have something more than I do to hope for. I can't ever be with my children again so I have to find new ways to be happy, new people, like you and your mum. You will have to do that too but your mum is still here, she's alive, and so are you. So long as that's the case, you will always have the hope that you can be with her again one day. Isn't that worth surviving for?'

'I guess so. I don't think I will like the city though. Why won't they let my mum live there?'

'It's complicated. It's the same reason I can't stay with you. The people that run Central City, they don't like the people who refuse to live there under their rule. I chose to leave the city because I found out things about those people that I didn't like.' Danny thought it best not to mention that had Eilidh been pregnant with Lucas in Central City five years ago and they had found evidence of his susceptibility to developing Type-1 Diabetes, the State would have preferred the baby to be terminated as part of the trial he had unearthed. 'Your mother's parents, your grandparents, they felt the same. But there are good things about the city too, like getting the care you need from doctors. There will be lots of children for you to play with and lots of cool places to visit – they have museums, play parks, swimming pools, you can play sports and you will get to go to a proper school and learn all sorts of things.'

Lucas didn't say anything more. They carried on eating in silence. Danny knew his answers were insufficient, and he knew that was because he didn't know the answers to Lucas's questions. Why had he, Danny, kept going after the twins had died and Rosa had taken her own life? Why had he kept going after he had learned the evil that existed in the State? Why had he spent three years scavenging, surviving, and wandering in the wilderness? What was he looking for? Some sort of spiritual awakening? Why had he not ended his own life if he could think of no reason to stay alive? Was he in denial about the whole thing, naively thinking that something better than what he had lost could be found? At least now in this moment he had a purpose and he knew he would gladly give his own life to protect the boy sitting next to him.

Danny finished his food and opened the door. 'Better see if I can move some of these rocks so we can get through.'

It took him half an hour to create a path wide enough for the car to pass. Two of the boulders were so heavy he was sure he would never get them to move but he dug deep and gradually, a millimetre at a time, they crept towards the outer verge of the road. He got back in the car and edged it slowly over the silt and rubble that remained. Twice the wheels spun on the loose surface and Danny pressed the accelerator to the floor to extract every last quantum of power the motor could muster. After twenty metres they were clear of the landslip and unobstructed road lay in front of them again.

'How are you feeling?' he asked Lucas before they set off again.

'Fine, I guess.'

'Time for your next injection.' Danny produced the syringe and vials of insulin. He emptied the remains of the first vial into the syringe, then pierced open a new one and filled the strings to the top as Eilidh had shown him. 'Pull your trouser leg up.' Lucas rolled one leg up to reveal his thigh, pale and thin and marked with pin pricks from years of previous injections. Danny found a clear piece of skin on the emaciated limb and inserted the needle, hoping that he had placed it far enough under the skin to reach the subcutaneous layer of fat, but not enter the muscle underneath. Lucas didn't flinch as the needle went in and came out. 'Okay. I need your help from here on in. Hassan said we might see security drones patrolling the sky the nearer we get to The Fort. You need to keep watching above and shout if you see one.'

'Okay.' Danny felt like he had lost Lucas somewhere on the journey. The playful kid who was always smiling and laughing on his porch, even when he was weak and ill, had been replaced by a sullen, uncommunicative boy who had drawn into himself. It was understandable. Hassan had warned them that if they were spotted by a drone it would be too late. All they could do was try to see them first and get the car off the road and under tree cover until the coast was clear to carry on. The sun finally began to dip towards the west as they continued on their way.

Even before they reached the outskirts of The Fort, Danny knew that Hassan's plan was doomed to failure. He had nodded along as Hassan had detailed the chances of securing a new battery motor at The Fort, or finding a way to charge the battery already installed, but in his heart he knew it was not something he would be capable of achieving. Perhaps Hassan, with his military background and expertise in leading raids into the cities, could circumvent the security of a defended military outpost, locate a battery unit, steal it and get back to the car undetected, but Danny was not confident that he would be able to complete such a task. It was for that very reason that Hassan was too valuable for the commune to lose. As they neared the limit of the motor's range, Danny pondered their alternative options. He considered simply handing himself in to the first State soldier that they came upon. He would be shipped back to the City to face the full weight of the State justice system but there was no guarantee what would become of Lucas. Danny had learned first-hand how cruel the State could be, even to children. If Lucas was found in the wilderness he would be treated as a traitor of the State regardless of his young age. He had to be delivered to the hospital inside Central City where they would treat him and enter him into the State care system. Eilidh had explained to the scared boy that he could on no account tell those who looked after him in the city where he had come from.

Option two was slightly more realistic than finding a new battery and managing to install it with his limited mechanical knowledge. If they could get close enough to The Fort to find a military or civilian car unattended they could simply drive off in it. It would be night time and there was a chance the missing vehicle would not be noticed until the following morning, by which time they would have a head start on any pursuers. The downside was that modern cars, especially those used by the State military and police were equipped with personnel databases. If the identity of the driver was not on an approved list the car would refuse to start and alarms would start ringing somewhere in The Fort. Danny had seen and used similar identification programmes in his time with the State Police but had no idea how to override them.

That left only one option that Danny contemplated with any likelihood of success. When Danny had still lived in the City the intercity shuttle service ran daily between The Fort, HighLand City and Central City. It was energy efficient, clean transport that provided a lifeline for the northern half of the State, allowing people and goods to be ferried around despite the continuing energy crisis. Despite Hassan's caution about the erratic timetable, Danny reckoned it must still run at least once or twice every day. The station at The Fort at which the shuttle stopped was located on the perimeter, so access could be achieved without having to sneak through a military barracks. No doubt there would be some security presence at the station, but less than within The Fort. If they could find an opportunity to get on board the shuttle they would be in the middle of Central City within a few hours. In the worst case scenario of this plan they may well be detected and Danny would be caught, but Lucas may still be taken care of.

The sun was beginning to lose its power as the day waned away when the car crawled to a stop in the middle of the road. They were at the crest of a hill and in the valley below they could make out a few lights that indicated the position of The Fort. The battery whirred sporadically before the range counter hit '0' and the motor died. Danny let the car freewheel through a few dips in the undulating road before a steep uphill slope brought them to a complete halt.

'That's that then.'

Lucas had drifted off to sleep next to him during the final half hour of smooth driving and now stirred as the car gave a final shudder. 'I wasn't much of a lookout,' he said, through heavy eyelids.

'Don't worry about it,' Danny reassured him, 'didn't spot anything anyway.' There had been no sign of any drones or other surveillance on the road, although that didn't rule out satellites looking down from their space orbit or any hidden State Security cameras along the road.

No other car had appeared pursuing them or blocking the road ahead, which was the surest sign Danny could have that they had not been detected on their journey so far. 'I'm afraid it's time to get out and travel by foot for a bit though.' Danny pointed to the lights and buildings in the distance, 'That's The Fort we need to get to tonight. Think you can walk some of the way?'

'I suppose so.'

Danny gathered up his bag. He left behind anything that wasn't essential. Once Lucas was out of the car Danny managed to push it off the road, down the natural slope of the hill. It tipped over the verge and travelled for a few metres before coming to a crashing halt against the tree line.

'We'll follow the road for a bit,' he said and they set off. Danny took Lucas and put him on his back, carrying the bag across his chest. The even road made the going bearable and soon they had covered half the distance to The Fort. Here Danny stopped and roused Lucas, who had drifted into another light sleep while clinging on to his back. 'We'll have a bite to eat here and then we need to leave the road and carry on through the undergrowth.'

The sun dipped behind the mountains as they resumed and the air cooled. Lucas had to walk some of the way as the flora grew thick around them. Danny went first pushing away grass and branches, making a path through which Lucas was able to follow. Progress was slow. They came to a clearing in the trees and over the top of the forest canopy they could see The Fort in more detail. Off to one side stood the track of the intercity shuttle. The shuttle was an electrified monorail that ran a hundred metres above the ground on a series of pillars. It only sloped down to ground level when it entered the main cities of the State, using the railway stations as terminals. The great height of the track allowed the carriages to travel over the wilderness unimpeded and preserved the ecology of the land beneath, while swerving around the mountainous uplands and curving past numerous lakes. The Fort was the only stopping point on the route between Central City and HighLand City. The monorail didn't drop down to meet The Fort, rather a platform had been added to the top of an existing skyscraper, the towering offices of the military outpost. Danny took the binoculars from his bag and looked through them. The line of pillars and track swooped through the valley in a graceful curve. He followed the line until it reached The Fort. As he had hoped on the nearside of a pillar, outside the limits of The Fort walls, there was a service shaft, a circular ladder of metal bars that climbed up to the monorail track. There was no sign of a shuttle at the station this evening but Danny had not anticipated there would be. Every morning when Danny had lived in the city a shuttle left in the early morning and headed north, while a shuttle from the northern city made the opposite trip south. They intersected at The Fort, where the single track split and dualled just outside the station, allowing the shuttles to pass each other. After arriving at their destinations they then made the return journey and kept criss-crossing between cities until curfew. With luck this was still the timetable they stuck to, which would mean Danny and Lucas could sneak aboard the first train heading to Central City the following morning. All they needed to do was get to the top of the service shaft undetected.

He pointed to the pillar and gave the binoculars to Lucas, lifting him up so that he could see over the

103

treetops. 'That's where we have to get to in the morning and climb to the top. Then we get to ride on a shuttle train.'

'Is it safe that high up?' Lucas asked. Danny remembered this was like nothing the boy had ever seen before.

'There's never been an accident in all the years it's been running. Pretty exciting, isn't it?'

'I guess so.' There was just a hint of enthusiasm behind the binoculars.

'We'll camp out here tonight under the trees and make an early start.'

Danny led them back under the cover of the forest canopy and from the bag took the spare clothing he had brought from the car. He gave it to Lucas who wrapped himself up in an oversized jumper and coat. Danny made him a soft pillow of earth and put the bag on top of it for a makeshift pillow. Within a few minutes Lucas had drifted off to sleep. Danny knew the boy was exhausted. A few more hours tomorrow, Danny prayed, and he would be in a city hospital and recovering from the long journey. He measured out another five units of insulin and injected it into the boy's leg while he slept.

9

Danny spent the night sitting against the trunk of a large tree. The sounds of the forest at night kept him on edge. There was a different aural tone here compared to that of the village which he had become used to. Wild animals had learned to avoid the settlement, whereas here it was Danny and Lucas who were trespassing onto their territory. It brought back memories for Danny of those first days and nights when he had left Central City, weeks spent wandering by day and sleeping rough at night, unsure if he was being pursued or not, unsure if he had put enough distance between him and the city. He had feared the sound of the drones overhead, each time that ominous buzzing crept up on him he dived under the nearest available cover. He had headed north at first and after a few days had found the small village he had spent the night at before, when they had been searching for the assassin Gabriella. A State hit squad had been close on her trail when they had finally caught up with her. Danny, Phillips and Gabriella had escaped, his partner Henrik had been shot but survived. As they had made their getaway the State soldiers had been rounding up the villagers, refugees from the City living peacefully in the wilderness. He never knew what became of those people but he now found the village deserted. The main street, a series of small cottages and bungalows with an old church building and village hall, was like a ghost town. There were signs of the gunfight that had taken place, empty bullet cartridges littered the ground. On the side of one building, Danny saw brickwork that had been pockmarked with several rounds of ammunition, surrounded by dry red smears running to the frosted ground. He found no bodies, but in the field next to the buildings there was a large patch of charred grass, the remains of a large fire. He kicked through the ashes and saw fragments of white bone. This was how the State chose to deal with those who defied it and harboured it's enemies. They had died for protecting Gabriella.

He stayed in the old hotel Phillips, Henrik and he had spent the night in before. There was some leftover food in the kitchen, decaying but still edible, and chopped wood that he used to build a fire in the lounge room. But Danny knew he would have to move on. The State Security Forces would have found the unconscious guard and they would know he had headed north. They were bound to pass the village he was known to have visited once before. He stayed two nights, knowing it was a risk to stay a third and set off again. He took a canvas sheet with him which became his accommodation each night, propped up into a rough bivouac supported by branches and sticks. He learned to live off what the wilderness provided: leaves, mushrooms, nuts, seeds and berries. When he stopped by a lake he chiselled a stick to a sharp point and tried his luck fishing. There was an abundance of fish and he soon became adept at spearing his dinner. Rabbits proved a trickier foe and it took him a while to fashion a trap of twigs and sticks that occasionally provided him with a rare treat. For the first six months he saw no other humans in the wilderness. Then one day he stumbled upon the coastline and in the distance saw a bridge that ran out into the sea, connecting the mainland to an island. He approached it and, as he set foot on the bridge, out jumped the first person he had seen since he had knocked out the guard at the City gate.

'Who are you?' the boy had shouted at him. He couldn't have been more than thirteen or fourteen years old. He pointed an old-fashioned carbine hunting rifle at Danny's midriff.

Danny instinctively raised his hands. 'I'm nobody. Just a traveller.'

'You from the City?'

'I used to be.'

'You work for the State?'

'Not anymore.'

'What you doing out here?'

Danny had no answer, 'I was just walking along and saw the bridge, so I thought I'd cross it.'

'You can cross it alright, but you'll need to keep those hands up where I can see them.' Danny was marched over the bridge with the boy following him a few paces behind. They walked for half a kilometre before reaching the shore of the island. As they neared he saw a party was waiting to meet them.

'Good work, Casper. Return to your post until your relief arrives this evening.'

'Yes, sir,' the boy turned and marched back over the bridge, rifle held upright against his shoulder. Danny watched him go.

'Welcome, stranger,' the man who had given Casper his orders now addressed him. 'You must understand our caution when we find a person wandering into our domain.' Danny thought about his appearance for the first time: his hair had grown down to his shoulders, though still balding on top, he was unshaven and his clothes were dirty and tattered. No wonder he was being viewed with suspicion.

'You have no reason to fear me, I am alone.'

'And what are you seeking?'

Danny shrugged, 'I was just passing.'

'We all are, in one way or another,' the man answered enigmatically. 'Come, you are welcome to join us as our guest.'

That was how Danny had first met Skylar, the leader of a small band of islanders who lived together on the edge of the State. He learned that the State had agreed to leave them alone on the island on the condition that they never set foot on the mainland. This they had done for over fifty years now. They practiced a strange sort of spiritual religion, something that Danny had heard about only in the dark history of the State. Each day everyone spent some time on their own simply sitting with their eyes closed, resting and seeking their own inner peace. Danny was to spend months living with them but he always remained as he had been on that first day: a guest. He tried their meditation ritual with the advice of Skylar, but Danny knew he would struggle to find any inner peace. He learned from them more basic survival skills for living in the wilderness: crop growing (they ate no meat), carpentry and weaving. Although they would harm no animal and lived peacefully, time was set aside each day to practice their own form of martial art. In the City these arts had been used as a form of exercise. Here, they took it seriously, in the same way that they practiced their religion. 'It teaches you control, concentration, balance and power,' Skylar intoned. There was real peace among the island commune. They numbered around fifty people who each took part in these daily rituals. All lived in a simple hut with thin walls and all helped with the work around the camp. Danny noticed that none of the people were older than about sixty, with the exception of the wizened Skylar, who, though sprightly and nimble, appeared to be in his eighties.

Danny acclimatised to this new style of living. He grew to accept what had happened to him, to Rosa and the twins, and he finally began to deal with the devastation of his past life. One evening he spoke of this with Skylar. No one had asked about his past when he had arrived. Now he opened up to the leader of the island. He told him of Rosa and the love they had once shared, of their joy at the imminent arrival of their children and their despair when Hanlen and Isla had been taken from them so soon. He told him of Rosa's suicide and the depression that he had suffered. Skylar nodded along to his story and offered counselling and solace.

'Who knows what the Gods have in store for us? Perhaps it was all part of a larger plan in order to bring you here to us. Life, fate, they can be cruel to us all and sometimes there is no explanation no matter how hard we may search for one. The only solution is to find acceptance and trust in those above us that they will lead us to enlightenment.'

The summer passed into autumn and winter followed. One evening, as the first hint of spring could be tasted in the air, Danny noticed a change in the mood of the camp. There was excitement among them, an atmosphere of anticipation. At first he thought it was due to the welcome signs of leaf buds and birdsong returning to the island. It was Casper, the boy who had first marched him across the bridge, who came to fetch him after supper, just as dusk was setting and the orange glow of the campfires began to crackle into the darkening sky.

'The master would like to invite you to the ceremony,' Casper announced.

'The ceremony?'

'Agnetha has made her choice,' was the cryptic reply.

Danny followed him through the camp. Other villagers, with wide, expectant smiles and chatter walked alongside them on the path which led to the far side of the island, facing out to the vast ocean beyond, the very edge of The State boundary. He noticed the face paint they had all decorated themselves with: red, black, yellow colours in various patterns on their cheeks and foreheads. Danny knew Agnetha was one of the older women in the camp: her creased, rugged face and long rusty-coloured hair radiated good health and energy, and a life spent living in full subjugation to the natural elements. They crested the large hills that ran through the middle of the island and below them Danny could see a large collection of wood gathered together to make a huge bonfire. Sticking out of the centre of it there was a large wooden pole, and there were steps leading up to a small platform on top of the pile of wood. As they descended, others had already gathered around the campfire. On one side sat Skylar, perched on a rock that resembled a throne. Casper led Danny to his side and pointed to a space that had been reserved for him next to the leader. Skylar greeted him with a smile but said nothing. Around him the villagers were wide-eyed, almost like they were hypnotised. Casper offered Danny a thick cigarette that was being passed among them. Danny refused, his lifelong aversion to smoking, illegal in the City, held him back from accepting. There were bottles of liquid being

110

passed around too. When one was offered to Danny, this time he accepted. He gulped back a mouthful and immediately regretted it. His stomach lurched, his gag reflex threatened to send the drink straight back out of his mouth. He had only tasted alcohol once before and the strong taste was unmistakeable. He felt light-headed instantly, his senses became heightened, his vision blurry.

From a gap in the rocks opposite them Agnetha appeared. She was naked, her skin pale in the moonlight. She greeted her fellow villagers with smiles and warm handshakes and embraces as she walked towards the bonfire. She climbed up the stairs and onto the platform. Her hands were then tied behind her, binding her to the pole.

Danny could see what was about to happen. 'What is going on?' he asked Skylar. He could hear his own voice slurring the words.

'This is the ritual that we have enacted here from the very beginning of our life together on the island. At the first full moon after one of our number has reached their sixtieth year, they are given the choice that we all must face about our future.' He paused. From around the campfire a strange, animal sound began to emanate, a bass chant that grew in strength. The seated villagers took to their feet and began swaying rhythmically to the noise. Higher, louder shrieks began to fill the night, howls that seemed to surround the group as they bounced off the rocks above them.

'What choice?' Danny called above the din. He was swaying where he sat, struggling to keep a clear head.

Skylar answered him without taking his eyes from the spectacle unfolding in front of them. 'They have three options: they can set sail out into the great unknown

111

ocean to meet whatever fate may await them; they can choose to return to the mainland and take their chances with the State; or, they can choose the rapture.'

From the rocks there now emerged four men wearing only loincloths on their bodies and masks decorated with large fangs and horns. They each carried a lit flame on a wooden torch. Their bodies convulsed and gyrated to the sound of the chants that carried them forward towards the base of the bonfire. Each took up position around the circle. Agnetha looked down on the crowd below her, a benign smile on her face, her eyes beaming with warmth. There was no sign of anxiety or panic or fear.

Skylar now stood and raised his hands. Abruptly the chant stopped. 'My fellow brethren, we are gathered here to celebrate the life of our dear friend and comrade, Agnetha. She has chosen to take the right path, the path of the rapture, the path that will lead her to her spiritual awakening and the life that follows beyond our limited mortal boundaries.' With that he threw his arms into the air again and the chanting and howling resumed with more intensity. The masked men stepped forward and put their flaming torches into the base of the bonfire. After a minute the flames took hold, licking at the foot of the structure and then gradually growing. Within minutes Agnetha was engulfed by intense flames and billowing clouds. Her shrieks rose as she began to burn, loud and pained, eclipsing the ongoing cacophony of sound from the dancing people below her. With one final blood-curdling scream the platform and pole vanished, collapsing into the fire with a crack and splinter of wood and a rising mushroom of black smoke. Danny tried to stand but was too dizzy, he fell backwards, landing on the soft ground. Above him flickers of orange danced like fireflies, rising into the heavens above him, his blurred, hazy vision seeing them as comets trailing across the night sky above him.

The next morning Danny found himself back in his tent. He had no recollection of how he had got there. His head thumped with a dull pain. The nightmare vision of the previous evening gradually emerged through the deep fug of his memory. He staggered out into the fresh spring air and splashed water from the trough over his face. No one else was up, no doubt they were still sleeping off the effects of the alcohol and drugs they had been intoxicated with the night before. He found Skylar sitting on his own outside his small hut.

'I think I shall be moving on today,' he told the old man.

'If that is what you wish. I sense you are never to be persuaded to become a true believer here.'

'I left the State because I found out they were killing children to resolve an over-population problem. You don't see that you are doing the same thing here?'

Skylar looked at him in puzzlement, 'We force no one to do anything. We are honest and open about what their future will hold.'

'You force anyone older than sixty to kill themselves, one way or another, so that the remaining population can be sustained.'

'The trouble is you do not believe. The rapture is not a death, it is a rebirth.'

'You don't honestly believe any of this nonsense,' Danny countered, feeling himself getting angry. 'Religion based on these nonsensical beliefs died out decades ago.'

'A lack of followers does not mean the Gods died, only that we humans lost our way. This haven is a guiding light to bring people back.'

'And you, how did you avoid the choice?'

'One is chosen in every generation to sacrifice themselves, to carry the burden of living on in their mortal form in order to guide the flock.'

Danny could have said more, but what was the point? 'I would rather take my chances in the wilderness on the mainland.' With that he left the old man, who did not stir from his morning contemplation.

It was Casper who marched him back across the bridge that afternoon and watched him until he had drifted out of sight along the coast of the mainland. As he turned back one last time before disappearing, Danny saw Casper wave to him before marching back to his lookout post.

He lived as a nomad for another year, the cycle of the seasons once more controlling how he survived in the wilderness. Sometimes he settled in one spot for a few days, sometimes he returned to previous places where he had set up camp before. Despite the horror of what he had seen on that last night on the island, he tried to keep up the teachings he had learned, spending time each day in contemplation and continuing to practise the martial art drills he had been shown. His life could have carried on that way until old age and the unforgiving wilderness had taken him, but for the vagaries of the extreme weather in the northern part of the State. It was a particularly bitter winter that had driven him further north than he had travelled before. Seeking refuge from driving sleet and snow in the hills he had come down onto the leeward side of a range of mountains he had never crossed before. There he had seen the small group of buildings huddled in the shelter of the valley. He had been found in the morning, covered in frozen ice drops, shivering inside the large barn. It was Jia Li who had discovered him. In his fevered state Danny had thought he was hallucinating, her elegant, dark features at odds with the rugged snowbound world she inhabited.

That was how he had arrived at the village which had become his home over the following months. He had drifted along for three years and somehow survived with no reason or purpose. Now he looked at the small boy, huddled in rags, stirring at his feet. Here was his purpose, here was something worth fighting for, here was some sort of answer to his question of why he had bothered to keep going for so long. If the universe had a plan for him, Danny felt sure it must be this, to save this child.

As morning broke new sounds filled the air. A familiar hum that had once been the backdrop to life in the City rose above their heads. The drones began arriving and leaving The Fort at first light and continued in a steady stream through the day. Danny dared to peek up to the sky from the edge of the clearing. He saw they were delivery drones, each carrying a package of some kind as they flitted overhead. That didn't mean they couldn't be surveillance drones as well. From now on they would have to remain under the tree cover to remain undetected.

He scurried back to where Lucas lay rubbing his eyes and yawning as he woke. 'How are you feeling?' Danny asked. 'Ready for one final effort?' Danny gave him his morning insulin injection, pricking him through the thigh once more. That finished the second vial, they had one remaining. 'I reckon the shuttle should arrive in the next hour or so. We need to be there when it arrives.'

'You mean climb that pillar?'

'Think you can make it?'

'I'll try.'

They ate breakfast, finishing the last of the remaining food they had brought with them. There was no point in rationing now: by the end of today, one way or another, they would have made it to the city. They set off through the undergrowth once more, Danny again leading the way, clearing a path as much as he could to make it easier for Lucas to follow behind him. There could be any number of alarms rigged in the forest that would detect their presence: pressure sensors, trip wires, laser beams and surveillance cameras. Danny had only hope and fate on his side to avoid them. The Fort had not been constructed to defend against an enemy from within the State, but to protect against potential attacks from across the water and from the air. The inland side of the outpost was less guarded than the sea-facing side. If they were detected then a squadron of soldiers with large guns would soon confront them to let them know they were trespassing on State military property.

It took them half an hour to reach the base of the concrete pillar onto which the service ladder was bolted. Lucas had stumbled occasionally. As Danny had picked him up from the soft forest floor after each tumble he could tell the boy was weakening, the exertions of the last day and night were taking their toll.

'I don't think I can climb that ladder,' Lucas told him as they peered through the circular bars that stretched upwards above their heads. About halfway up they could see a small landing that would provide them with a resting place.

'I don't expect you to. I will carry you. Do you think you can hold onto my shoulders?'

'I'll try.'

'Okay,' he gave the boy a reassuring smile, 'come here.' Danny took off his rucksack. From it he removed the syringe and the one remaining vial of insulin and the small cloth pouch with wooden marbles in it. Everything else he left behind, hiding his father's old bag under some branches and leaves. He bent down and allowed Lucas to clamber onto his back, his arms around Danny's neck. He was light, one symptom of the drain of diabetes on his body that for this task at least would be an advantage. The first rung of the ladder was level with Danny's chest. 'Hold on tight,' he said and managed to jump high enough to get one foot on the first rung before pulling himself up. From there it was a long, monotonous climb, one rung at a time. Despite Lucas's slight frame after a few steps the weight of carrying an extra body began to drag against Danny. He gritted his teeth and carried on. He tried to keep reassuring Lucas over his shoulder. 'You doing okay?'

'Yeah,' came the response. Danny could feel Lucas's grip weakening. He took hold of the boy's clasped hands with one of his own and carried on climbing using his other hand. He could see the platform halfway up gradually drawing nearer. The higher above the forest treetops they climbed, the stronger the wind blew around them and gusts forced Danny to stop and hold on tightly to the metal bars. The drones flew above the height of the monorail, so were still well overhead, but the constant buzzing from them grew louder and more menacing.

117

Danny felt the tremor in the pillar as his hand drew level with the landing that would provide them with a rest. It started small, a quiver that grew into a pulsing beat. The frame of the ladder began to shake, a wobble at first developing into a violent shudder. Danny looked up. Further along the monorail he saw the shuttle carriages approaching from the north – it was the first intercity shuttle of the day from HighLand City heading south. He had no idea how long it would stop at The Fort before setting off again. There was no time to stop for a rest.

'You okay back there?' he called. There was no reply. Danny knew Lucas was drifting in and out of consciousness. High or low blood glucose, it didn't matter which, he had to get him onto that shuttle and to the City. Danny redoubled his efforts. He didn't look up but focussed on each rung of the ladder in front of him and climbed as fast as his body would allow him to. The rocking motion of the pillar and ladder decreased and then stopped as the shuttle arrived at the station above them. He could hear the whirring motors turning over and the static of electric current running through the metal monorail. Danny was soaked through with sweat. His hands became slick, slipping on each piece of cool metal as he grasped it. He couldn't wipe his forehead without letting go of the ladder or Lucas and stinging drops of sweat began to drip into his eyes. Still he kept climbing.

Finally he could see the end of the ladder a few rungs above him. His hand reached the solid grey concrete at the top and he heaved himself and his human cargo onto a narrow ledge. Lying on his back, Danny breathed heavily, letting blood flow back into his tired limbs. He looked to the side, between the underside of the carriage and the rail that it rested upon. He saw a series of automated loaders running up and down a ramp, stacking crates of provisions onto the shuttle. There seemed to be an endless line of the metal boxes waiting to be loaded. There was a symbol on the side of each one. It was a yellow triangle with a black image of an exploding shape. Underneath it were clear words in bold yellow stencils: DANGER EXPLOSIVE.

He had no time to wonder why the military outpost would be shipping armaments and explosives to Central City. He picked up the half-asleep Lucas and dragged him along the ledge. He didn't look over the side, where there was a hundred metre drop to the ground below. There was no sign of any soldiers or personnel on the other side of the shuttle, everything was being done by machine. So far their luck seemed to be holding out. He reached the end of the ledge. Just within reach was a manual service entrance: a small, square panel at the bottom of the carriage just wide enough for a person to squeeze through. Even in these modern times of driverless shuttles there was still the need for an engineer to gain access in the event of a mechanical or power failure. He lay Lucas down and began to pull at the handle on the panel. It was stiff but Danny had come too far to be stopped at this stage. Grasping it with both hands he used his entire body weight to wrench the lever downwards. It began to inch round, then suddenly came loose, almost sending Danny sprawling off the narrow ledge. He opened the panel that was hinged on one side and stuck his head through it. Inside the carriage was packed with crates with the same labelling as those he had seen on the platform. There was a small space between

119

the wall and a tower of crates that was just big enough to accommodate them.

He hauled Lucas up and began to push him through the gap headfirst. When he had got the boy inside he noticed the increase in the pitch of the whine from the motor and the change in tone of the electric current under the carriage: the shuttle was about to depart. He jumped forward, getting his head and shoulders through the gap and finding a metal bar inside that he grasped just as the shuttle began to move. His legs were still dangling outside the carriage and his feet dragged along the concrete ledge as the speed of the shuttle increased. He clung on and then felt the ledge disappear from beneath him as the shuttle left the station behind. He was now travelling at a hundred kilometres an hour with a hundred metre drop below his trailing legs which were being buffeted from side to side in the shuttle's slipstream. Gradually he pulled himself inside the carriage. Too late he felt the syringe and vial tipping out of his pocket. He had no way to stop them. They fell into the chasm below. Once inside the carriage Danny reached out and heaved the panel closed, pulling the lever up on the inside to lock it. Then he lay down next to Lucas as the shuttle glided along the monorail towards the city.

The slowing of the shuttle brought Danny round from his slumber. There were no windows in the carriage and he had no idea how long he had been dozing but he guessed it had been for more than an hour and they were now arriving in Central City. Lucas was awake beside him, he looked pale and his hair was matted with sweat.

'Are we here?' he asked, looking up at Danny.

120

'I think so.' The motor slowed and there was the sound of brakes squealing. Danny knew the shuttles only used physical brakes when arriving at the terminals. They were crawling now, coming into a platform at the Central Station. The air in the carriage was arid, Danny could feel a dry scratch in his throat. 'Thirsty?' he asked Lucas, who nodded, 'We'll get a drink as soon as we can.' He could see the boy fading away before him. The previous weeks without a stable supply of insulin had been bad enough. The strain of the journey, the lack of food, water and rest were more than his frail body could take. There was no option now but to get him to the hospital as fast as he could. If it meant his own capture along the way then so be it. He had imagined a scenario, however unlikely, where he had managed to avoid being detected in the city and had escaped back to the village in the north. He had always known it was a long shot. He rubbed the grizzled stubble on his face and looked at his shirt and trousers sprayed with dust, dirt and sweat from their trek through the forest. They would stand out among the well-kempt citizens, a bedraggled man carrying a sick child through the streets. Danny pictured the route he would take from the station to the hospital. It had been a long time since he had set foot in the city but he could still clearly see the streets and buildings that would line their way.

There was a dull thud as the shuttle came to a complete stop, followed by a beep and the doors on the opposite side of the carriage opened. They were hidden by the tower of crates but would be exposed as soon as the loaders began removing them. Danny hauled on the lever and the service panel popped open. He looked through. On this side of the platform they were facing a white wall and there was no one in sight. The towers of

121

crates swayed as a machine collected the first crates and withdrew them. Danny dropped out the access panel and landed on his feet. He was able to reach back in and grab Lucas's feet and pull him down. He closed the panel and carried Lucas along the platform, the carriages of the shuttle gave them cover. At the end of the platform was a barrier that they wouldn't be able to get through but to the side there was a service door. It was their only way out. Danny tried the handle, the door pulled open and he carried Lucas through into a dark corridor beyond.

On the surface the city that Danny emerged into, holding Lucas in his arms, looked the same as the one he had left three years ago. The buildings were still homogenous white cubes arranged in a grid pattern. The sights, smells and sounds were all familiar. Memories of Rosa, his parents, his former life as a police officer, came flooding back to him. Lucas stirred at the barrage of noise created by the numerous drones overhead. A couple of buses whirred past them. On the streets there were more people, more faces, than Danny had seen since the day he walked out of the City. He realised how used he had become to the quiet and solitude. Lucas opened bleary eyes to take in some of his new surroundings. It was all foreign and confusing to him, a mad rush of voices and activity that he had never experienced before. He clung on to Danny tightly as they started moving through the streets.

As they walked Danny began to notice the things that had changed. There were hardly any cars on the roads. He knew about the ban on non-essential travel but had left before experiencing what the city would be like without constant traffic. It left an eerie gap in the landscape of the city. The other thing that stood out were the pieces of graffiti and fly-posters that adorned some of the white walls. There weren't a lot of them, perhaps one or two blighting each city block that he crossed, but in the past there had been none at all. Not only was it illegal to deface State and private property but the punishments were severe and the City clean-up machines would usually dispense of any vandalism within minutes of it appearing. Danny was in too much of a hurry to stop and read exactly what the posters were saying, but he could see that it was the same as the posters that Hassan and his team had brought back to the village. It appeared there was a genuine uprising, however small, against the Central Alliance Party and a campaign to see them defeated at the upcoming elections.

If the State Surveillance cameras still operated as they had when he had been a police officer, then his presence would surely have been picked up by now. He saw the cameras affixed to walls along the streets and on traffic lights and signposts at junctions. Even with weight loss and added stubble his features would still be picked up and matched to his file. All he could do was keep going until someone stopped him. He passed the main square and the ornate City Parliament building and carried on up the steep hill that led to the hospital. He was aware of perplexed looks from citizens they passed. After the variety of people and faces he had become accustomed to in the village it was strange to be back among so many who all looked and dressed similarly: a city of slim, smooth, healthy, well-preserved people. Overhead the expressway that used to be filled with traffic was empty and some citizens were walking across it. Danny staggered up an on-ramp onto a flyover and used it as a shortcut to get to the front doors of the hospital.

The doors slid open and he stumbled through them. There didn't seem to be any security on the doors, no scanning machines or face recognition. He made it to the reception desk. A bank of monitors faced him. He looked around for a human face. Across the foyer an elevator door slid open and a young man stepped out wearing the white scrubs and coat of a doctor. He looked up in surprise from his TouchScreen as Danny shouted and crossed the polished floor towards him, wild-eyed and carrying a small boy in his arms.

'He's got Type-1 Diabetes. He needs insulin,' Danny said. Almost throwing Lucas into the arms of the doctor, whose TouchScreen clattered to the ground as he reached out and took Lucas.

'Diabetes?' the young doctor asked.

'Yes, trust me.'

'Okay, what's his name?' The doctor spun back towards the elevator.

'Lucas,' Danny called. His knees were weak, the adrenalin that had kept him going through the streets seeped away from him and he felt faint. The elevator opened and the doctor entered with Lucas. Danny remembered one last thing. 'Wait,' he called out. The doctor held the doors. Danny staggered forwards and took the small cloth pouch of wooden marbles from his pocket. He pressed them into Lucas's hand. The boy's eyes flickered open and looked at him. 'You made it Lucas, they'll take care of you now.' Danny backed away and the elevator doors closed.

Danny fell backwards and sat on the cold floor of the foyer. What now? He needed some food or a drink but he had nowhere to go and no money. He had been so focussed on getting Lucas to the hospital that he hadn't contemplated what he would do next. His eyes closed as the room began to swim around him, exhaustion taking hold of his body and mind.

When he opened his eyes again he was looking straight into the barrel of a State Police stun gun. On the other end of the gun a young female officer stared at him. Gradually he realised they were not alone, there were several guns pointing at him and several officers aiming them.

It was the young female who seemed to be in charge: 'Daniel Samson, you are under arrest on the charges of treason against the State, abandoning Central City without a permit, dereliction of your duty as a State Police Officer and assaulting a State Officer.'

Danny crumpled into a heap in front of them.

PART THREE:

CENTRAL CITY

3rd JULY

10

It had been tempting to disembark when the shuttle had pulled in to MidLands. She had been in that city before, she had contacts there, it was not the complete unknown that continuing further north represented. Although the State ruled over one unified island, each of the huge megacities represented a unique, individual society. In these days of curfews and restricted travel, the majority of citizens never ventured beyond the walls of their own conurbation. Max was one of the lucky few with work credentials that allowed her to see the rest of her country.

The ticket had arrived in her account two days after the meeting with the man called Phillips. An intercity shuttle journey from the Capital City to Central City. She had had no further communication with Phillips and had not signalled her acceptance of his offer. Her reluctance to be dragged further into the shadowy world of corruption and the potential of worsening her standing with the State authorities held her back for another few days, which she spent confined to her apartment, wrestling with her ambition and journalistic instincts. Eventually, after a week had passed, she could no longer ignore the persistent nagging in her mind. This could be the one chance she had to report on something that truly mattered. There were three days to go before the elections. Hoping her indecision had not ruined the opportunity and she had not left it too late, Max packed a bag sparingly. She left a message with Buzz Mayfield saying she had decided to take his advice and visit her parents on the southern coast until the election was over and she could return to work. It was a lie Buzz could easily expose with one call to her parents' home, but Max felt she could not tell him the truth about her trip north. She sensed if her employer were to learn of her intentions she would find her travel privileges swiftly revoked.

Were the officials at the shuttle terminal eyeing her warily? Ever since the meeting with Phillips and his accusations about the behaviour of the State and the Party, Max had been unable to shake the feeling of paranoia that crept over her. How much of it was in her head? Was she really being kept under surveillance? She breathed easier when she boarded the shuttle that morning and her progress was unhindered. She took a quiet seat next to the window. The carriage, built to seat a hundred people, was empty apart from her and one other man, who smiled courteously at her and moved away to sit at the opposite end. It had been a long time since the intercity shuttle had been filled to capacity, it was used more to carry goods between cities now, rather than people. They left the Capital terminal on schedule and within minutes the crowded white cubes were behind them. The track rose, crossing the perimeter walls and passing the fields of agriculture and farming that ringed the city. Soon they were crossing a green wilderness below. The journey was smooth and uneventful. Max was content to sit and stare at the scenery for the hour it took them to speed over the country and arrive at the MidLands terminal. Every time she had travelled on the shuttle before, this is where she would have disembarked. She fought her instinct to do the same on this occasion. The thought of a few days with her parents by the beach became an attractive proposition once more. Another woman entered the carriage. Max looked round and saw that the man had departed. The woman took his place at the far end. As she passed Max there was no friendly nod between them. Her conflicting thoughts were abruptly ended and her decision made for her by the beeping alarm that signalled the doors were closing and departure was imminent. There was no stop now until they arrived at Central City, there was no turning back from the path she had chosen.

As they headed north the landscape continued to be green, with forests and wilderness stretching to the horizon on both sides of the route. Gradually the topography began to shift from the relatively flat blanket of vegetation to undulating slopes separated by valleys through which the monorail weaved. Large expanses of water became more frequent and the gentle hills developed steeper inclines. Broad-leaved trees changed to coniferous pines. The air-conditioned carriage kept them cool as the sun continued to beat down across the length and breadth of the State. The shuttle climbed over the range of mountains that marked a physical border between the southern and northern halves of the country, before beginning its descent to the lowlands in which Central City nestled. Max had seen images of the scenery from this part of the State before, but now realised how foreign it was compared to the Capital in the south. They may all inhabit the same isle, but this felt like a different place, rugged and untamed in contrast to the gentle rolling terrain of the south.

Max wondered what awaited her in the City. When she had previously visited the MidLands she had noticed how similar the city appeared to her own: the buildings and infrastructure looked identical to that of the Capital and the people dressed and styled themselves identically to their fellow citizens in the south, but the atmosphere was not the same. The people seemed warmer, friendlier, more willing to chat to a stranger. They were less guarded, perhaps purely because they were geographically further away from the overbearing presence of the State machinery and power centred in the Capital. The language, although technically the same, using the same vocabulary, felt different. She was always able to understand the pronunciation and dialect, but words were delivered differently. They seemed to be spoken with a warmth lost in the cold, stiff southern accent - although she detested the way her surname was mangled: the soft purring 'r' replaced by a harsh 't'. It reminded her of how John Curran pronounced her surname. Perhaps she should have asked him for some advice before leaving, he had been born and raised in Central City after all, before he moved to the Capital. It saddened her that she felt she could no longer confide in her old mentor.

Around midday they crested a hill and in the valley below them was the familiar sight of structured farmland, fields of green crops and vast areas of grazing occupied by cattle and sheep. The fields rolled away until they hit a vast wall that rose incongruously from the sea of green. Beyond the wall the uniform white buildings familiar to all the State cities sprawled out. The monorail descended down the hillside, rushing over the farmland and city walls. The buildings passed by in a white blur until the shuttle finally began to decrease speed. They crossed the main river, dominated on one side by two tall chimneys that towered over the rest of the city which Max recognised as the State Arms Factory. Without ceremony they arrived at the terminal and the doors opened. It had taken the shuttle only three hours to transport her to her destination.

Along with the shuttle ticket, Phillips had made a reservation for Max at a hotel in the centre of the city. She picked up her small carrier case and left the shuttle, stepping out onto the platform. The station felt familiar, the design and signage uniform to the décor of the Capital terminal from which she had departed that morning. Large monitors around the station were broadcasting the State news channel. The image of State Chancellor Lucinda Románes loomed out from the screens, her voice echoing around the terminal building, as she gave another speech ahead of the upcoming elections. Beneath her the citizens of Central City carried on without paying much attention to the propaganda that filled the air. The speech ended and a virtual newsreader took over, informing everyone of the election that was now only two days away, and reminding all that voting was compulsory.

Emerging from the main entrance she stood among the architecture of the State. Citizens walked past, buses and taxis travelled along clean, wide streets and drones buzzed over the rooftops. There was no hint of election fever or a rising rebellion on the street. It felt like a normal uneventful day in any State city. Max realised she had been expecting something more and actually felt deflated at the mundane scene that she now saw. She took out her TouchScreen and looked up directions to the hotel.

It was not far and it took her only five minutes to walk the short distance from the station. The hotel looked ordinary, a typical three floor rectangle of white

131

walls dotted with square windows. The slide doors to the hotel were wedged open, Max assumed to allow fresh air into the foyer, although the air on the street was humid and still. The Registration Scanner was located just inside the door. Max placed her hand on the black screen and waited for the laser beam to confirm her identity. Nothing happened. On closer inspection she saw that the machine had no power. She looked around the empty foyer. It was shabby and in need of freshening up. There was a desk at the far end with a note stuck to the side which read: 'Ring Bell For Attention.' Max pressed the small gold bell on the desk. A sharp 'ting' called out and she heard motion in the small room behind the reception desk. A door at the back opened and out walked an elderly man, smartly dressed in a short-sleeved shirt and navy blue suit trousers. In one hand he carried a small battery-powered fan that he held under his face for the entirety of their conversation.

'Yes, madam, how can I help you?' He spoke to her like a grandfather speaking to a child. Being referred to as 'madam' took Max aback, the archaic form of address with gender assumptions had long been out of use.

'The scanner at the front door seems to be broken.'

'Not broken, love. No power,' he eyed her warily now, peering over the top of his SmartLenses at her. 'Your accent – not from around here, are you?'

'I travelled up from the Capital today. I have a reservation. Maxine Aubert,' she offered.

'Must be important if you're allowed to travel across the State like that. Bigwig, are you?'

'I'm a journalist.'

The old man grumbled something unintelligible under his breath, 'Well, not sure how you've ended up staying here,' he gestured disparagingly to the surroundings. 'We have a timetable operating throughout the city now for power. Our grid is switched off between ten in the morning and five in the evening, so if you want hot water or hot food you have to get up early enough or wait until the evening. Same with the doors on the rooms and in and out of the hotel. They are fitted with electronic scanner locks, so they only work when they have power. Rest of the time, don't leave anything valuable lying around.'

'This happens every day?'

'For the last six months now. Rumour is it'll be the food and water that gets rationed next, but they won't announce anything about that until after the elections. No wonder people are starting to complain. Now, what did you say your name was, dear?'

'Maxine Aubert,' Max repeated. The man took out a pencil and opened an old style ledger. He scribbled her name down. 'With a 't' on the end,' she corrected him.

'Room 2C, up two floors at the end of the corridor. You'll have to take the stairs, no power in the elevators either. It'll be stuffy in there with the heat. No air-con and the electric windows will be shut until the power comes back on too.'

'You say people are starting to complain. I heard there were protests happening in the city.'

The hotel owner raised his head and stared at her. Max's soft smile and empathetic eyes reassured him. 'There have been some small gatherings. A few posters around the place. Not that it will do much good,' he shrugged. 'Maybe a couple of independents will be elected, maybe it will make the Party listen. Probably won't make much difference. I reckon I shan't be around to see much change.'

'Where do they have these gatherings?'

'The main square, in front of the City Parliament building.' He looked at her with kindly eyes, 'I would watch out if I were you. I wouldn't be going down there looking for trouble.'

'Has there been much trouble?'

'Not so far, but you can feel the tension all around. This heat doesn't help. Tempers are getting frayed. It will only take one spark and the State will respond.'

Max could see the worry in the man's face as he contemplated what a State reprisal against unruly citizens would entail. He must be in his nineties, she thought, he would have lived with the unchallenged power of the Party for his entire adult life. She thanked him and he shuffled away, through the door at the back of his small office, wafting the handheld fan across his sweating brow.

She climbed the unwelcoming concrete grey stairs, designed only to be used as an emergency exit, and walked along a threadbare carpet to her room at the end of the corridor on the second level. The view out of the window was the white wall of the neighbouring building. As the proprietor had predicted, the room was stifling, hot and smelled of musty sweat. There was a sink in the corner of the small ensuite toilet room and she splashed cold water onto her face. Her instructions were to wait until she was contacted, presumably by Phillips or one of his group. She sat on the hard bed and idly flicked through the latest election coverage on her TouchScreen. The face of Lucinda Románes stared back at her. She seemed to be haunting Max's every move. Even this far north, there was no escaping the reach of the Central Alliance Party and the State.

Henrik James sat with his head in his hands. He had known better days. As if the growing unrest among the citizens of Central City wasn't bad enough, the prisoner in the cell several floors below his office in the State Police headquarters was an added complication he could have done without. Apart from the question of what to do with his ex-partner next, the reappearance of Detective Daniel Samson brought back memories of how Henrik had come to be Chief Commander of the State Police in the city. His father, Lars James, had once held the same office until he had become embroiled in the investigation into the death of Consul Donald Parkinson. It had ended with the assassin Gabriella Marino brutally killing the Chief Commander and escaping from this very building. Henrik had been in hospital at the time, recovering from a gunshot wound. He rubbed his chest now, sensing where the bullet had entered his lung, although cosmetic surgery had removed any trace of scar tissue. When the dust had settled Henrik was given a choice: continue to serve the State with a guaranteed promotion within the police force, or do what his ex-partner had done and desert the State and the city and face a life in exile. In accepting his new role as Superintendent, Henrik signed a non-disclosure contract that forbade him to ever discuss the circumstances around the death of Consul Parkinson. The punishment for breaking this contract was written into it: death. Henrik had discovered the evil that had been committed in the name of the State and the Party. His own father had been implicated in the cover-up of the murder of

135

innocent children. He was determined to stay and make sure such a thing never happened in Central City again. Within a few months his old boss, Chief Commander Michaels, was transferred to the Capital and Henrik found himself occupying the most powerful law enforcement position in the city. It had not come without its challenges. It had fallen to Henrik and the State Police to keep the populace calm as the energy crisis worsened, power rationing was rolled out and cutbacks began to impact on the citizens' way of life. He felt he had managed the situation well. There had been a small rise in crime statistics, mainly theft related to energy production and the odd anomalous arrest for civil disobedience, but generally the city had continued to function in an orderly manner.

That was until the decennial elections had loomed over the horizon. The protests had been minimal at first. It was not illegal for citizens to stand as independent candidates in the elections and to run campaigns in order to attract votes. Gradually, the rhetoric of the campaigns began to turn into attacks on the Central Alliance Party and the State, something that was expressly forbidden. The dissent had grown louder and then the gatherings had started. They were small in the beginning, forty to fifty people with placards and signs appearing in the main city square each day. Henrik had contacted State Command in the Capital City seeking their guidance in dealing with the matter. He was relieved when they had replied that no direct action was to be taken against the protestors. Instead he was to mount an intelligence gathering operation, learn who the individuals were, identify the ringleaders, and then once the elections were out of the way, appropriate legal punishments would be enforced. Henrik was in favour of any course of action that avoided violence and bloodshed on the streets of the city. It wasn't the response he had expected from his superiors, but he wasn't about to disagree with them.

However, when the citizens saw the police were not halting the protests and were allowing the gatherings to continue without reprisal, the protestors had been emboldened. The size of the gatherings grew: now there were over a hundred people camped outside the City Parliament. Messages of defiance began appearing on buildings and signs around the city and, due to cutbacks and energy saving measures, the cleaning machines were unable to erase all of them. Again he contacted his superiors, again their answer remained the same – gather intelligence, wait until after the elections before acting. Thus far his detectives had been unsuccessful in gathering any useful intelligence about the protestors. They knew who the legitimate independent candidates standing in the elections in two days were, but they appeared to have no links to the group of protestors. The original gathering involved a few like-minded citizens who came together organically, but the subsequent escalation appeared to have been organised, planned by someone who wished to see the protests grow. The police had been unable to infiltrate the group with any degree of success in order to determine who this individual or group was.

The protests continued unabated and Henrik counted down the days until the election was over and, he hoped, the whole situation would dissipate, running out of steam as another victory for the Central Alliance Party would reassert the authority of the State. If the protestors retreated so too might the threatened recriminations of the State towards them. When his ex-partner had wandered in from the wilderness, Henrik's already troubled mind had a new conundrum to contemplate.

***

He had been at home when he had received the call. A traitor from the wilderness had been captured after entering the city. Henrik complained there was no need to disturb him at his home for such a trivial matter. He chided his captain and instructed him to follow the established procedure for dealing with such criminals. Although not a common occurrence, it was not unknown for a citizen to try to enter the city illegally, particularly a deserter who had discovered that life in the wilderness was not as noble or gratifying as they had expected it to be. The crime was considered serious and carried with it a punishment of life imprisonment or the death penalty in order to dissuade any other citizens from making a similar choice.

The captain managed to interrupt Henrik, 'I thought you would like to be informed about the identity of the traitor, Chief Commander.'

'Why should I care about the identity of such a person?' Henrik asked indignantly.

'Well, Chief Commander, we have a positive identification that this traitor is your former partner, Daniel Samson.'

Such a high-profile deserter reappearing forced Henrik to contact the Capital City headquarters once again, and this time their response was unequivocal: Daniel Samson was to be executed, without trial, without questioning, and without being allowed to come into contact with any other citizen of the city.

It had been a week since Henrik had received his orders and still Danny Samson sat in solitary confinement in a holding cell. He could not remain alive there for much longer before the Party would lose patience and start to ask questions, or even take direct action.

An hour after his captain had called to inform him of Danny Samson's reappearance, Henrik James entered the interrogation cell in police headquarters, dressed in full uniform, and sat down opposite the traitor he barely recognised as his former partner. They had never been close friends while working together, they had only been partners for a brief time, but they had been partners nonetheless and for that reason he felt some empathy for the man slumped in the chair, his hands cuffed to the table.

'Have you been given some food? Something to drink?' Danny shook his head. Henrik pressed a call button on the desk and asked for water and food supplements to be brought in. He took off his hat and laid it down on the table, on top of his TouchScreen. 'You've lost weight.'

'New fitness regime,' Danny managed a weak smile and nodded to the braids and stripes on Henrik's uniform. 'I see you've moved up in the world. Following in your father's footsteps?'

Henrik heard the touch of malice in Danny's comment. 'Some of us chose not to run away but to stay and do our duty to protect the citizens of this city.'

'With a nice little promotion to keep you quiet about daddy's dodgy past. I hear he was buried with full State honours.'

'I'm not my father,' Henrik said, his jaw tightening. There was more he wanted to share with Danny, but he was aware that the interrogation room was monitored and recorded at all times. 'So tell me, why have you come back to the city?'

'The boy I brought with me, where is he?'

'He's in the hospital, they're taking care of him.'

'What will happen to him?'

'He is now under my personal protection. He will be looked after until a suitable home can be found for him.' Danny stared hard at Henrik, looking directly into his eyes, trying to discern if he was being told the truth. 'You may not believe it,' Henrik continued, 'but in my position I am able to do some good. I have the power to help citizens who need protection.'

There was a pause as a glass of water and two food pills were brought in and placed in front of Danny. When the door closed behind the messenger again, Henrik stood and walked round the table. He unlocked the handcuffs that chained Danny to the table, enabling him to swallow the pills and gulp down the full glass of cool water. Henrik resumed his own seat and waited for him to finish.

'I'll ask again. Why have you come back to the city?'

'The boy was ill.'

'No one else could have brought him to the city?' Danny didn't reply. Henrik picked up his TouchScreen and flicked it on. He opened up a folder of photographs and selected one before turning the screen and showing it to Danny. 'Did you really think you would have got this far without being spotted?'

Danny looked at the image. It was a picture of himself and Lucas taken outside The Fort, at the base of the monorail pillar. Henrik flicked the screen and Danny saw another image, this time Lucas and he were lying inside the carriage of the intercity shuttle. Another swipe of the screen and Danny was walking through the city streets carrying Lucas. Another swipe and there was the hospital foyer, with Danny on his knees as the doctor took Lucas from his arms.

'Your identity was confirmed soon after the shuttle had left The Fort. Our intelligence department was notified and kept a close eye on your progress, ready to intervene if it looked like you were a threat. Have the years in the wilderness really made you so naïve that you thought you could walk undetected into the centre of the city?'

'It was for the boy,' Danny repeated.

Henrik sighed, 'That may be so, Danny, but it's the State elections in less than a month. You see how your sudden reappearance will make some people nervous.'

'Why should I make them nervous, Henrik? Are you suggesting I may know something that they would like kept secret?'

Henrik ignored the sarcasm, 'Don't make this any worse for yourself than it already is, Danny. You know that there are those who will want you to face immediate punishment.'

'So kill me. Do their bidding like a good loyal soldier.'

'Believe me, if I wanted an easy life, I would do exactly that.' Henrik tried to communicate to Danny with a look that he hoped would not be picked up on the surveillance cameras. Was Danny getting his meaning?

It had been while Henrik was driving from his home to the headquarters an hour earlier that he had received the message, not on his official TouchScreen device, but on the other, unregistered one that had been delivered to him not long after he had returned to active duty as a police officer three years ago. Since he had received the device he had only been contacted sporadically. Usually he was only asked to provide information or statistics. Nothing he had been asked to do had made him question his conscience. He served the State with distinction, while secretly providing facts and figures that undermined official State press releases to the small group of agitators. He had no idea how they had learned about Danny's arrest so quickly but the message was simple: keep Samson alive, they would make arrangements. Unlike any of the previous messages he had received, this one was not anonymous, it had a signature: Phillips.

Henrik had long suspected that the secretive agent he had only known for a brief time was behind the fledgling protest movement. He was well aware that he had been targeted by the ex-State agent because of his position and rank within the force, and because, like Phillips and Danny, Henrik had learned the true nature of those in power within the State. Unlike Danny, Henrik had remained, to fight for change from within the institutions that enforced that corrupt power, and that made him valuable to someone like Phillips. Now his true test was beginning. He had done what he could to help the citizens of the State, now he sensed the time was coming when he would have to choose where his real loyalties lay.

'You understand that I am all that lies between you and the full weight of State law?' he tried to make his point to Danny again without incriminating himself to those who were sure to be listening in.

'You mean this State law?' Danny reached out and took the TouchScreen from Henrik before he could react. He scrolled back through the images Henrik had shown him, stopping at the photo of Lucas and Danny crouched in the shuttle carriage. He pointed at the crates in the corner of the image. Henrik peered at the screen. Danny handed the TouchScreen back to him. Henrik's eyes widened. He used his fingers to zoom in to the edge of the screen that Danny had pointed out to him. On the crates there was a symbol and some words. They were blurred but still readable. 'I'm not the only thing that arrived on that shuttle this morning that you should be worried about.'

***

He had kept an eye on Danny discreetly over the following fortnight. He was sure the State would try to silence Samson if Henrik had not already done so. He couldn't compromise himself further by insisting on special protection or treatment for a traitor to the State. Further contact between him and his ex-partner would only attract more suspicion. He ensured the cells were guarded by officers he could trust, but the State commanded more loyalty than he ever could and before long they would find someone or someway to snuff out the threat that Danny posed. He kept checking the

143

unregistered TouchScreen, waiting for some sign that Phillips had a plan.

After Danny's revelation, he had ordered a check on all manifests for deliveries into the city in the previous days. There was no record of any explosives or weapons being moved on the intercity shuttle or by any other means. It was a legal requirement that any such goods should have approved documentation and that the local State authority should be notified. In Central City that meant the Chief Commander of the State Police. He knew the crates had been loaded at The Fort, which meant State Security Forces were transporting weapons into the city, his city, and they were doing so without telling him. The orders could only have come from the Capital, from the Senate, from the Defence Ministry and with the knowledge of those at the very top. Henrik couldn't be sure for what reason they would be arming forces in Central City, but his gut told him it would not come to any good.

Finally, this morning another message had arrived on his illegal TouchScreen. It was vague and unsigned. He assumed it was from Phillips. All it said was to make sure he was absent from police headquarters that afternoon. Picking up his uniform hat, he exited his office. He informed the captain he was heading to the City Parliament to inspect the demonstration. There was nothing suspicious in him making a visit there.

11

Early afternoon passed without any word. Max grew bored sitting in the stuffy hotel room, constantly checking her messages to see if anyone had been in touch. There was nothing to stop her heading out to explore the city on her own. If Phillips wanted to get hold of her, she was sure he would be able to find her. She changed into a fresh light t-shirt and linen trousers. She took her TouchScreen with her, but apart from that had nothing of value that couldn't be left in the unlocked room.

The old man was not at the reception desk when she left the hotel, but it didn't take Max long to find a sign directing her towards the City Parliament. As she picked her way along the straight streets that sloped downhill, turning at right angles at each junction, she began to notice the hints of protest Phillips had told her about. In a State where no one ever questioned those in power, it didn't take much for a protest, however small, to be noticed. The posters were not massive and they were not widespread, but they were there, and it was more open dissent towards the Party than Max had ever seen before. She used her TouchScreen to photograph a few of them as she passed.

The nearer she drew towards the City Parliament, the more she sensed the unusual tension in her surroundings. There was a low murmur of sound ahead that grew with each city block she traversed. Although she had been told about the demonstration, Max was unprepared for what she saw when she turned the corner and found herself in the main square of the city.

On the far side, standing tall and ornate over the scene below, was the Georgian-era building that housed the parliament. In front of the steps that led up to the entrance was a scene that the old building would not have witnessed for decades, if not centuries. It was such an unusual sight that Max would only have believed it was a re-creation of a past event, as though she had travelled back through history. It was hard to estimate how many citizens made up the crowd that stood in the square. In the centre was the core group of protestors. They chanted slogans, being led by someone with some sort of loudhailer or megaphone. They held homemade signs, crafted from everyday material like cardboard or bedsheets, with slogans painted on them: 'The Party has Left Us Powerless'; 'End the War, Save the Planet'; 'Romános – *Cui Bono*?' They faced the parliament building and called for change. Surrounding this diehard group were other citizens who stood apart but appeared to be sympathetic to the message being sent towards the ruling chamber. Cowed for so long, and aware of the illegality of what was occurring, some clearly backed the sentiment of the protest but were reluctant to cross the Rubicon into open criminality. What amazed Max further was the presence around the square of the police cordon: officers, in full riot protection suits and holding shields, who simply stood and watched the crowd in front of them flagrantly break State laws that banned civil protest, gatherings of this size and dissent towards the ruling Party and Senate. They could easily overwhelm the unarmed group in front of them, silence their voices and clear the square within minutes, so why didn't they?

146

Max's experience as a journalist told her the answer: politics. At the moment this situation was contained, State news wasn't reporting it anywhere, the protest did not extend beyond those who saw it in the centre of the city. With the election looming, the Party would be more than happy to keep the situation under control in this way. If the police were to attack unarmed citizens, causing injury and perhaps death, it could escalate into a major story, one that the mainstream State media could continue to ignore, but which would inevitably spread throughout the other cities of the State. Max had seen the polling data: the Party did not wish to invite any more negative coverage two days before the election. The protest could continue so long as it remained at this manageable scale, non-violent and limited. Any crackdown could wait until such time as the Party had returned to a sure-footing following the election.

What Phillips had told her in the car park basement was true. This was more than the rumours and murmurings she had reported on in the MidLands. This was an underground resistance in its infancy, this was open revolt on the streets against State rule, fuelled by disgruntled citizens who had reached the end of their patience with a Party that was failing them. She had already witnessed how the energy crisis had affected Central City in a way that the Capital had been sheltered from. Support for the First Strike War was still reported by the State News media to be strong but there was no evidence of that outside of the Capital. The feeling was less unequivocal among citizens living where shortages in food and power were taking their toll. How much this crowd of gathered citizens represented the larger populace of Central City remained for Max to investigate, but it was clear that she was witnessing something that was unimaginable in the south of the State, near to the seat of power.

She weaved through the crowd. She was met with smiles. The protestors seemed to be enjoying themselves, buoyed up by being able to express their opinions without reprisal. There was almost a carnival atmosphere within the group, though there was no doubting the seriousness of their complaints and the earnestness of their intent. The mass was made up of individuals of all ages and types: men, women and everything in between; old and young; families who had brought children; workers in uniforms and fashionable students. She made her way to the middle, where she could see the cheerleader, fist raised as she belted out another chant against the State and encouraged those around her to follow her lead. There were whistles and drums – musical instruments that had completely fallen out of use in the age of digital music creation. They provided a live, raw soundtrack to the noisy scene.

She dared to snap some images with her TouchScreen, aware that both the State and the protesters would probably prefer there was no record of this incident, but no one objected and she noticed others doing the same, some were even recording movies of the event. Craning her neck she could see over the front few rows, beyond the black helmets of the police cordon and up the steps to the front of the parliament building. At the main entrance she spotted a group of onlookers. One in particular caught her eye. She raised her TouchScreen and captured an image of them. Zooming in on the still she found the man she had spotted. It was the excess of braid and stripes that caught her eye. Now she could see the face of the man wearing the uniform and she recognised the Central City Chief Commander Henrik James. The story of his father's murder and his subsequent rise to fill the same position within the police force was a story that had filtered its way down to the Capital City. Much of what happened in the north went unobserved and unreported, but news of a heroic State servant rising above personal tragedy to do their duty made for good propaganda. The Commander appeared to be in discussion with security personnel from the Parliament. There was nothing suspicious about his presence there and Max moved on, circling around the group once more. Her next task was to try and speak to some of the people brave enough to defy State law, and get them to talk to her on the record.

She waited until she had seen Henrik James leave the police headquarters before approaching the main entrance. This was the riskiest part of the plan. It relied on good fortune, which she never liked to be in thrall to. She placed her hand on the scanner. The laser beam swept across the screen: 'Identity confirmed: Cassandra Ford. Proceed' flashed across the panel. She stepped forward to the next scanner and the procedure was repeated with a laser sweeping across her eyes. Again, Cassandra Ford was identified and cleared to enter. The fact that she wasn't Cassandra Ford and had used fake skin to cover her palm and synthetic contact lenses on her eyes proved any security system based entirely on computer software and artificial intelligence was fallible. Her plan would succeed or fail now based entirely on the facial recognition ability of human beings. If anyone knew what Cas Ford really looked like, they would spot the imposter in seconds. The desk sergeant barely looked up as she passed. He had become too trusting of the computer's ability to screen arrivals at the main desk. When he did cast a glance in her direction he saw only the familiar blonde, shoulder length hair and the uniform of a pathologist as she advanced down the corridor.

Now she had to work fast. Facial recognition would be scanning the camera feed from the main entrance and when that check revealed the face that was supposed to belong to Cas Ford was in fact someone completely different, alarms would start to sound. She followed the floor plan she had memorised. She had been in this building once before and knew where the cells were. She proceeded along the corridor to the elevators. Once inside the lift she shed the lab coat and removed the gun from her belt. Phillips had assured her that Henrik had been told nothing except to make sure the guards around the cells that afternoon were not people he valued highly.

The bright white walls of the prison cell and the stark light from the single bulb above were giving Danny a searing headache. He was losing track of how long he had been held in isolation now. A week? Ten days? The only interruption had been the short interview with Henrik soon after he had first arrived. Apart from that he had been kept confined to the same room, with food and drink delivered to him through a hatch in the metal door. He had no idea what fate awaited him. Did anyone even know he was being kept there? The State could simply make him disappear and no one would ever be aware of what had happened to him. He was rested after his journey through the wilderness, but still felt weak from the frugal diet and inhospitable environment in which he was kept. The guards around his cell had not spoken to him, but neither did they appear vindictive or hostile towards him. All he could do was sit in the cell and contemplate the likelihood that the rest of his life would be spent living this way, for however short that life may be.

The midday meal was brought round. Danny could hear the trundle of the robotic trolley approaching along the corridor and the slots to the neighbouring cell doors opening and closing as trays of food were delivered. When the machine reached his door the slot at head height flicked open. Danny caught the eyes peering in at him. He felt a chill run down his spine. This was not the established routine. The robotic porter was usually unaccompanied. The eyes that looked at him did not belong to any of the guards who had been monitoring him over the last few days. Instead of the food slot opening there was a heavier metallic sound. The locking mechanism of the cell door opened. Something was wrong. He backed into the far corner of the cell as the door swung inwards. A huge man stepped through the doorway. Whoever he was, he did not look like a kitchen worker. He towered over Danny and his uniform strained to contain his broad muscles. In his hand he held not a tray of food but a cord of flex cable. It took him only three paces to cover the length of the cell. Danny tried to anticipate the first attack, countering with a weave and throwing a punch that landed against the unyielding jaw of his assailant. The man swatted him aside like a bothersome fly. His huge paw gripped Danny's head, pushing his face into the wall of the cell. Danny could feel the pressure on his skull as it was crushed by the vice-like grip. He felt the loop of cable slip over his head.

Desperately he scrabbled at it with his hands, trying to stop it from coiling round his neck. With a firm slap, Danny's head rocked backwards. He felt the noose start to tighten.

Stepping out of the elevator she crouched low and began methodically moving through the corridors until she reached the secure unit where the prisoner cells were located. The building seemed empty, perhaps because manpower was stretched by the protests happening in the city, or a sign that Henrik had done as he was asked. However, there could be no compromise with personnel numbers on prisoner guard duty. That was outwith even the Chief Commander's control. She removed the blonde wig and took a deep breath. Phillips's instructions ran through her head one final time: no unnecessary casualties, use the minimum force required. Military planners and officers always used language like that. Those in the field knew the reality during any operation was never so straightforward. There was no window in the door that led into the secure unit, she would be going in blind. She checked the code written on her sleeve and punched the series of numbers into the entry panel. The door buzzed and clicked open – again Henrik had delivered. She stepped through the door.

The duty sergeant had only a second to look up before the bullet entered his clavicle, shattering the bone and sending him sprawling backwards from his desk onto the floor. She moved past him without looking back. She had expected more of a guard presence, something didn't feel right. She began to run along the passageway. Closed doors were on either side of her. She turned a corner and saw a man standing outside an open cell. He had his weapon raised and ready, pointing through the door. She knew this was the cell she was looking for. The man in the corridor turned towards her and started to shout something but was silenced before he could finish a word. Two bullets burst through his kneecaps and he crumpled to the floor, rolling in agony. In the seconds it took him to fall she was upon him, delivering a hard kick to his face for good measure, rendering him unconscious. She looked into the cell. She saw the broad back of a man towering over a smaller person. The huge man was looking over his shoulder, alerted by the gunshots and confused by his fallen colleague, but he had not stopped trying to complete his task. He still held the cord around the prisoner's neck, strangling him.

Danny could feel his face about to explode as the pressure increased. Blood was unable to flow in or out of his brain. He knew he would blackout soon. Just as his eyes were closing he felt the hesitation and a slackening of the cable. Then it fell away completely. The weight of the huge man landed on top of Danny at the same time as he felt the spray of warm liquid cover his face and splat against the back wall of the cell. Gasping in the welcome oxygen he pushed the body away from him. The red blood and grey brain matter were pooling around him.

'Come on,' a voice urged him, 'we need to move.'

He looked up from the beckoning gun being waved at him into the woman's face. 'You!' he exclaimed.

'Let's go.' Gabriella replied. She leaned forward and pulled him up. Danny swore there was a smile on her face as they raced out of the cell.

12

Max saw the State Police car arrive and the officer approach Chief Commander James with urgency on the steps of the parliament. After a few words Henrik James jogged down the steps with the officer and into the car, which set off in haste. Something had happened, the face of the Commander looked tense.

She felt a hand on her arm at the exact same moment as the police car disappeared. 'Glad you finally made it,' Phillips said into her ear, 'I was expecting you sooner. Been taking in some of the sights?'

'Gathering evidence,' Max replied without looking round and trying not to sound startled.

'There is still a chance for you to write something before the election, although if you had started gathering evidence a couple of days earlier it would have made it easier to get it published in time.'

She allowed herself to be led through the crowd. 'You wouldn't happen to know why the Chief Commander of the police has just rushed away, would you?' she called to him as he pulled her along.

'You're very observant, Ms. Aubert. I hope those sharp eyes have been taking in everything you have seen so far.' They reached the edge of the square and disappeared into a narrow alleyway, separating an old sandstone building from a smooth modern office cube. Phillips glanced backwards to ensure they had not been followed. At the end of the alley was a brick wall which appeared to be a dead end. When they reached it Phillips placed his hand on a patch of brickwork that was slightly discoloured. A section of wall with unnoticeable edges receded and slid to the side. They slipped through the gap and the opening slid shut behind them.

'Where are we going?' Max asked as they walked along another passageway.

'I promised you the chance to talk to an ex-officer who will go on record for your story.'

'The one trapped inside a police cell.'

'Not anymore he isn't.'

Only when they were clear of the police building could Danny catch his breath. Gabriella hadn't needed his help to clear a path for them to flee. From the cells she had dragged him down the fire escape staircase. She had blown off the lock of any door that barred their way with a volley of bullets from her semi-automatic, before battering it down with one or two shoulder charges. At the bottom of the stairs they had stumbled across two officers who had the misfortune to be on a break when Gabriella had burst through the door. Both would regain consciousness soon enough and the broken bones in their legs and arms would heal in time. She knew her exit route exactly, Danny assumed she must have had some inside help. She helped lift Danny and toppled him over the metal fence at the rear of the building before effortlessly vaulting over it herself. They landed next to what looked like a plain AutoTaxi, a uniform grey coupé with a yellow light on the roof. When they got inside it was apparent that it had no AutoDrive function and was a manual car that existed without any link to the computerised world. Gabriella took the wheel and drove off calmly, merging into the street and joining the other

155

AutoTaxis of identical colour and appearance that transported citizens around the city. Danny took in the face that had featured in his dreams in various guises since their last meeting. Sometimes the olive-skinned face was a calming presence in his subconscious, the sea-green eyes beamed at him, comforted him, supported him, sometimes she was on his side. On other nights she appeared like a demon, the eyes on fire, the face taunting him. She was dressed in combat clothing and had pulled a black baseball cap over her short chestnut-coloured hair. She looked the same as when he had last seen her, handcuffed to a desk in police headquarters after he had arrested her three years ago.

'Why are you here?' he asked.

She kept her eyes on the road, 'Someone told me you needed rescuing.'

'Who?'

'A mutual friend.'

'Are we going to meet them now?' Danny only received a smile in response. He tried changing the subject to another of the hundred questions that was racing through his mind. 'What happened to you?'

'You mean after you left me chained to a desk to be murdered by your old boss?'

'You killed him.' Danny thought of Commander Lars James. His body had been found in Danny's office in police headquarters where Gabriella was being held. She had disappeared into the night like a ghost, never to be seen again, until now. He had known, as the State did, that Gabriella had killed Lars James and escaped. Danny recalled the butchered body. He had been a big, powerful man. His corpse was reduced to a bloody, mangled pulp, his skull pummelled and misshapen. It was hard to imagine Gabriella had been responsible for all that damage, but Danny had seen how brutal and violent the assassin sitting next to him could be.

'It was self-defence,' Gabriella said, 'not that I would expect any State official to accept that as a legal position.' The office had been destroyed, desks and chairs upended and smashed, signs that a violent fight had occurred. Who had started it was never determined.

'And then you just disappeared? Was it you who killed Nelson and Donovan?' Danny had read about the murders of the Vice-Chancellor and the Defence Secretary in the days after Gabriella's escape.

Gabriella thought before deciding to answer. 'Someone had to do something.'

'And Phillips?' Danny asked. The agent, who had saved Danny's life the same night that Gabriella escaped, had also disappeared at the same time as the assassin.

'He also felt something needed to be done.'

They had left the centre of the city now and were heading east along the highway that connected the two coasts of Central City, lined with row after row of white buildings.

'Why did you rescue me?'

'Just following orders.'

'You're still an assassin-for-hire?'

'I haven't killed anyone yet.'

'Tell that to the guy lying in my prison cell.'

'You're complaining?' Danny felt the welt that had formed in a ring around his neck where the flex cable had been. 'My orders were not to kill anyone,' Gabriella looked at him now, 'aren't you glad I used my initiative?'

With a sudden movement the car dived off the highway and through a narrow maintenance gap in the

157

wall that bordered the road. They followed a narrow, paved track that ran parallel to the main road until it dipped down into a valley. The highway continued above them, a bridge on concrete pillars carrying it across the river that lay at the foot of the slope. The track ran down to the edge of the river. Gabriella continued along it as it became rougher before disappearing as it reached the water's edge. She turned the car and drove parallel to the river, across long grass and foliage until they were directly under the overpass. The vehicle skidded to a stop next to the base of a large concrete support that carried the road overhead.

'Out,' she ordered. Danny got out of the car. He looked around. The ubiquitous white houses were still visible in the distance, but they had not encroached onto the river's flood plain. There was another car, identical to the one Gabriella had driven, parked under the bridge. 'Follow me.' She walked towards the concrete base. Danny had assumed they were solid, but he now saw there was a door in the side of it, some sort of maintenance hatch, he thought. It had an old-fashioned handle on the outside which Gabriella turned to pull the door open.

They stepped inside. The thick concrete of the outside walls was replicated in the grey interior, a corridor ran through the rectangular base. At the end of that was another door which Gabriella led him through. They were now under the rock that formed the hillside of the valley. The corridor sloped downwards at a shallow angle, gradually taking them further underground. It widened into a curved archway formed by corrugated iron panels. They had entered some sort of bunker made from connecting tunnels, dug into the natural landscape. Along the side of the tunnel were various doors. Gabriella stopped and waited. Further along a door opened and they walked towards it.

'What is this place?' Danny asked, trailing behind her.

'An old State military installation, built before the First Strike War began. It was designed to be used as a base if there was an attack on Central City. It was mothballed years ago when it became clear that was never going to happen.'

'How could they be sure Central City wouldn't be attacked?' Danny had always believed his city was a strategic target for any of their adversaries in the war. That was what the State had told them. It was home to the biggest arms factory in the State which supplied their military forces with the majority of its armaments. Gabriella declined to answer his question. They reached the door that had opened and stepped through it, entering a vast hall. Desks and chairs covered in sheets and a coating of thick dust filled the room. A solitary lightbulb was working, hovering over a desk in the far corner. At the desk sat a young woman with her arms folded. She was slim, her light-brown hair was tied up in a ponytail and she wore a blouse. In front of her on the table lay an old-fashioned spiral notepad and pencil.

'Enjoy,' said Gabriella and stepped back out of the room, closing the door behind her before Danny could ask what was happening.

Max stared at the balding, grizzled man who had been left standing at the door. He looked bewildered, his mouth open, gaping at her. 'You look as puzzled as I was,' she said, her voice carrying across the empty echo chamber. He didn't answer. 'Please tell me you are Daniel Samson and this hasn't been a complete waste of time?'

Danny found his voice, 'I'm Danny Samson.'

'Well, why don't you come over and sit down?'

'Who exactly are you?' Danny asked.

'Max Aubert.'

'Is that supposed to mean something to me?'

'Probably not, I'm a journalist.' Max almost said 'was' instead of 'am'. She had a feeling her career was already unsalvageable, certainly with the main State media companies. Danny still hadn't moved from the doorway. 'You want some water? There may even be coffee.'

'Water's fine,' Danny replied and began approaching the desk behind which the woman sat. 'Why am I here?'

Max gestured to the seat opposite her. Danny sat while she stood and poured him a cup of water from a dispenser. 'Don't worry, it's fresh,' she said, placing the paper cup in front of him. 'I get the impression some of the other rooms in this shelter are used more frequently than this one.' She let Danny take a long sip before answering his question. 'We have a mutual acquaintance who thought we should meet.'

'Who would that be?' Danny asked.

'He calls himself Phillips.' Max saw the reaction in Danny's face, his eyes widened and flickered in recognition.

'I barely know him,' he replied.

'Me neither, and I suspect, like you, I wouldn't trust his word if my life depended on it.'

'*Especially* if my life depended on it,' Danny corrected her.

'But he approached me in the Capital a few days ago and told me there was a story I might be interested in. A

160

story that the Central Alliance Party would not want to become known.'

'Why would he tell you that?'

'He has his motives. I think he would like to bring down the Party and he is using the upcoming elections to further his cause. I managed to get myself into a bit of trouble by asking a few questions the Party did not like. Phillips thinks I could help him by reporting on a story that the citizens deserve to hear. He told me an interesting and far-fetched tale about children being killed in Central City.'

'I don't know what you're talking about,' Danny lied.

'He told me there was an eye witness, an ex-police officer who investigated an assassination and ended up on the run because of what he had learned.'

'Sorry,' Danny tried to appear nonchalant, 'you must be thinking of someone else.'

'He told me this ex-officer was stuck in a prison cell and once he had been broken out would understand the debt he owed.'

'And in order to pay that debt I have to tell my story to you?'

'Something like that.'

'I didn't ask to be broken out of jail.'

'That's a very ungrateful attitude.'

'Suppose I do know something that might interest you, what then?'

'If I believe you and can corroborate certain facts, I write it up.'

'No one would touch it, let alone publish it.'

'Not the mainstream media, but Phillips assures me he has a way to distribute it.'

'Would my name be mentioned?'

'I need someone to talk to me on the record.'

'So I would be signing my own death warrant.'

'Perhaps,' Max shrugged. 'Although from what I understand, your death warrant has already been issued. My name would be on the report too. You have to decide if you want to make a difference or not. 'Pick a side' was how Phillips put it to me.'

'And if I refuse to talk?'

Another shrug, 'Then I have wasted my time, but it will be for Phillips to decide what happens to you next. According to him you were only kept alive in your cell long enough to be rescued thanks to his protection. He does seem to be very well connected. I don't think he would hesitate to return you to police headquarters if you were of no use to him. I get the impression he doesn't become emotionally attached to people very often. Easy come, easy go, if you like.'

Danny mulled over his options, or rather, the lack of them. The skin around his neck was still raw. He knew what a return to the hospitality of the State authorities would mean for his short-term future. Now more than ever, he wished he was back in his small shack in the wilderness, leading a simple life tending to his crops and sitting in the warm summer sun. The sounds and smells of nature that he had become accustomed to already seemed like a distant memory. 'Do I get to talk to Agent Phillips about any of this?'

'I think the answer to that depends on how much you talk to me first.' Max picked up the pencil and held it poised over a clean page of her notepad. They had reached the crucial point in their conversation. Either Danny was going to decide to talk to her now or the whole thing had been a wild goose chase and she would be returning to the Capital with a career writing celebrity puff pieces to look forward to. She could see the ex-State officer trying to decide what to do. He stared hard at her, trying to find some inkling of motive, trust or assurance in her face. She only smiled back in what she hoped was a reassuring manner.

Finally he sat back in the chair and gulped down the rest of the cup of water before he started speaking.

'It all started with the woman who just delivered me into this room,' Danny began.

Henrik stared at the image from the State Surveillance Camera. He couldn't believe what he was looking at. Detective Archie Cancio sat opposite him, waiting for Henrik's response.

'Is it her, Chief?' Cancio asked again.

The High Commissioner of the State Police had already been in touch from the Capital City. Henrik had been severely reprimanded for the escape of a traitor from within his own headquarters. He had professed his regret, offered his word that Danny Samson would be rearrested without delay and assured him that the officers to blame would be identified and punished accordingly. The matter was further complicated by the body of one Günter Foch, found dead in the cell of the escaped prisoner, with his brain spattered against the wall by a single bullet. Foch, it turned out, was a decorated member of the State military and a serving police officer in the Capital. Much of the file that Henrik had seen about Foch was redacted beyond his initial police training and induction, which suggested, in Henrik's experience, that he was now Special Forces, and more particularly, part of the State hit squads that Henrik knew existed

163

despite official denials. One such hit squad had delivered the bullet wound that had injured his shoulder and punctured his lung. As well as Foch, another officer, Kyle McEwan had been found in the corridor unable to move thanks to bullet wounds in both his kneecaps. McEwan was one of their own, a young detective who had gained swift promotions through the Central City police ranks. Henrik had thought him an intelligent, diligent and trustworthy officer with a bright future. He had to now accept that McEwan had been a plant by State Security within his force. It didn't come as a surprise to him, only a disappointment.

A full external enquiry was to be set up by State Security Forces into the escape of Daniel Samson, the murder of Foch and the attempted murder of McEwan. The murder had already been added to the list of offences that Danny Samson was charged with, but it was clear that he had been helped in his escape. Archie Cancio, as the senior detective on duty, had immediately been assigned to lead the internal investigation. He was a man Henrik trusted and admired. He was older than Henrik, a veteran with an exemplary record. He was gruff, disarming and unassuming and believed in hard work and sticking to established facts in order to get results. In the chaos and shock that immediately followed the break-in and escape at headquarters, he was exactly the experienced and organised head needed to restore calm. He set about working the case in his usual way, without flair or drama, but carefully and by the book. He'd identified the victims, established a chain of events and collated all the available surveillance footage within the first hour.

Henrik had returned from the demonstration at the City Parliament to find the headquarters in lockdown. He had been allowed entry and given access to the prison cell. Cancio was already there. Secretly, Henrik wished the case had fallen to someone else. It would be difficult to lie to a good officer like Archie. After briefly scanning the crime scene, Henrik retired to his office and asked Cancio to update him with his initial findings.

Although Henrik had been warned by Phillips that something was going to happen, he was not at all happy about the way the situation was developing. First came the revelation that his old colleague, Cassandra Ford, one of the department's leading forensic pathologists, seemed to be mixed up in the inquiry. Her identification had been used to gain entry to the building, but the security footage seemed to suggest the woman who had entered had not been Cas Ford and had not gone to the laboratories in the basement of headquarters. Whoever had stolen her identity had entered with a semblance of a disguise that made her look like Cas Ford – a blonde wig and a white lab coat – and had avoided showing her face to the cameras at the entrance and in the corridors and elevators within the building. It was hard to believe that Cas Ford was not complicit in allowing her identity to be used. Henrik knew she had a strong bond with Danny Samson. She had known him much longer than Henrik had, she had helped him through some tough times in his personal life. The imposter had access to Cas Ford's palm and eye prints. Unless Cas had been forced against her will to give up these identifiers, she must have provided them to Phillips or someone close to him. There was a small black market in selling identities within the State, but Henrik knew Cas would not need money to be persuaded to help her old friend.

Cancio requested permission to pick up Cas and bring her in for questioning. Henrik delayed giving him an answer until he was fully informed of the rest of his initial findings. That was when Archie handed him the TouchScreen with the image on it that Henrik now looked at. It showed two people running out of the rear entrance of the police building. It had been captured by a camera situated across the street. One of the people, a few steps behind the woman in front, was clearly Danny Samson. The woman had shed her blonde hair and white coat and now wore black fatigues and had short chestnut hair, cropped around a taut, chiselled face with olive skin and sharp green eyes.

'It's her,' he replied to the waiting Cancio.

'Gabriella Marino, the woman who murdered your father.'

Henrik nodded, still staring at the picture. He thought back to that time. He, Danny and Phillips had arrested the assassin and brought her back to the city. His father had been interrogating Gabriella when she had broken free from her restraints and a vicious fight had followed. She had beaten his father to death, cutting his throat so deeply it had almost severed Lars James's head from the rest of his body. The officer whom Danny had entrusted to babysit Gabriella Marino that night had been Cassandra Ford. An investigation had cleared her of any blame. She was only a pathologist after all. She had let Gabriella run and claimed she had been powerless to stop her. Henrik had learned about his father's past, the cover-ups and corruption he had been party to, and what kind of man Lars James had been. Henrik tried to disassociate

166

himself from his father, he had tried to prove he was a better man. But Lars James had been his father, he had cast a long shadow, and Henrik was staring at the image of the person who had murdered him. Despite everything he knew, he could only feel anger as he looked at her. She had robbed him of the chance to confront his father, to learn the truth for himself, to hear first-hand what had driven a good man to stoop so low in order to serve the State. It was hard not to feel the desire for revenge against her.

Now they were all back and all connected again: Gabriella, Danny, Cas and Phillips. The unrest in the city that he had tried so hard to prevent from escalating could not be a coincidence. Danny's return to the city may not have been linked to Phillips, but his rescue was. Henrik felt powerless. He was inextricably linked with that quartet. As soon as those higher up learned of their involvement, Henrik's previous attachment to them would be flagged. The external inquiry into the escape would be thorough and Henrik would not be able to influence it in any way. It would unearth his convenient absence from the building at the time of the escape. It would discover his order to change the guards in the cells that morning. Henrik would be trapped in his duplicity. He could see no way out.

'Anything else?' he asked the patient Cancio.

Archie placed the evidence bag on the desk. Henrik picked it up and looked at the piece of flex cable inside, it's white cover smeared with red blood. 'Found next to the body of Foch.'

'He was trying to strangle Samson?'

'That would be our guess. Marino arrives just in time, takes out McEwan and Foch and flees with Samson.'

167

'She saves him from death.'

'Chief, we're in murky waters here. I don't like the idea of a State Security Officer coming into headquarters to murder a prisoner.'

'I agree, it doesn't reflect well on the Security Forces,' Henrik replied.

'It's not just that, Chief. Soldiers like Foch don't act on their own. Someone must have ordered him to get rid of Samson. The question is who?'

Henrik knew who. Not the identity of the individual who gave the order but the group of people at the top of the Party who would delegate such a task. He knew what Danny Samson knew about the Party and the State. He knew these people would stop at nothing to prevent those secrets from being made public. He knew because he had been on the receiving end of their subtle menace in the past.

'Okay. Get the word out that Gabriella Marino is back in the city and is to be considered a threat.'

'And Cassandra Ford?'

'I know Cassandra well. Let me try to reach out to her first.'

Cancio hesitated. It wasn't standard procedure for a senior officer to interfere in this way, and he knew about the Chief's previous involvement with Samson and Marino, but he could see the logic in a friendly face trying to make a soft approach to the pathologist.

13

Two hours and several cups of water later Danny had told Max all that he could remember about the assassination of Consul Donald Parkinson and the subsequent investigation. Max scribbled notes on her pad while he spoke, stopping him occasionally for clarification or with a question. The link to the higher echelons of the Party and the Senate were what interested her most, rather than the original crime. She pressed him on whether he thought Phillips and Gabriella had been responsible for the killings of Defence Secretary Nelson and Vice-Chancellor Donovan.

'It would be a logical assumption,' was as much as Danny would admit.

'You say that any recordings of meetings where this trial of child euthanasia was discussed were destroyed?'

'The only evidence left is the bodies. The State managed to cover up any links between the deaths here and those of Nelson and Donovan in the Capital. The murdered children were never mentioned. The doctor who was involved was sent abroad to the front line of the war. The State blamed it's favourite scapegoats: the unspecified terrorists.'

'And you ran away?'

'What could I have done? I fled because my life was on the line.' Danny stared at the young woman who simply stared back. He wouldn't allow her to make him feel guilty for running. It had been his only option.

'And now you've come back. Why?'

Danny thought of Lucas. He wondered how the boy was doing after a few days of proper medical care. 'I had a reason.'

'Is it linked to Phillips and whatever he has planned?'

'I have no idea what he has planned. I didn't know he was going to break me out of jail and I didn't know about you interviewing me.'

Max sighed and leaned forward, tapping the end of her pencil against the notepad and scanning what she had written. 'It's a great story. The citizens have a right to know about it, but I don't think I can publish it.'

'You don't believe it?'

'I do, but it's far-fetched and without any evidence to back it up, the Party will be able to deny everything.'

'It would damage them. That's why they don't want me to talk.'

'It would do some short-term damage, but the Party would recover in time. If only there was some tangible piece of evidence, anything at all.'

'There was one thing that wasn't destroyed,' Danny said cautiously, wary of trusting the reporter across the table from him. 'The original State University thesis that Donald Parkinson wrote detailing how the euthanasia of disabled children would help to solve the population crisis.'

'It's not enough. It doesn't prove they actually did anything.'

'It was co-signed by his sponsors: Donovan and Nelson. It proves they all knew each other and had discussed such a plan. Put that with the known facts of their deaths and surely that is enough to print a story and let people make up their own mind about the connections.'

Max put the end of the pencil in her mouth and chewed it between her teeth. 'Okay, it would help. It wouldn't do any harm. So where is it?'

'We had a hard copy printed on paper. I left it in my office the last night I was there. Cassandra Ford took our case notes home with her. She knew they would be destroyed if they were left in the hands of the police.'

'That sounds like a dangerous thing to do.'

'She's always been a good friend to me, especially after…' Danny stopped himself. He hadn't spoken to the reporter about his own personal tragedy and there was no reason to go into it. Cas Ford had looked after him in the days and weeks after Rosa's death. She was the closest thing he had to a friend when he was on the Force. 'She may still have it.'

'Do you know where we could find her?'

Danny shrugged, 'I've been away for three years, I've got no idea where she will be now. She might still be at the same address.'

The door to the corridor opened at that moment. Gabriella walked in, this time followed by a tall man that Danny recognised immediately.

Phillips walked across the room towards the desk at which Danny and Max sat. 'Come with me,' he told them.

There were about fifty people in the room, each busy concentrating on their own task and creating a bustling sense of purpose. Despite the serious atmosphere, bursts of laughter and shouts across tables showed a bond of camaraderie between the workers. Some were painting banners and large posters with traditional paints and cloth, others were designing official-looking leaflets and posters on TouchScreens. All the messages being created were in support of independent candidates, encouraging citizens to vote for change in the election that was now less than two days away. Another bank of desks was filled with people wearing SmartLenses with microphone attachments. As Phillips led Danny and Max past them they could hear snippets of conversation. They were cold-calling citizens on behalf of independent candidates. This room was the hub of the campaign against the Party. It had the look and feel of an old student union with volunteers pitching in where they could. For such an operation to exist within the State was an achievement in itself, regardless of how professional or not it appeared. Max thought she recognised one or two faces from the protest in the main square of the city earlier. At the far end of the room was a separate office with a window looking onto the work floor. Phillips opened the door and ushered them inside. When he closed the door the noise from outside disappeared behind soundproof walls.

'Take a seat, please,' Phillips said. Danny and Max sat on the sofa under the window while Phillips sat behind a desk. Gabriella remained standing by the door.

'What is this place?' Danny asked. 'Are you running a political campaign?'

'Merely facilitating. Compared to the machinery of the State it's not much but we're trying to give the independent candidates some sort of opportunity.'

'You're doing all of this? You're the one organising the protests and putting up the posters. You're running all the independents as though they were one political party,' Max said.

'That would be illegal and you know it. The Central Alliance Party is the only political party allowed to exist.

We are simply an interested group giving individuals a helping hand.'

'Why are you hiding underground then?' Max persisted.

'I think you are smart enough to answer that question for yourself, Maxine.' Phillips gave her a withering look before moving on. 'So tell me, how did your conversation go? Are you convinced?' He directed his question towards Max.

'I believe his story.'

'You will report on it? Something we could distribute? As you can see, we have the infrastructure to get such a story out in time before people cast their votes.'

Max shook her head, 'I promised you I would treat this as a journalistic assignment and there is still a lack of proof, even if Danny was to go on record. I have no corroborating witness willing to go on record.' She paused and looked pointedly at Phillips and Gabriella, but knew that neither would be willing to see their name appear in her story. 'And no concrete evidence.'

Phillips nodded, 'So I understand, but Cas Ford may be holding something that could change your mind.'

'You were listening to our conversation?' Danny said.

Phillips smiled, 'Still the same old Danny, far too naïve for this world.'

'Do you know where we could find her?'

'Yes, Cas is someone we can trust.'

'Does she still work for the police?' Danny asked.

'Unlike you, Danny, she chose to stay, like your ex-partner, Henrik. They have been trying to make a difference while you have been wandering about in the

173

wilderness on some sort of spiritual quest. It was thanks to both of them that we were able to get you out of jail.'

'How did they help?'

'Henrik kept you alive and gave us your exact location, as well as ensuring the guards were underprepared. Cas allowed Gabriella to assume her identity with fake skin and eye grafts to gain access to the building. These people still care about you.'

'Can you take us to her?' Max asked.

'Gabriella will accompany you this evening. Your deadline is midnight tonight. That will still give us time to publish and distribute tomorrow, if you are willing to write something. You can freshen up and eat before you head out.' Phillips dismissed them and turned to his TouchScreen. Gabriella opened the door, Max stood and walked out. Danny remained sitting until Phillips looked up. He waved Gabriella out and she closed the door behind her. The two men sat looking at each other.

Danny spoke first, 'What are you really doing here?'

'Exactly as I told you, Danny, helping independent candidates campaign.'

'Rubbish, you have no trust in any politicians or any State process.'

Phillips stood and perched on the end of his desk, looking down on Danny, 'You're right. This election is just the beginning. You started something three years ago, Danny. You might not realise it, but you did. Some people took notice of what you uncovered, people in positions of power. They started to question the Party and the State. Not in public, not so anyone would hear about it, but behind closed doors. Meanwhile the citizens have begun to show discontent: the energy crisis, the population crisis, the climate crisis, the war, the lack of employment, the lack of purpose in people's lives, loneliness – it all adds up. These things lead to opportunity, Danny, a chance for change, a chance to challenge those that have misgoverned for too long. While you were messing about in the wilderness, we have been busy.'

'You can't seriously believe you can topple the Party?'

'Why not? You've been away for too long, Danny. These elections could be the catalyst for something far bigger.'

'Losing a few seats in the Senate will make no difference whatsoever to the Party.'

'You're right,' Phillips moved back behind his desk and sat down. 'But what if they could be used to trigger a bigger change.'

'What? A revolution? Civil war? What are we talking about?'

'It just requires a spark, Danny, something to ignite the people, awaken them from their complacent slumber. You can't imagine what I have learned since we last met, Danny. Your little discovery here in Central City was just the tip of the iceberg. You remember what Elisabeth Sand told you?'

Danny knew what Phillips was referring to. Right before she had been killed, Sand had asked him: 'You think this is the worst of it? Do you want to know the truth about the war?' At the time Danny was so caught up in his own investigation he hadn't wanted to know any more.

Phillips continued, 'While I was forced to leave the State, I did some investigating of my own. I learned a few truths about our governing party. Truths that made me

175

angry, Danny, like you were. Truths that made me want to lash out and take violent retribution. Gabriella and I tried that when we killed Donovan and Nelson. It got us nowhere, and then we had to flee. We realised that real change couldn't be achieved like that. We needed a plan, a long term strategy to take down the corrupt State that this country has become.'

Danny was not surprised Phillips had carried out the assassinations in the Capital City, but he was astonished to hear him admit it. 'What truths did you learn?'

Phillips shook his head, 'Not yet, Danny. You have to prove you want to be part of this.'

'You think I want any part of this? You're mad. They will hunt you down and kill you and crush your tiny resistance like squashing a bug.' Danny stood up and turned to leave, only then realising Gabriella had silently entered the room and stood blocking his path. He noticed her hand poised by the handle of a sheathed knife at her hip.

'Make sure Danny gets some rest,' Phillips said, looking down at his TouchScreen.

It was early evening when Gabriella drove them out from under the road bridge and onto the highway, heading back west to the centre of the city. Max sat in the passenger seat while Danny sat in the back. There was little traffic during what used to be rush hour, only buses cruised along. Gabriella stuck to the speed limit to ensure they didn't attract any unnecessary attention.

After staring at the uninspiring buildings passing by for ten minutes, Danny couldn't face the silence in the car any longer. 'So, a journalist. That's a pretty thankless task in the Capital, isn't it?'

'It's not easy,' Max answered without turning her head.

'Why do you do it?'

Max automatically started quoting: '"Congress shall make no law abridging the freedom of speech, or of the press; or the right of the people peaceably to assemble, and to petition the Government for a redress of grievances."'

'What does that mean?'

Gabriella laughed, 'It's the first amendment of the United States Of America.'

'It's a bit late to believe in that. Those ideas disappeared about the same time as that country.'

'It still holds true,' Max said defensively, 'it's still an ideal worth aiming for.'

'I take it you work for The Star Tribune?'

'What makes you say that?'

'I can't imagine Phillips confiding in a reporter that worked for any of the State media organisations, or one of their reporters deciding to side with someone like Phillips.'

'You guessed right.'

'So how did you end up here?'

'I ran into some trouble in the Capital. Let's just say I fell out of favour with the Party.'

'Who did you annoy?'

'The Chancellor.'

Danny whistled, 'Queen Lucinda herself. Not easy to come back from something like that in your line of work. So Phillips reached out to you as someone who could be persuaded of the merits of his latest enterprise.'

'He approached me, yes. So far everything he has said has been true.'

'Truth is a very fluid concept with our friend Agent Phillips.'

'Didn't he save your life once?'

'More than once,' Gabriella interjected.

Danny turned to her, 'And where do you fit in his grand plan? A paid henchwoman?'

'I gave up the assassin business,' Gabriella answered, focussing on the road ahead.

'You believe in this nonsense too?'

'I believe those who wield power like the Party need to be challenged.'

'Tell me about the First Strike War.'

'What about it?'

'Phillips said he had learned something about it. Something far worse than anything he had suspected about the State, far worse than what we uncovered in Central City.'

'Perhaps one day you will be ready to learn the truth, but if he thinks you shouldn't be told just now, then that's his final decision.'

Max turned to look at Danny and they shared a look of fellowship. Max was just as in the dark as Danny about the truths that Phillips claimed to have learned.

'Why did you decide to come back to the State?' he carried on questioning Gabriella, 'You're wanted for murder.'

'Events coalesced,' Gabriella said. Max remembered Phillips using the same phrase in the car park basement. 'I'm not scared of the State Security Forces. I've handled them before. Some things are worth fighting for.' Danny remembered vividly how well Gabriella could handle herself.

'You served in the State military, in the war?' Max asked Gabriella, who nodded. 'With Phillips?'

'Our paths crossed on a few occasions.'

'Whereabouts? I've been to the front line.'

'Laramidia, Appalachia, Zhonghua.' Gabriella rhymed off the names as though they were towns one could stop at on a touring holiday. Laramidia and Appalachia were the two inhabitable coasts of the Civil American States that remained after the First Strike had destroyed the centre of the continent. In prehistoric times they had been the names of two islands of the continent which were then separated by a seaway. When the Civil American States were again split, this time by nuclear fallout, the names were resurrected. Some of the fiercest fighting in the early years of the war had taken place in these regions as both sides sought control of the country and its resources.

'Zhonghua? You mean in an enemy country?' Zhonghua was the biggest and strongest of the enemy countries that had formed the Axis Powers after the First Strike. Though denying responsibility for igniting the war, the Zhonghua Republic was left as the only superpower in the world and saw an opportunity to expand its empire. The Union of Soviet Socialist Republics followed them, creating an army with the might to wipe the rest of the world off the face of the planet. The State, what remained of the Civil American States and the European and African Unions combined to fight a rearguard action. It was a military miracle that they had not been overwhelmed by the superior forces they faced. Instead, the battle lines became entrenched and had remained more or less unchanged for almost half a century. The fighting continued in Laramidia and Appalachia and

179

occasionally sprung up in other parts of the world. Most of it was done by machines now, a remote war with hardly any human casualties.

'I worked covert missions to infiltrate strategic military targets, gather intelligence and if possible disrupt their armaments programme. Where did you report from?' Gabriella turned to Max.

'Estados Unidos Mexicanos,' Max answered, naming the country to the south of Laramidia.

'Mexico,' Gabriella translated, 'the old country that still survives despite being right in the middle of it all. I'm impressed.'

'I wasn't, it was a mess.'

'Fifty years of war will do that to a place.'

'You've been there?'

'Phillips and I spent some time there recently, when we needed to disappear from the State for a while.' Max had many questions she wanted to ask Gabriella. Once the elections were out of the way maybe she would agree to an interview, even off the record.

They veered off the highway. Citizens casually strolling across the empty roads had to move out of the way swiftly as the unexpected car drove by them. The citizens looked different here, away from the very centre of the city. The effects of recent power rationing and falling standards of living were apparent in those aimlessly wandering the streets. The clothes were not quite as crisp and clean as current fashion dictated they should be. The men looked unshaven, the women less made up. Modern hairstyles were absent, replaced with uncared for tangles. The roads were dirtier, covered with cracks and potholes. The white buildings had turned a dusty grey. Max recognised the signs of social hardships.

She had seen similar things in areas of the MidLands where she had found discontent. Such sights were unknown in the Capital. The further north she went, the more the hardships seemed to proliferate.

'This used to be one of the more affluent areas,' Danny muttered, echoing Max's thoughts.

'You've been here before?' Max asked.

'We used to live here,' Danny answered, looking at the streets he had once called home. Connections and memories to his lost life crept to the forefront of his mind. He saw Rosa walking along the roads as if it was only yesterday, not an entire previous life he had once led. He tried to think of something else before the emotions overcame him. 'Did Cas know you were using her identity at police headquarters?'

Gabriella nodded, 'Phillips warned her. We sent over a couple of men to keep an eye on her just in case the State Security Forces tried to get in touch with her about it.'

'And they haven't reported anything? No one coming to question her about how you might have stolen her identity and used it to break a prisoner out of jail?'

'She told Phillips she hadn't heard anything.'

'When did he speak to her?'

'This afternoon, soon after your escape.'

Danny felt a sense of urgency. He knew if he hadn't been locked up in police headquarters, Cas would never have been dragged into any of this. 'Any chance we could get there a little quicker?'

Henrik had tried calling Cas Ford at her home but hadn't received any reply. Now he sat in a car across the road from her house. There were no lights on despite the power being on in this section of the city, and no sign of life. The entrance door was closed and the curtains drawn. It was a risk visiting her. The standard tracking implant would show he had been here, but he had little to lose now. It was only a matter of time before the inquiry into Danny Samson's escape brought an end to his career in the State Police. He got out of the car and crossed the road. He pressed the buzzer and knocked on the front door. There was no reply and no movement. Cas wouldn't ignore his calls. He had left a message to say he would be coming. He circled round the building. The neighbourhood had seen better days, creeping negligence was present in untrimmed trees and narrow patches of roadside grass growing to knee-height. There were unrepaired cracks in the pavements and roads and the fences needed a fresh coat of paint. Henrik approached the rear entrance of the house and tried knocking again. He pushed the door and it swung open. Instinct made him reach for his standard issue ShockBaton. He stepped into the hallway that ran the length of the house. 'Cas,' he called out, 'it's me, Henrik.' There was no reply.

He checked the first room on his left. The bathroom was empty. He crossed the hallway and entered the kitchen. He stopped in his tracks when he saw her. Cas was hanging from the ceiling, a cord of cable flex tightly wrapped around her neck. Henrik did not stop to take in any more of the details. He could see that she was dead, it was too late to do anything to help her. He had to get out of the building as quickly as he could. He could not afford to be caught there. The suspicion that would fall on him would be the final nail in his career and his reputation. The Security Forces didn't need another reason to dig deeper in search of his betrayal. He pulled his police handgun from its holster and ran through the house and out of the front door, leaving it open behind him.

He didn't spot the new arrival in the street until it was too late. They saw him as he barrelled into the road. The two men had parked next to Henrik's incongruous vehicle in the empty street and were just exiting their car in order to inspect it. They turned and Henrik saw they were holding weapons. Without hesitating or thinking, panicked by what he had just discovered, Henrik raised his gun and fired at them. He was quick enough to catch them off guard. Their car windscreen shattered and the bodywork took several hits as Henrik fired wildly. The two men were hit: one fell to the ground, the other toppled back into the passenger seat he had just emerged from, his body crumpled at an inhuman angle.

Adrenaline stopped Henrik thinking logically, he charged on. He didn't stop to investigate who these men were. He jumped in his car and drove away at high speed. The incident had happened so quickly that no neighbours had emerged to witness what was going on or to see him leaving. Later, once he had returned to his office, he realised how many mistakes he had made. There was only one person who would be able to help him. He took the unregistered TouchScreen from his pocket and sent him a message.

14

As soon as they turned the corner into the street they could tell something was wrong. Gabriella slammed on the brakes. The door to Cas Ford's house lay wide open. On the opposite side of the road a car sat with both the driver and passenger wing doors raised. Gabriella slowly drove forwards, creeping closer to the scene with caution, ready to accelerate away from danger in a split second. As they neared the stationary car they saw the red pool gathering on the road, blood dripping from a lifeless hand that was hanging out the open door.

'Your watchers?' Max asked. Gabriella nodded. Before she could say anything else Danny had opened the rear door and was sprinting across the road towards Cas's house.

'Wait,' Gabriella shouted, but Danny was already gone. 'Shit.' She pulled out her gun and jumped out. 'Stay here,' she commanded Max and set off after him.

The house was laid out as Danny remembered it. The hallway led from the front all the way to the back of the building. Off to the left was the bedroom, to the right the living room and at the back the kitchen and bathroom. He hadn't stopped to consider that whoever had paid Cas a visit might still be in the house. He looked in the living room, it was empty, but the table and chairs had been knocked over. The bedroom was undisturbed. There was an eerie silence in the house, like the atmosphere from the outside world was afraid to enter, creating a void. Footsteps behind him made him turn and he saw Gabriella entering the house, gun raised. He carried on. The bathroom was empty. He caught a scent of perfume that he instantly remembered as Cas.

'Dammit,' he heard Gabriella shout. He wheeled round and followed the voice. It had come from the kitchen. He rushed through the door. His stomach lurched. 'Don't just stand there, help me,' Gabriella shouted at him. She was in the middle of the room trying desperately to raise the feet that dangled in mid-air. Danny looked up at Cas's face, which rolled from side to side. The cable was tight around her neck, which appeared to be sitting at an odd angle, as though broken. Her eyes were open but lifeless, her arms hung limply by her sides.

'It's too late,' he uttered. There was a noise behind him. Gabriella let go of the body, which started swinging, and grabbed her gun from the table. She pointed it at the door over Danny's shoulder just as Max stumbled in. She stopped in the doorway, her mouth wide open in shock.

'Is that her?' Max asked.

'Yes,' Gabriella answered as she ushered them back out of the kitchen. 'Come on, we need to get out of here.'

Danny refused to move. 'You killed her,' he said to Gabriella. 'You did this with your stupid plan to break me out of jail. For what? Nothing. So Phillips could try and impress some reporter to further his ridiculous cause? And now this, another death on your hands.'

'Let's argue about that later, it's too dangerous to stay here.'

'What about the essay?' Max asked.

'We don't have time,' Gabriella insisted, trying to get them to move.

185

'It's the reason we came. If we can find it then at least she didn't die for no reason at all.'

'She didn't die for no reason, she was killed for helping break me out of jail,' Danny shouted, his anger boiling over.

'By who?' Max asked.

'By the State,' Danny shouted at her in exasperation. 'You still don't get it, do you?'

'Alright, calm down,' Gabriella insisted, holding up her palms. 'Do you know where she might have kept the paper you're talking about?'

Danny relented. They were right. If they left without what they had come for then Cas's death would be even more pointless.

The dust began to settle. It had taken Gabriella fifteen minutes to break through the concrete block behind the false wall. They hadn't brought any tools with them, so she had to make do with what she had with her. The tip of the steel serrated knife had broken off, but the blade had proved strong enough to act as a chisel when hit with enough force by the handgun that had stood in for a hammer. Now they could see the metal container buried in the concrete. Gabriella began chipping around the sides of it, every so often pausing and trying to prise it free with her hands.

While Gabriella was busy in the bedroom, Danny and Max cut down the body of Cas in the kitchen. They laid her on the floor. Danny found an old towel and covered her face. When the body was discovered a forensic officer would have to do a complete examination. It would be someone who knew Cas, who worked alongside her and had learned from her. Cas would be subjected to the battery of tests that she had so often prescribed for the deceased of the city. 'You see now?' he asked Max, as they sat at the table, staring at the body in front of them.

'You're sure the State Security Forces are behind this?'

'You're not convinced? Her identity is used to break me out of jail and within hours she's found dead.'

'Why would they kill her?'

'You've never been a crime reporter, have you?' Danny asked.

'There aren't many murders to report on.'

Danny knelt down by the body and picked up one of Cas's hands. 'Look here.' He pointed at the ends of the fingers. On each of them the fingernail had been pulled out, they were caked with dried blood. 'And here.' He pointed at Cas's knees. Only now did Max see the odd angle at which the lower part of her legs were bent. The feet too had fallen to the side, bending outwards, the ankles had been broken. 'They tortured her,' Danny explained, his investigative mind reawakening. 'They wanted to know who was behind my escape. Maybe she told them, maybe she didn't. It doesn't matter. She was dead as soon as they found out she had helped break me out. This is what the State does. They have hit squads. Then they hang her to make it look like suicide. Any competent examiner would be able to spot the signs of murder straight away, but all they need is for the appearance of suicide and reports will be filed that way.'

'It seems so unbelievable,' Max said unconvincingly.

'You're a reporter,' Danny urged, 'what does the evidence tell you?'

'And the men in the car outside?'

187

Danny shrugged, 'They either killed them on the way in or on the way out.'

There was a flurry of angry blows on brick and metal from the bedroom, followed by Gabriella shouting, 'I've got it, let's go.'

Danny took one last look at the body of his friend, another victim lying dead on the floor. He wanted to tell her he was sorry, but it was pointless. He hurried out of the door after Max.

Gabriella jumped behind the wheel of the car. 'We've probably already been spotted,' Gabriella said as they jumped in beside her. She gunned the engine and took off at high speed.

Danny picked up the metal box that had been thrown on the back seat. 'Give me your knife.' He inserted the blade in the opening and prised the lid open until he felt the lock inside snap. All that was inside were a few sheets of paper. Among them Danny found the print-out of Consul Donald Parkinson's undergraduate dissertation entitled 'Thesis on Possible Solutions to the Eradication of the Overpopulation Problem within The State.'

'Read it,' Danny thrust the paper in front of Max as the car swung sharply round a corner. Max took the papers and began scanning them. As they sped along the road, Gabriella now ignoring the speed limit, Danny shouted to Max, 'Now will you write?'

They ditched the car a few miles away in another part of the city, leaving it in an empty parking garage. They took off on foot, Gabriella leading the way, Max poring over the document as they hurriedly walked.

'Where are we going?' Danny asked, jogging a few paces to keep up.

'There's a safe house nearby.' It was starting to grow dark now. The streets were quiet and there were no lights thanks to power rationing. They turned down an alleyway. Danny recognised the path that led down towards the river. They reached the walkway that ran alongside the water. On the other side, lit and reaching up into the growing gloom, the tall chimneys of the arms factory dominated the night sky. When Danny had been a police officer this path had been part of his daily commute. Gabriella urged them on until she stopped in the middle of a road. She looked about her, making sure they were not being watched.

'What?' Danny asked, confused at the sudden pause. Gabriella bent down and pulled up a metal manhole cover. 'Down there?' Danny asked.

'You're welcome to see how far you get on your own,' Gabriella said and dropped through the hole and out of sight. Max stuffed the paper into a pocket and followed her. Danny came last, pulling the cover back into place above his head as he descended beneath the city. Coming down the ladder in the shaft they emerged into a tunnel. Gabriella pulled a small torch from her belt. They were in an old sewer that had been out of use for years, replaced by the modern, sophisticated environmentally-friendly system. The smell of sewage still lingered. Danny retched as Max covered her nose and mouth with her sleeve. They followed Gabriella as she set off down the tunnel. She seemed sure of which direction she was going, they had no choice but to follow her.

They walked for what seemed like an hour, but was only fifteen minutes. In some places they had to wade through rancid, foul pools of water that reached knee height. They could hear creatures scurrying and squeaking around them. Finally, Gabriella stopped under another ladder shaft and began climbing. When she reached the top she used her shoulder to lift up another metal cover. They emerged into the cool night, sucking in lungfuls of fresh air. 'Come on,' Gabriella pulled and pushed them out of the middle of the road while Max and Danny coughed and spluttered. The smell and taste of the sewer would linger for hours to follow. They were in a different part of the city now, not far from the main square and the City Parliament. They approached a block of apartments. As they neared a door clicked open and Gabriella shoved them inside.

Max stared at the TouchScreen, the blank page stared back at her casting a bright white shadow across her face. The apartment had power while the street outside and the surrounding buildings sat in darkness. Somewhere there was an independent energy source which produced the low hum of electricity that was amplified in the quiet stillness around her.

Phillips had been waiting for them in the safe house. Gabriella had taken Danny into another room while Phillips led Max into what would once have been someone's living room. There were standard blinds on the windows, closed but slanted to allow a view of the street. While he had been in the room with her, Phillips kept glancing between the slats, ensuring no one had followed them. On the wall hung an old painting of a tall ship, and there was an empty shelving unit. Apart from that the room was empty and every footstep Phillips took echoed against the cold wooden floor. In the middle of the room a small folding table and chair had been set up with the TouchScreen.

'Decision time,' he told her. 'Will you write?'

She walked forward, pulled out the chair and sat at the table. 'How long do I have?'

'Two hours, if we want to get it out by the morning. Do you need anything else?'

'No,' she answered. Phillips left her alone. She heard him walk across the hallway and join Danny and Gabriella in the other room. The walls seemed to be soundproof though and once the door had closed she heard nothing else. She tried to collect her thoughts. The immediate revelations of the past day swirled around her head. She struggled to put them into the context of her life, and the lives of all the citizens who lived in the State, who trusted the Party to take care of them, to protect them and to lead them through the trials that the world threw at them. She couldn't dismiss the Party as pure evil in the same way that Phillips or Danny viewed them. The journalist in her wanted to be fair and balanced, to try and see both sides of the story, to justify the things she had discovered. She thought about the good the Party had done for the country and the people. It was too easy, too simple, to dismiss the achievements that the Party had succeeded in delivering. Could the end of poverty and homelessness be weighed up against a misguided solution to a crisis of overpopulation and the exhaustion of resources it brought with it? She tried to detach her emotions from the horror of the killing of children. She was remote from the individuals involved in that case, with the exception of Danny, but when she tried to think impersonally about what she would write, the image of Cassandra Ford hanging from her kitchen ceiling kept appearing in her mind. She had no doubt the police pathologist had been tortured and killed. It was hard to disagree with Danny that it had been a State hit squad that had carried out the attack. Her thoughts drifted, unfocussed. She pictured her parents in their home by the sea. They would be having another pleasant evening, sitting together in their living room, reading or watching a programme. They might decide to go for a stroll along the coast to take in the dusk or watch the stars blinking in the night sky while the waves rolled soothingly onto the sandy beach at the foot of the cliffs. She felt a pang of sadness that she was not there with them. The sadness turned to anger. Anger that they, like so many others, knew nothing about what was happening in the rest of the State. Anger that they had been lied to by those elected to serve them, fooled by cover-ups and misinformation spread to keep the masses in line. She could keep her emotions in check, but she could not ignore the facts that she had discovered. The citizens had a right to know what had been happening. The reasons she had wanted to be a journalist in the first place, when she was an innocent, naïve teenager, still held true, even if no media company would be brave enough to carry the story. This was her chance to prove what she had always believed, the unfashionable, historic truth that had once been the foundation on which democracies had been formed: the right to freedom of speech and of the press to hold those in power to account.

She took out her notepad. It was crumpled and stained after the evening's exertions. She started scanning over her notes, flicking back through page after page until she reached her scribblings from the press conference at The Palace two weeks' ago. That was her starting point.

She called up the virtual keypad and began typing. The words came slowly at first as her thoughts circled round a structure on which to pin her muddled ideas. Then they started to fall into place, forming sentences, then paragraphs. Her ideas became sharper, clear and organised. The noise of her fingers tapping on the TouchScreen was the only sound that broke the silence of the night.

Danny felt better after a shower and change of clothes. When he entered the living room he found Phillips and Gabriella waiting for him.

'I'm sorry about Cas,' Phillips offered.

'You realise it is your fault she is dead.'

'She knew the risks she was taking by helping us.'

'Did you promise her you would protect her? The same way you promised Maxine?' Danny pointed to the room across the hallway where he had seen Max being taken.

'If you want to blame me for what happened, that's fine. I don't have time to argue with you.'

'Is she writing your story for you?'

'We'll see,' Phillips shrugged as though it hardly concerned him one way or the other. 'I have learned about something more pressing, more disturbing, from your old partner.'

'Henrik?'

'He sent me a message. Information that you provided to him in your interview but which you neglected to tell me about.'

'Maybe you didn't ask.'

'Is it true? Did you see State Forces transporting weaponry into the city?'

'I saw crates on an intercity shuttle. What was in them, where they were going, I have no idea.'

'Even you aren't that naïve. You've seen what's happening here. They're preparing to retaliate against the protestors.'

'They wouldn't,' Danny replied. He couldn't imagine the State openly attacking its own citizens in the streets with violence. 'They have allowed your demonstrations to take place without any reaction so far. Why would they start now?'

'Once the election is over they will retaliate. They will have ten years until their authority can be challenged again. In that time they will spin the events, deflect blame and allow memories to fade. Henrik has kept the State police on a tight leash, but he has no control over the State Security Forces.'

'Are there State Forces gathering in the city?'

'We have no confirmation, we're checking with our sources.'

'You may be worrying about nothing.'

'I can't afford to think that way.'

'I can't tell you any more than what Henrik has already told you. I saw crates of weapons, beyond that I know nothing.'

'You still choose to deny it, deny what this is: a corrupt one-party state where murder, oppression and persecution are allowed to flourish, implemented by a Party that is free to pursue its whim without any checks or balance.'

'They will not murder their own citizens in the full glare of the public, that's not how they work.'

'Isn't it?' Phillips caught himself before he said anything more.

194

Danny could tell Phillips knew something that he still refused to reveal to him. 'What is it? What is the truth you have learned that is so devastating?'

Phillips shook his head, 'Not yet.'

Before Danny could press him any further the door to the room opened. Max entered with the TouchScreen. She handed it to Gabriella who briefly glanced at the typed words before handing it to Phillips, who also skimmed over the content. After a moment he looked at the journalist. 'You're sure?' he asked her. Max nodded, a grave look on her face. 'Very well.' Phillips tapped the TouchScreen a few times. He stopped with his finger hovering over it. 'You know there will be no turning back when this is seen by the State? You know the consequences this will have for you?'

'The citizens deserve to know what's been going on, someone has to write it.'

Phillips lowered his finger and pressed the screen with certainty. There was a small whooshing sound effect. 'It's sent.' He looked at Max. 'Welcome to the fight.' He dropped the TouchScreen onto the floor and smashed it under his foot, bringing his boot down on it several times until the machine had splintered and cracked into hundreds of small shards. 'Let's go,' he ordered them.

15

'Concerning the Corrupt State: An Exclusive Report by Maxine Aubert' landed on the streets of the main cities the following morning. Citizens awoke to messages delivered to their TouchScreens containing the report, printed copies were plastered on walls and bundles were left at travel terminals and in restaurants and cafes. Over breakfast, during morning commutes and while taking leisurely morning strolls, citizens all across the State read about events that had previously been unknown or covered up. Details about the murders of Vice-Chancellor Donovan, Defence Secretary Nelson and City Consul Parkinson were told for the first time. The State's trial which had killed defenceless children was exposed in harrowing detail. Excerpts from a State University thesis were quoted, written by Parkinson and sponsored by Nelson and Donovan. The subsequent cover-up story was debunked. As a piece of unbiased, factual reporting it failed. There was no counter-argument, no right-to-reply for the State press officer, no interview with a Central Alliance Party member. Daniel Samson was quoted as a key witness. The names of Gabriella Marino and Phillips were omitted. Corruption at the highest level of the State Police was also presented, with the posthumously-honoured Chief Commander Lars James shown to be a corrupt enforcer for the State. The supposed suicide of a City Parliament office worker Montana Childe, a key witness in the case, was exposed as murder. A world of underground clubs used for gambling, solicitation, drinking and social gatherings, as well as unrecorded off-the-record political meetings was detailed. The death of Cassandra Ford, the pathologist on the original case and ally of Daniel Samson was added as a footnote to the whole affair. Surrounding all these case details were reports of a citizen uprising gathering momentum in Central City, reports that the complicit State media in the south were ignoring or refusing to mention, along with the severity of the energy and food shortages outwith the Capital.

Max was proud of her story. She had tried to keep her personal emotions in check, although would admit that some had spilled onto the page. But she had kept to the facts as she saw them and as they had been presented to her. She did not embellish, she did not add emotive language. She did not need to in order to get the reaction her story attracted.

How Phillips had managed to get it distributed so far and wide in such a short space of time nobody knew. It was taken for granted that he had contacts in high and varied places. The exposé was not reported on by the State media news channel, nor on the pages of the other State-owned news organisations. The Star Tribune did manage to mention it briefly, commenting on the link to their reporter, Maxine Aubert, though stressing that she had published her report in a freelance capacity while on leave from her position with the organisation. Anyone who had read this article on The Star Tribune site would have been puzzled if they had returned an hour or so later – the story had disappeared without a trace.

There was no immediate reaction to the story on the day before the election was due to be held. Nowhere did citizens rise up in arms about the revelations, there were no spontaneous marches or protests, no State buildings were attacked by angry mobs and no State workers were confronted. The citizens of the State read the news and carried on with whatever business they had to attend to that day. No one cancelled meetings or appointments, the schools remained open as did the factories, warehouses and processing plants. The citizens had learned to be reserved with their emotions, they trusted those in charge to take the appropriate action and ensure their best interests were looked after. Until now this approach had served them well. But the story did not go completely unnoticed. As people met in the street or at work, as visitors arrived on friend's doorsteps, as families gathered for meals around dining tables, as groups met to play sports, conversations turned towards the report that had appeared that morning. Word began to spread, opinions began to form. Most dismissed it, they didn't believe a word of it. Look at the timing of the revelations for a start, they argued, clearly this was someone out to cause trouble, to destabilise the Party before the election. It was probably the work of one of our enemies in the First Strike War. Some chose to ignore the horror that was presented to them – the Party did what it must do to look after the State and the citizens, and overall the Party continued to make the right decisions for their benefit. But there were a few, a small minority, spread through each of the cities of the State, who absorbed what the article was telling them and reached a different conclusion. They did not shout about it, they did not reveal what they were thinking, they knew better than to draw attention to themselves from the ever-watchful authorities. They would have a chance tomorrow to express their displeasure at what they had learned when it was time for them to cast their mandatory vote. On the day, some of them would change their minds and vote for the Party as they had always done – voting was not anonymous and a record of how every citizen voted was kept by the State. There would be a tiny faction though, who would carry through their conviction and turn their vote into a protest by voting for an independent candidate, or by spoiling their ballot, or by abstaining – both of the latter two actions would result in a criminal charge if the State decided to enforce the strict electoral laws.

Henrik James turned up for work at his usual time that morning. He had spent an uncomfortable night pacing around his home, unable to contemplate sleep. He looked for signs in the faces of those who greeted him with the obligatory salute, a hint that they knew something, that rumours had started to circulate about the death of Cassandra Ford.

Detective Cancio had called him the previous evening to inform him of the discovery of Cas Ford's body at her home. He asked Henrik if he had tried to contact her.

'I tried calling her a couple of times after we had spoken but got no reply,' James answered. He waited for Cancio to continue, expecting to hear damning forensic evidence proving his presence at the crime scene, his fingerprints and DNA detected inside the house next to the dead body. He waited to hear about two dead men found in the street outside, killed with bullets from a gun registered to the State Police Force and belonging to Chief Commander Henrik James. Would he care to explain?

Instead, Archie Cancio only sighed and muttered that they had been too late. Perhaps it was friends of Günter Foch who had got there first. He didn't like the idea of a rogue group of State Security soldiers marauding through the city on a killing spree. 'We'll keep looking for Gabriella and Danny Samson,' he said and hung up.

Henrik let out a long deep sigh, only then realising he had been holding his breath. His message to Phillips had worked. Henrik was sure that Phillips already knew about Cas Ford's death when he had messaged him. There was no hint of shock or dismay in his reply. However Phillips had managed it, he had done what he had promised: he had deleted the tracking data that showed Henrik had visited Cas Ford's house that afternoon, cleaned up any forensic evidence linking him to the scene and he had disposed of the two dead men and their car before the police had arrived. Phillips was not happy though. He informed Henrik that the men he had killed were two of his most valuable people. However, he had agreed to overlook the unfortunate mistake on the condition that Henrik was now more beholden than ever to him. When Phillips wanted a favour in return from the Chief Commander of the State City Police, he would expect it to be carried out with no questions asked. Henrik agreed. In return he had told Phillips what Danny Samson had told him about weapons arriving in the city aboard an intercity shuttle.

Before he managed to make it to the sanctuary of his office, Henrik was made aware of the new development that would dominate his day. The article was shown to him by his personal assistant who was waiting diligently for him inside the main entrance. Maxine Aubert was not a name he was familiar with, but the story she told was

200

one he knew well, and the name Daniel Samson leapt out at him from the page.

Max slept until mid-morning, recovering from the drama of the previous day and the late finish. They had left the safe house once Phillips had sent her story. Another grey car was parked outside the apartment and Gabriella had driven the four of them back to the bunker under the highway. Now, she showered and dressed in fresh clothes. The bag of luggage that she had left in her hotel room the previous day had appeared next to her bed in the small box room in which she had slept. She lay on the camp bed staring at the concrete grey ceiling. There was a sharp knock on the door before it opened.

It was Gabriella, 'Not too late for some breakfast if you want something to eat.' Max followed her through to the canteen hall where there was a small selection of drinks, plain cereal and plain bread. Gabriella sat opposite her and watched her eat in silence until she was almost finished. 'Do you want to go into the city?'

'Why?'

'Thought you might want to see if your report was having any effect.'

'It's out there already?'

'Since first light.'

'Does Phillips think I should venture out? Aren't we wanted criminals now? Traitors of the State?'

'We don't need to ask his permission.'

'I was under the impression he was in charge.'

'I stopped taking orders when I left the State military.'

'You act like you're his personal bodyguard.'

201

'Just because I agree with a few of his principles and ideas, doesn't mean I'm his servant.' Max looked into the green eyes across the table from her. The face was youthful, but marked with life experience by deepening lines and numerous light scars. The short hair was tousled and unruly, the cheekbones firm and strong. Her neck and shoulders were narrow but muscular in her vest top. There was something boyish about her appearance, but Max could sense the ruthlessness of a killer. She did not find it hard to picture Gabriella as the cold-blooded assassin she knew her to be. She certainly believed that if Gabriella wanted to walk away from Phillips or choose her own course of action, he would be powerless to stop her.

Danny had not slept well. He was unaccustomed to the small, sealed dark room and the total silence that encompassed him in his cell of the bunker. He too found a change of clothes lying next to his bed when he awoke, another set of black trousers and a t-shirt which he had seen many of the volunteers in the base wearing the previous day. He slipped them on and left his room, surprised to find the door unlocked. He had already eaten his breakfast and left the canteen before Max and Gabriella had arrived. By that time he had entered another room in the complex of corridors that sprawled throughout the underground lair. He didn't see many people and assumed they were out performing some duties to prepare for the election the following day, including canvassing on behalf of independent candidates and continuing their protest in the main city square. He stumbled into the room he had been in the previous day, where Max had interviewed him. Phillips was sitting at one of the tables on his own. Danny noticed how tired Phillips looked. He was unshaven and wearing the same clothes as he had been in the previous night. His eyes were heavy and darkened from a lack of sleep. He was flicking through channels and sites on a TouchScreen. As Danny approached, Phillips looked up.

'I thought you would have been out doing some last minute campaigning or organising,' Danny said, pulling out a chair and sitting opposite him.

'Until tomorrow, I've done all I can.'

'You really think that story will make much of a difference?'

'Probably not, but at least we've tried to do something. In all the excitement and drama I haven't been able to thank you, Danny.'

'Thank me?'

'For telling Max your story, for going along with it, for believing that the people deserve to know what really happened.'

'It won't change anything,' Danny shrugged. 'I was facing a life in prison anyway.'

'It's still a brave thing to stand up like that though, against the powerful people of this country.'

'What happens now?'

'For you?' Phillips asked. Danny nodded. 'Well, you'll have to lie low for today certainly, better not leave here in case you are spotted. Once the election is over we will be able to get you out of the city again.'

'Back to the wilderness?'

'I don't think you will be able to survive anywhere else from now on. If the State Security Forces weren't looking hard enough for you before your name appeared in Max's article, they certainly will be now.'

Despite the threat, Danny felt a calmness come over him for the first time since he had left the village in the north three weeks' ago. Perhaps there was still a chance he would be able to return there. He pictured the meadow, his shack, his field of crops and the stool on the porch sitting empty in the summer sun. He thought of Eilidh: how was she coping without her son? She had no idea that Lucas had made it to safety in the hospital, that he was alive and getting medical care. He imagined her huddled in her lean-to, clutching the blanket that Lucas had slept in next to her as she lay on the mattress. Danny knew he wanted to return there as soon as possible, to leave behind the city, the politics and the oppression that he felt inside these city walls. The clouds lifted, the trials of the last week may yet have a positive outcome. He could put up with a couple of days sequestered underground if the promise of a return to the wilderness was his prize.

The Press Secretary was the one charged with presenting the article to Lucinda Románes. She cursed the spineless Vice-Chancellor and other cabinet senators who had all passed the buck and insisted that it was her job to inform the Chancellor of anything that appeared in the press, State-authorised or not. After a morning photo-call at one of the Capital's military bases, the Chancellor's motorcade swept back into The Palace grounds precisely on schedule. As the driver stepped out of the car and opened the rear door, Press Secretary Alice Anderson stepped forward.

'Give it to me,' snapped Lucinda Románes as she exited the car, before Alice had a chance to speak.

'You've heard about it already?'

'I am the Chancellor, I do hear about what is happening in my State.' Alice handed over the TouchScreen on which the article by Maxine Aubert was displayed. 'This is the same reporter who asked me if I was going to resign at the press conference?'

'Yes, Chancellor.'

'Have Davies summoned to my office this instant.'

'Yes, Chancellor.'

Edward Davies, Teddy to his friends, had been expecting a call from the Chancellor since the story had broken early that morning. He had been in his post as Head of the State Security Forces for a little over two years – not long in an administration that tended to allow people to stay in post until they chose to retire or passed away. In those two years things had generally gone well. There had been no crisis beyond the everyday work of the ongoing First Strike War, the usual counter-terrorism objectives and the various other bits and pieces that his department fulfilled as part of its role in keeping the State safe. He was not remiss in his job. He understood perfectly well the importance of a strong State, of ensuring the citizens were kept in line and their enemies were kept at bay. The State Security Forces were so powerful and feared that it was not often that anyone chose to try and take them on. He picked up the file from the officer, who had been handling the case of the young female reporter, and walked from his office in the west wing of The Palace to the Chancellor's office which was housed in the centre of the building on the top floor.

Romános was in her office on her own when Teddy was admitted by her personal assistant. He had always got on well with the young man who guarded the entrance to the Chancellor's office, so he could tell from the frosty atmosphere and unusual lack of small talk what awaited him inside. This was going to be an uncomfortable meeting.

'Sit down,' the Chancellor ordered him without looking up from her desk. Teddy sat in front of her. He felt like the school boy summoned to the principal's office. 'You've seen it, I take it?'

'Yes, Chancellor.'

'How far has it spread?'

'It seems to be in all the cities: printed copies, posters and on numerous sites online.'

'How is that possible?'

'It seems whoever is putting it out there has some inside help. We're investigating.'

'And the girl, this Maxine Aubert? Why wasn't she being watched as I requested?'

'She was under light observation. We assessed her to be a minor risk.'

The Chancellor gave him a withering look, 'She was allowed to travel out of the city?'

'As all journalists are who have the appropriate credentials. We had watchers follow her on the intercity shuttle to Central City. You will remember I raised this issue with you when I first took over. Freedom of the press should not equate to freedom of travel. I recommended all members of the press have their travel credentials revoked and they should have to apply for necessary permits on a case-by-case basis. Once in the city she ventured to the ongoing demonstrations there. We lost her in the crowd, but had no reason to believe she was an immediate threat. She was on leave from her role as a reporter.'

'Is The Star Tribune involved?'

'According to Buzz Mayfield, Ms. Aubert had told him she was going to visit her parents on the south coast for a few days. He seemed as surprised as us when he discovered what she had really been up to. We persuaded him to stop carrying the story on their site.'

'It should never have been there in the first place. After the election the Tribune is finished.'

Teddy wondered if he would face a similar fate after the election, but now was not the time to inquire about his own situation. 'What now?' he asked.

Romanés turned in her chair, staring out of the window onto the rooftop of The Palace. Beyond it the Capital sprawled out into the distance. 'We continue as planned. Are your assets in place?'

Teddy nodded, 'The inventory has arrived. Personnel is assembling. By the morning everything will be in place.'

'We have to make a response, but we must not add fuel to the story. I will address the State through the media denying the story and assuring the citizens that those behind these lies will face the full justice of the State. Have your men assemble in the morning at the protest, have them clear the protestors from the square, but I want no violent scenes, no retribution, while citizens still have time to vote. A show of force, an expression of the law being enforced, but nothing else until after the election is over. Is that clear?'

'Understood. And after the voting has finished?'

'Then proceed as before. Put the protestors down.'

'The journalist?'

'Leave her. If we do anything now it looks like we are admitting that what she has written is true.'

'And the ex-police officer, Daniel Samson?'

'He is a wanted criminal, a traitor to the State and an escaped prisoner. If you find him, kill him.'

16

Gabriella parked the car in another basement of a parking lot, out of sight from the street. They walked down an alleyway which opened out onto a street. Max recognised the hotel she had visited the previous day. She wondered about the old man behind the reception desk, if he had read her article this morning. Would he have noticed her name on the byline and connected it to the name in his hotel register belonging to the woman who had booked a room, arrived, left and then never returned?

They walked towards the City Parliament but before arriving at the square, Gabriella detoured towards the main railway terminal. At the main entrance she stopped and pointed. Max looked at the bundle of papers sitting in an old rack. The rack looked out of place, an antique from the age when printed newspapers had still been commonplace. There was only one paper in each of the slots of the rack. It was her article, set in black and white with a bold red banner across the top. Letters across the banner shouted out the headline: 'THE CORRUPT STATE'. Underneath, in a slightly smaller font size was her name: 'An Exclusive Report by Maxine Aubert'. There were no pictures, just text, neatly arranged in two columns across the page. Max picked a copy up and flicked through it. It was thin, only running across six pages and unadorned with anything else apart from her words. As she stood reading the text she had written the night before she noticed others picking up a copy for themselves, ordinary citizens curious to see what this obscure item was. Some headed into the terminal, they would sit and read it while waiting for their train to arrive, or on the journey to their homes. Others were exiting the station, perhaps they would browse over this curiosity during a lunch break or with dinner at home. Phillips had kept his word, he had got her story out as he promised he would do.

'Is it just here?' Max asked Gabriella.

'Every city,' Gabriella answered. 'Follow me.' She led Max inside the station and towards the TouchScreen hire desk. She picked up one of the TouchScreens that were free for any citizen to use in the station. She tapped a few words into the search bar and turned the screen towards Max. The results of her search filtered down the screen. There was entry after entry, page after page, mention after mention of her name and links to her article. Max tapped on the first one. The article appeared, set out in the same style as the printed version they had just seen outside the station. As Max scanned the words the screen flickered and an alert appeared: 'Content Removed'. She clicked back to the original search and tried another link further down the list. Her article appeared again. She tried a handful more. Sometimes the article appeared, sometimes it had been removed.

'They can't remove all of them,' Gabriella said, 'it's too late. Your article is out there.'

Max replaced the TouchScreen. They walked through the station and back out onto the street. Every time Max spotted a citizen with her article in their hands she felt herself swell with pride. This was it, this was what she had wanted when she had started out as a young reporter. Something she had written was making a difference. The danger that she may face in the future was not unknown to her, but for now it felt like it was worth the risk. Phillips had delivered where the media companies had failed. Unlike Buzz Mayfield and the State Media Compliance Department, Phillips had published her story in full, her words, uncensored and unedited, the truth as she saw it. This was what a free press could achieve, this was why the freedom to publish without State censorship was so vital to any country. She, Maxine Aubert, was holding the State and the Party to account when no other authority dared to. Tomorrow when citizens came to vote, many would make a decision informed by the words she had written and the scandal she had exposed. She had no qualms about what she had done. Her integrity was intact, she had not been forced to write something she did not agree with. She wondered if her mother and father would see it, and what they would make of it. No doubt Buzz and John Curran would be aware of it. She imagined they would not be pleased, although she liked to think they might raise a wry, knowing smile to each other, a reminder for them of their younger days when they had been hungry reporters determined to resist State power, before the system had beaten them down.

They carried on walking into the main square. The crowd of protestors was still there in the middle of the civic space, surrounded by a cordon of police officers. There were more protestors than there had been the previous day. Whether that was due to Max's article or not they couldn't be certain, but Max did notice the paper copies of her article in the hands of many of those who had gathered. Some stood in small groups sharing a copy, reading over the shoulder of a citizen. Others were in heated discussion, pointing at the text and animatedly

211

expressing opinions. The drums and chants were louder, the confidence of the demonstration emboldened by what they had read, their cause justified beyond doubt. No longer were they only making a point about the handling of an energy crisis or overpopulation. Now they were protesting against a corrupt State that was not looking after their interests, as it had always claimed. The State had been proved to be brutal, callous and uncaring, putting the interests of the few at the top above those of the many. The fresh impetus added dissent to the atmosphere. The protestors were no longer afraid, they directed chants directly at the police who surrounded them. They shouted insults towards the parliament and the State representatives who worked inside it.

Still the police stood unmoved. There was no sign that they were about to take any action. Max understood why. Politically, it would be a disaster the day before the election. The Party would win the election there was no doubt about that. Her story would fade away, the protests would run out of steam. If the State kept its cool, the whole situation could be contained and would blow over. The thought dispirited her. The elation she had felt moments earlier receded as she saw the scenario play out to the end. Without sustained scrutiny, the Party would be allowed to continue as it had through the previous decades. Her article would be dismissed and consigned to history, forgotten altogether. Suddenly, Phillips's plan seemed ridiculous. Danny had been right. How could they hope to take on the State? It was too powerful. As she looked at the crowd around her, Max finally understood the futility that Danny had spoken of. No journalist could change the course of history just by writing the truth and letting people read it. It would change nothing. What could anyone do to make an actual difference?

Gabriella stood next to her, sharing restrained greetings with a few in the crowd who seemed to know her. They must have been part of the group that was based in the underground bunker. The long hot summer was continuing with another blistering day. As the afternoon wore on the numbers in the square decreased, while those that remained began to seek a spot of shade around the edges of the square. The chanting became sporadic and listless. The effects of the morning's revelations dwindled with the diminishing energy. Max wanted to get out of there. She wanted to be back in the Capital City, back in her flat or with her parents, back where she had grown up, where she belonged, where she had happy, innocent memories. A world she knew she could never return to now.

The TouchScreen projected the large image onto the wall so that everyone in the mess hall could watch the broadcast at the same time. The holding card had been there for five minutes, ever since Phillips had gathered everyone in the room. Finally, with a blink and a burst of unintended static noise the picture changed to show Chancellor Lucinda Románes sitting in the familiar surroundings of her office in The Palace. Danny sat at the back of the room. He was surprised at the amount of people who had gathered to watch. There must have been another section to the bunker that he had not seen, another corridor of rooms where all these people were housed. He noticed they all wore the same black combat clothing he had been given to wear. The men and women varied in age, but the majority of them were young, between fifteen or sixteen and thirty years old. As the image on the wall settled, a hush descended over the room.

From behind her desk in The Palace, Lucinda Románes clasped her hands in front of her and leaned forward, staring straight into the camera and looking her subjects squarely in the eye. 'Citizens of The State, it has come to my attention that there is an article in widespread circulation around our cities that makes several wild and fantastic accusations about myself, the Central Alliance Party, the Senate and your elected government. I address you now, on the eve of our free and democratic elections, to assure you all, every single one of you, our citizens, our family, that the allegations printed in this libellous document are completely false. I repeat, unequivocally and completely false. There was no trial on children in Central City, there was no cover-up, no State hit squads and no illegal nightclubs. This article is a complete fabrication. Our dearly missed comrades Ishmael Nelson and Patrick Donovan were killed by an assassin at the behest of terrorists, our enemies in the First Strike War, who will stop at nothing to destroy our way of life. It would not surprise me to learn that it is the very same perpetrators who are behind this latest attempt to destabilise our State and influence the election of your new Senate and Chancellor tomorrow. The author of this article, Maxine Aubert, is a disgraced journalist who has a history of betraying the goodwill of this State in allowing a free press to criticise and attack the Party at every opportunity. Only a few days ago, her employment at The Star Tribune was suspended due to her personal vendetta against the State. The police officer cited as a witness in the article is a convicted traitor and deserter, a man of low morals, a fantasist who blames the State for unfortunate tragedies in his own personal life.'

One or two heads turned to find Danny at the back of the room. He greeted them with a wry smile and a shrug. The Chancellor continued for another five minutes, moving on to the well-versed political statements she had been regurgitating for the last three months in the lead up to the election. The article was not mentioned again until the end of the speech, as the Chancellor wrapped up her special address to the nation.

'Rest assured, my fellow citizens, your elected government will find those responsible for this false propaganda, this tissue of lies and inventions. We will hunt them down and bring them to justice. They will become an example, a warning to our other enemies who would do us harm. Our State is strong, our bond unbreakable, together the Party and her people are invincible. Tomorrow you will vote for me and my Party in your millions. We will not let you down. Goodnight.'

The screen went black before the familiar news anchor of the State broadcaster reappeared. Phillips switched the TouchScreen off and addressed the silent room.

'There was nothing there we did not expect to hear. We knew they would deny it. We know how they work. They have turned the truth around and are using it as another call for unity. They call us the enemy. This is what we are up against.' With that he exited. Slowly the people in the room stood and wandered away, speaking in small groups as they left. Some gave Danny a nod of recognition as they passed him, faces he had never seen before who seemed to know who he was. On the far side of the room, one young male caught his eye, exiting by

215

another door. The face looked familiar but vanished before Danny could place him. He was young, only sixteen or seventeen. When Danny had seen him before the face was even younger. His short and neat hair had been wild and unruly. His shoulders had filled out and he was a few inches taller, becoming a man now as opposed to the boy Danny was sure he had once met. Danny stood and walked after him.

Leaving the canteen hall behind, Danny entered a corridor identical to the one he had been in previously, a mirror image with several doors on either side of a tunnel. Those whom Danny followed filtered into two doors across the corridor. As he pushed through them, a few of them stood aside to let him pass, treating him with reverence. Through the door he found himself in a large hall, bigger than any of the others he had seen in the underground base so far. It was filled with rows and rows of wooden workbenches. On top of the benches there was a selection of weapons. Many of them Danny recognised: old, antique rifles and handguns and rudimentary grenades. There were rows of glass bottles filled with clear liquid and topped with cloths, improvised explosives that were being carefully placed into crates. The workers were returning to their places and picking up weapons in front of them, cleaning and preparing them. He saw the boy that had caught his attention sitting at one of the benches and made his way towards him.

'Casper?' Danny said as he approached him.

The young man looked up at him. 'Hi,' was all the young man whom Danny had last seen waving to him from the end of a bridge in the wilderness said.

'What are you doing here?'

'The same as you. Joining the fight.'

'The fight? What fight?'

'Against those that oppress us.'

'What about Skylar? What happened to the commune?'

'He died. The village turned against him and burned him at the stake. It was what he deserved.' Casper said it matter-of-factly, without emotion.

'And the villagers, what happened to them?'

'Most took boats and set out over the water, hoping to reach the Southern Americas or the African Union. A few of us came back to the mainland, some stayed in the wilderness. I came to the city to join the fight.'

'There is no fight,' Danny said.

'There will be. This is just the beginning. We have to prepare.' Danny saw with despair that Casper's impressionable young mind, once devoted to the maniacal Skylar, was now under the control of a new leader.

Before Danny could ask what they were preparing for, Phillips appeared from nowhere at his side. 'I see you have found each other. Young Casper mentioned he had met you in the past.'

Danny turned and grabbed Phillips by the arm, leading him away from the workbench. 'What the hell is this? Are you building some sort of army?'

'Does this look like an army to you? It is hardly worthy of the name.'

'What would you call it then?'

'You saw for yourself how the State is preparing to deal with us,' Phillips brushed Danny's hand away from his arm. 'You saw the weapons being brought to the city. What do you think their purpose was for? I suspected something like this may happen. They will come for us after the election. As well as weapons I have heard there are military personnel gathering near the city.'

'And you want to take them on with antiques and homemade firebombs? These are just kids, Phillips.' He pointed at Casper who watched the two of them while he cleaned and assembled a rifle. Danny thought back to the remote bridge where Casper had stood sentry, a similar rifle flung over his shoulder.

'We don't choose to fight, but we must be prepared and do what we can to defend ourselves.' Phillips's calm demeanour as he spoke down to Danny only infuriated him more.

'You want this to happen. You want them to attack you. You don't care about these kids so long as your plan succeeds. You are goading the State in order to provoke a response. You used me, you used Maxine and you're using these people.'

Phillips's face twisted, like a switch had been thrown. He stepped close to Danny, drawing his face aggressively near and grabbing Danny's t-shirt in a fist. 'If that's what it takes, then so be it.' His spittle sprayed Danny's face. Danny had never seen him snap in this way before. There was real passion behind those cool eyes. 'Don't you see? The Party is at its weakest in decades but if nothing changes after these elections it will recover, it will bury the past like it has always done, it will continue to fool the citizens and use them to serve its own purpose. They will do whatever they must to cling onto power.'

'What is it?' Danny pleaded, 'what is it that the Party has done that is so bad? I know they have made some serious mistakes, I know there is corruption, but I have also seen the good that the Party has done. What is

218

driving this? What do you know that you are not telling me?'

Phillips didn't answer, he turned and walked away, leaving Danny standing at the front of the room. Danny saw the young men and women staring at him. He walked after Phillips and the workers returned dutifully to their tasks. He understood now that Phillips wasn't motivated by politics alone, nor was he motivated by what they had uncovered in the city three years ago. There was something else, something worse. Whatever the reason it was driving him to take extreme measures, to risk lives in pursuit of some crazed goal to drive a wedge between the citizens and their government.

He caught sight of Phillips retreating down the corridor, 'I want out of here,' he called after him, 'I want no part of this.'

Phillips stopped and turned back to face him. His normal, unruffled appearance had returned. 'Not today. After the election you are free to go wherever you please.'

Danny stayed in the confines of his small room for the remainder of the day. It was a cell just like the one he had been held in by the State Police. He contemplated what he could do. Should he try to contact Henrik James and warn him about Phillips and the lengths he was willing to go to? He was uneasy about informing on anyone to the State authorities, but he was sure Henrik did not know the true nature of what Phillips was planning. If Henrik knew about it surely he would stop it? He may have helped Phillips up until now but he had sworn his allegiance to the citizens of Central City and protecting their safety. If he was to learn of a militia forming within his own city, Henrik would have to act to stop it. There

219

was always the chance that Henrik would also re-arrest Danny and put him back in a police cell. He thought of Maxine and how Phillips had used her, manipulated her into producing his propaganda. It didn't matter if it was true or not. Perhaps that mattered to Maxine, but to Phillips it just mattered that the news had been spread around the cities before the election. Gabriella and Maxine had not returned that day as far as Danny knew.

He was brought dinner by one of the young soldiers dressed in black who left it inside his door. 'He said you should eat, even if you will not join us. Tomorrow will be a busy day,' the girl had said as she laid down the plate. Danny left the plate untouched. In the stillness and quiet of his room he lay on the bed. He lost track of time with no clock and without any natural light to guide him.

At some point he drifted into an unsettled sleep. He dreamt of a black-shirted army marching through a city, firing weapons and throwing firebombs indiscriminately. He saw innocent victims, bodies lying in the street, as he walked through the aftermath. A small child was wailing, he approached the sound and found himself looking at his son, Hanlen, cradled in the arms of his dead mother. Out of an alleyway a small boy staggered, bloodied and blinded. It was Lucas, groping into space, seeking someone to help him. A loud gunshot echoed around them. Lucas dropped to his knees and toppled over. Danny turned and saw Phillips. 'We must all make sacrifices for the greater good, Danny,' he said with a sinister, inhuman smirk. Danny ran away, spinning round the corner into another street. He came face-to-face with masked Special Forces soldiers. His hands outstretched in front of him, Danny pleaded for them to stop. They marched towards him mercilessly. He turned again to run away but was distracted by something hanging from the streetlight overhead. It was Cassandra Ford, her tortured limp body was carved open, her intestines dripping from her stomach. Next to her, hanging from the same light but still alive, kicking and struggling with a noose around her neck, was Maxine. Her strangled cries were silenced by another shot. This time he saw Lucinda Romànes, the Chancellor herself, holding the smoking gun. She repeated the words that Phillips had just spoken: 'We must all make sacrifices for the greater good, Danny.' Another alleyway appeared where there had once been a brick wall. Danny sprinted into it, a silent scream emanating from his open mouth. His path was blocked. It was Gabriella. She held another newborn baby in her arms. It was his Isla. 'Don't hurt her,' he pleaded with the assassin. 'Why would I hurt her? I want to protect her,' Gabriella answered, 'I need to protect her because you failed to do it.' Gabriella pulled a gun and aimed it straight at Danny.

'No,' Danny cried and sat upright on the uncomfortable iron frame bed. The sweat was pouring from his brow. There was a knock at the door.

It was Casper who appeared, 'It's time for you to get ready and join us. We leave in ten minutes.' He closed the door behind him and left Danny alone. His breathing returned to normal. The serene dreams of a peaceful end he had become used to living in the wilderness were gone, now the nightmares that had once plagued him in the city had returned.

PART FOUR:

ELECTION DAY

5th JULY

17

In the cities of the State millions of citizens awoke and prepared to cast their vote. For many it would be the first time they had experienced the privilege, for those who had lived long enough it would be their tenth or even eleventh time. Some would fulfil their duty before continuing with whatever they did to pass the days: walking, running, cycling, gaming, interacting socially online and even in the real world. Others, the thirty to forty percent who were still in regular employment would cast their vote before resuming their regular routine, be it working in a farm laboratory, in engineering factories keeping the fleet of city robots onstream, in one of the superhospitals, or in the huge weapons factories. Half of those who still had jobs were civil servants, employed by the State directly – their votes were guaranteed to the Central Alliance Party, unless they wished to be fired from their job with immediate effect. The roads remained quiet, the private travel ban was still in place for Election Day. Almost all the votes cast would be done on personal TouchScreens from the comfort of home, which helped the State as each vote could be easily traced. In a nod to tradition and for those select few who still favoured the old ways, a handful of polling stations were set up within State buildings. Here politicians, ever seeking publicity, would arrive in order to be seen smiling and voting. In the Capital City, a polling station was set up in The Palace and a select few photographers from the media were admitted to watch the Chancellor make her vote with staged efficiency.

In Central City, the skies were a brilliant blue again and for once they were quiet: no drones flew on Election Day, a security measure that had survived from the days when large crowds had gathered at public buildings in order to vote. One physical polling station was erected in the lobby of the City Parliament, just outside the security gates one needed to pass through to gain admittance to the interior of the building. Citizens were not permitted in the Parliament, even on Election Day. So far that morning, no one had turned up to cast their vote in this antiquated way. The election officers charged with supervising the booth had left their posts by now, far more interested in the events happening outside the front door. They stood, along with many others who worked in the building, political and security staff, on the top of the steps looking out across the road to the centre of the square. They had become accustomed to the protest crowd over the last week or so, but today it had grown into something else. There were at least treble the amount of protestors and as a consequence the volume of the chanting, shouting and general atmosphere had also risen.

From a window above the square, on the corner next to the Parliament building, Phillips, Gabriella, Danny and Max looked down on the demonstration. They were in a disused office, made redundant now administration work could comfortably be done by people working in their own homes. The room had white walls and a grey linoleum floor. At one end several desks and chairs were stacked up. Phillips was wearing SmartLenses, using them

224

to magnify the image below them. Gabriella used an old-fashioned scope from a sniper rifle to achieve the same view. Max and Danny had to rely on their own eyes to watch what was unfolding.

'How can you be sure something will happen?' It was Gabriella who was questioning Phillips for a change. It was reassuring for Danny to see that he treated her question with the same dismissiveness he often used with Danny.

'After Max's article they are stepping up security in the city. The Chancellor wasn't making idle threats in her little speech yesterday. Pretty soon this,' he looked at the protestors and the State Police who continued to surround them, 'will be out of Henrik's control. Then, who knows what will happen?'

'I should be down there if something is going to happen,' Max cut in.

'It could become dangerous very quickly,' Phillips cautioned.

'You said yourself there won't be any violence until after the polls close, the Party wouldn't attack its own citizens until it had safely secured another decade in total power,' the reporter argued.

'Very well, I can't stop you. Gabriella, you should go with her.' Max opened her mouth to protest, but Phillips raised his hand to stop her. 'Just as a precaution, she won't interfere with your journalistic integrity.'

'Fine,' Max acquiesced and walked across the room, picking up her TouchScreen and notepad.

Gabriella turned to Phillips. 'You really think it could become violent? They will attack the protestors?'

'You bring weapons to a standoff and it only takes one moment to set off a chain of events no one anticipated.' Gabriella looked him in the eye with suspicion. Danny was caught between them. Gabriella was trying to figure out what Phillips was really edging around. After an awkward moment he turned back to look out of the window. Gabriella followed Max, who had already left the room.

'Tell me,' Danny asked when the two men were left alone in the room, 'is it the Security Forces or us that are bringing weapons into this situation?'

'We have to be able to defend ourselves,' Phillips repeated the mantra from the previous day. Before Danny could challenge another evasive answer, Phillips stepped forward with renewed interest in the events taking place in the square. 'It's happening,' he said. Danny saw the State Police, who had provided the human cordon around the demonstrators for the last month, smartly and as one, drop their riot shields and take a step backwards, all the individuals moving as a well-drilled whole. The noise from the protestors dropped as they became aware of the unexpected movement.

Over the quietening atmosphere, Danny could hear the clear, clipped commands being issued. He searched the square and saw where the voice was coming from. At one corner an officer was issuing the instructions to which the State Police officers were responding. 'Fall back slowly on my mark!' He bellowed, 'And, step! Step! Step!' With each repetition the line of riot police took a further step backwards until they had moved across the road and were backed up against the surrounding buildings. 'On my mark, right turn and fall out! Mark!' The well-drilled personnel turned to their right, then began stepping forward in marching time. They

226

disappeared from Danny's view as they reached the corner to the right of the building in which he stood.

'They're retreating,' Danny stated, for a moment thinking that for once Phillips had got it completely wrong. They had backed down and removed the cordon. The State wanted to avoid conflict as much as the citizens did. The Party could win the election and forgive and forget, pretend it never happened, knowing they were secure in power for another decade. Phillips had made a massive miscalculation.

'They're not retreating,' Phillips answered calmly, 'they're being replaced.'

Henrik was in the Situation Room at police headquarters when he was alerted to the unusual action occurring outside the City Parliament. He should have known it was coming. A message had arrived from Phillips the previous evening. It had warned him about the arrival of State Special Forces on the outskirts of the city. Airforce carrier planes had been spotted leaving the Capital. Henrik had checked with the two main airports situated in Central City. No military planes had landed. There was an old airstrip on the coast that had long been out of regular service but was still maintained as a back-up for the military. It was staffed by State Security personnel. He was still waiting for a reply to his enquiry about any military aircraft arriving there in the previous seventy-two hours. Combined with the statement from Danny that weapons had been arriving in the city, it was hard to believe that Phillips's warning was not genuine.

No more headway had been made by Detective Cancio in his investigation into the prison escape and the death of Cas Ford, other than Archie had categorically ruled out suicide as the cause of her demise. There were signs of torture on the body that could not be ignored, even if the killer had wanted the death to be framed that way. Henrik felt guilty about withholding what he knew from a loyal colleague, but he was doing Archie a favour. He didn't want to see a good man being dragged down into the gutter the way he had been, the way Danny Samson had been, or the way his own father had been.

The election came as a blessed respite. All usual police business, including open investigations were on hold for the day to ensure the smooth running of the vote. That included continuing the safe policing of the demonstration outside the City Parliament, which had grown in size since the article by Maxine Aubert had appeared and stoked up a fresh outcry against the Central Alliance Party. As a result, Henrik had deployed double the amount of officers to the square. Other officers were seconded to the Online Fraud Department who would monitor votes made over the State internet and search for any anomalies that suggested vote rigging or identity fraud. Archie Cancio had been sent there and had accepted it as an understandable order. Henrik had arrived early and taken his place in the Situation Room from where he would oversee events from all across the city. Although many seemed to forget, the State was still at war with countries around the world in an ongoing conflict, and elections always presented a tempting target for terrorists.

The first couple of hours had passed without incident until he noticed the rising murmur from one of the desks at the front of the room. A hand was raised. The taskforce leader went over to consult. She turned to Henrik and waved him to join them. Henrik didn't need to be told what he could see was happening on the bank of monitors at the desk. They showed the square outside the parliament building from various angles. Every angle showed the same thing: the State Police Force was withdrawing from the scene.

'Who gave this order?' Henrik demanded.

'No one in this room,' the taskforce leader replied, looking genuinely perplexed.

'Get me the onsite commander on the line now.'

Max felt the tension and confusion in the square. Some of the protestors took the withdrawal of the State Police as a sign of victory. They began to sing in celebration, jeering at the retreating officers. There was a minor surge towards the parliament building entrance. There was now nothing to stop the protestors storming the building if they wanted to. Something held them back though, they were unable to overcome the mindset that had kept them cowed for so long. The State wielded its power over the citizens by more than force, it had a psychological grip that was harder to break down than any physical barrier. Others in the crowd sensed that it may not be such a welcome development. With Gabriella following her, Max pushed her way into the middle of the crowd, where there was a statue that provided a raised dais to stand upon and see over the top of the people. Gabriella stood alongside her.

'What's going on?' Max shouted over the din.

'I'm not sure.'

'Does Phillips know?'

'I don't know.'

'What is he planning?'

'He hasn't told me anything. I thought he was just here to see how the election panned out.'

'No, something else is going on,' Max said with certainty. She was sure Phillips had foreseen that something was about to happen. She was sure he had an angle to make it work to his advantage.

Over the noise of the crowd a new sound grew. It was like a drum of some kind, a regular beat that kept an even pace as it drew nearer and gained strength. The chanting and singing ceased as heads swivelled towards the oncoming noise which echoed around all sides of the square. The constant beat was unrelenting. The source was revealed as hundreds of soldiers in boots appeared marching towards the square in perfect uniformity. Alongside the marching feet another sound joined them, the hum of engines and squeak of wheels created by tracked unmanned vehicles rolling along the roads. The cheers that had died away moments before were replaced with the first cries of panic as the full might of the State Security Force converged on the square from all sides. There was no escape for the citizens caught in the centre.

Danny watched in horror from the window. Row after row of soldiers filtered into the square and began spreading out, replacing the cordon that the State Police had previously provided. There the similarity ended. Whereas the police cordon had been maintained at a respectful distance, providing a watchful but unthreatening presence, the soldiers pressed closely up to the edge of the protestors with riot shields and ShockBatons raised. At intervals there was a gap in the cordon of soldiers into which rolled an unmanned drone tank. Danny had only ever seen these machines in news footage from overseas of battlefields in the First Strike War. They were the size of a family car, steel-plated with a turret that could swivel through three hundred and sixty degrees. On the front were two mounted machine guns and on top of the turret was a grenade launcher. They were controlled remotely from a base that could be hundreds of kilometres away. Many of the parts that went into building these machines were produced at the weapons factory by the river, only a few streets away from the city square in which they now lined up.

'You knew this was going to happen,' Danny said to Phillips, who was still viewing everything through his SmartLenses.

'You saw the artillery being delivered yourself, Danny, you must have had an idea something like this was a possibility.'

'You said they wouldn't do anything until after the election.'

'It appears Maxine's article has had an effect on those in the Capital. They obviously feel a show of force is required to make people think twice about who they might vote for today.'

'They're not going to start killing their own citizens on the streets in cold blood.'

'No, I think you're probably right. Not intentionally anyway, I'm sure they wouldn't want to do that. If, on the other hand, things got out of control, an itchy trigger finger, a stray bullet, a misheard instruction, then who knows where this might end.'

'This is madness,' Danny exclaimed, growing increasingly desperate.

'No,' Phillips withdrew his SmartLenses and looked at Danny, 'this is the true nature of the State. This is what

I have been trying to tell you. This is what true power looks like and this,' he pointed out the window for added emphasis, 'is what we must fight against.'

'What is it?' Danny insisted. 'What is it that you won't tell me? Something about the war?'

'That's just it,' Phillips raised his voice to match Danny's, 'there is no war. There never was.'

There was no question now that Phillips had been right. Every surveillance camera angle Henrik could see showed the State soldiers lining the square. He finally heard the voice of the onsite commander, Superintendent Dollan in his ear receiver. 'Who ordered this?' Henrik shouted. Heads in the situation room turned towards him.

Dollan's reply was difficult to make out above the noise he was in the middle of. Henrik could see the source of the noise when he looked at the monitors and saw the panicked crowd in the square. 'It came direct from the High Commissioner, Chief. You were not informed?'

'No, I bloody wasn't,' Henrik fumed. If the order had come direct from the Capital to the onsite officer in charge it was clear they had decided to cut Henrik out of the loop. Whatever the Cas Ford investigation discovered in the next few days, regardless of whether Samson and Gabriella were caught or killed, he was finished in the State Police Force. All that remained for him was to learn the severity of his punishment. If they unearthed the full truth about his betrayal, Henrik had no doubt he would end up facing the same fate as Cas.

'There's nothing we can do, Chief,' Dollan continued, shouting over the cacophony behind him.

'We're pulling back to a safe distance and awaiting further orders.'

'Your orders are to get in there and take back control of our city,' Henrik shouted.

'With all due respect, Chief, your position has been superseded in the chain of command. I cannot order my men to disobey the High Commissioner. And on top of that, there is no way we can challenge the manpower and weapons they have at their disposal. It would be suicidal.'

Henrik knew perfectly well Dollan was correct. 'Understood, Superintendent. Do what you can to diffuse the situation and keep the citizens and your men safe.' He pulled out his receiver and threw it to the floor. They were powerless to do anything other than watch the events unfold. Henrik retreated to his position at the rear of the Situation Room without issuing any instructions to the expectant team. He slumped in his chair. He was out of options. He couldn't turn to Phillips for help now, it was too late. His fate was sealed and he knew it. He could try running. In the confusion of Election Day he might even be able to get out of the city. But then what? He thought of Samson and his years in the wilderness. Perhaps that wouldn't be so bad, but Henrik had never been one to retreat and abandon his responsibilities. He had to live with his decisions, and face up to the consequences.

Then he saw her. That same face that had broken into his headquarters and freed Samson a couple of days ago, the same face that belonged to the murderer of his father. A camera in one of the corners of the square had zoomed in to the centre of the crowd, focussing on a raised platform on which the leaders of the protest had gathered, standing above the swarm of people around them. Next to her, he recognised the journalist Maxine Aubert, the subject of a 'restrain and detain' order that morning, issued to all police forces in the State. However, it was the face of the woman standing just behind her that Henrik concentrated on. Gabriella Marino was looking at the scene unfolding around her. As he watched the live pictures he saw them jump down from the dais and begin fighting their way through the mass of bodies that were all trying to move in opposite directions at the same time. The Security Forces were gradually moving forwards, tightening the cordon around the protestors, corralling them into a tight, crushed unit that could be guided out of the square and into the surrounding streets. They were breaking up the demonstration.

Henrik made up his mind. 'I'm going to the City Parliament,' he announced to the task force leader. 'You're in charge. You have my authority to give whatever orders you see fit.' With that he strode out of the room, turning his back on his command and his force. He knew he would never be able to come back into the building to which he had dedicated so much of his life as an officer of the State.

He waved his personal assistant away, 'It's too dangerous,' he assured him, and left him standing in the parking garage, as he got into the AutoDrive car and shut the door. 'City Parliament,' he ordered the vehicle.

'That area is out of bounds to all personnel at this time due to an ongoing security situation,' the vehicle's onboard computer told him in her soothing, calm voice. Henrik beat the wheel in frustration and then bypassed the computer controls using his authority as Chief Commander. Taking manual control he turned into the

234

street at the top of the ramp and took off along the deserted road towards the main square.

Max and Gabriella became separated in the heaving, tightly-packed crowd. Panic had manifested itself in frightened pushing and ill-judged decision-making. People were falling and being trampled, groups and families had become separated and were desperately calling out to one another. The crush only intensified as the soldiers and their drone tanks pushed the crowd tighter and tighter together. Max had seen from the raised position what the soldiers were doing. Gabriella had noticed it too and ordered Max to get out of the crowd as quickly as they could, but it was too late. They were caught in the stampede.

Bodies were pressed together, dust and dirt swirled round them. The heat in the crowd was overwhelming. Some fainted in the press. Max stumbled over something on the ground. Looking down she saw it was the arm of a woman. She was unconscious on the ground, bruised and battered from the footsteps that had trampled over her. She may have already been dead, Max thought. They could kill us all, she realised. Why don't they stop? She felt a tug on her arm and turned. It was Gabriella reaching between the bodies surrounding her and pulling her forward.

'Come on,' she shouted in Max's ear, 'we have to keep moving and get away from the centre.'

'People are being hurt in the crush,' Max shouted back.

'There's nothing we can do about that here.' Gabriella pulled her sharply and Max was free from the immediate scrum she had been squeezed into. Now

235

Gabriella was behind her and pushed her forcefully through the crowd.

'What does that mean? 'There is no war.' Of course there's a bloody war, it's been going on for fifty years.' Danny was no longer watching the events below him. He was staring at Phillips as though he was insane.

'There's fighting,' Phillips replied. 'There are two nominal sides. It has all the hallmarks of a war, but from day one the First Strike War has been a lie, fought under false pretences, because it suited leaders on both sides to be at war.'

'You're saying the First Strike was faked?'

'In a way,' Phillips continued to watch out of the window, closely monitoring something that Danny could not make out. 'Did you never ask yourself this question: why Billings? Why Montana? There's nothing there, no military bases, no arms factory. The big cities on the coasts have army bases, airports, naval bases. Why would the Axis Powers deliberately target a city in the middle of the country with no strategic value in a war? Why would you start a war and not try to take out your enemies most valuable assets? The obvious answer is that the Axis Powers did not fire any nuclear missile at the Civil American States.'

'Then who did?'

'A nuclear device detonated in Montana and Wyoming but it was not launched by any of the Axis Powers. It was not planted by any terrorists. It was an accident, a mistake. The exact cause is anyone's guess, no investigation has ever been conducted to determine what really happened.'

'The Civil American States blew itself up with one of it's own weapons?'

'With so many nuclear devices proliferated around the world the only surprise should be that it took so long for an accident to happen and only the Civil States suffered such an accident.'

'But why then go to war? Why blame terrorists or another country?'

'The government couldn't admit to killing half of their own population and rendering half of their land uninhabitable. Such a scandal would have resulted in the remaining parts of the country tearing itself apart. Instead, they claimed it was an attack in order to pull the country together. Nothing stirs up patriotism like a common enemy against which to do battle. Every war in history tells us that.'

'And the Allied Powers just went along with this without asking any questions?'

'You have to think of the wider politics. The First Strike changed the dynamics of power around the world. Suddenly the Zhonghua Republic, backed by the SSSR and other neighbouring states had no challengers to their power and dominance of the globe. The only way the Civil States and her allies could protect themselves was to come together with unwavering support. The combined forces of the European Union, the African Union and our State, together with what remained of the Civil American States force, still faced odds stacked against them, but there was a chance we could resist the superior Axis Powers. The Civil American States needed her allies by her side to protect what it had left, and to do that they lied about the cause of the nuclear strike.'

Danny struggled to remember his history lessons about the early years of the First Strike War. 'But didn't we launch nuclear strikes in retaliation for the First Strike?'

'Of course we did, that is what you do when you have been attacked. You retaliate.'

'You said we hadn't been attacked.'

'Exactly.'

'We bombed innocent countries to cover up a nuclear accident? Hundreds of thousands of people died.' Danny refused to believe it. He knew the State was corrupt, he knew they had done bad things, he had been warned that the war was not what the citizens had been led to believe, but he could never have believed that this was the truth.

'Economically it suited everyone. Manufacturing, heavy industry, they were dying out all over the globe thanks to the restrictions of climate change and dwindling resources. The war gave fresh impetus. Mothballed factories could be repurposed. Workers who were being replaced by robots were needed again. At the time, the State didn't know it was all based on a lie of course. Whether that would have made any difference is debatable. Only later did the Party learn the truth. The Europeans decreased their involvement in the war when they discovered what had really happened, but agreed to maintain public support for the Allies. All governments agreed that no citizens of any State could ever know the truth.'

'How do you know all this?'

'Over the last three years, while I was away, I travelled through various places in the European Union, the African Union, even the Southern Americas. I tracked down people who had been in and around power at the start of the war. I persuaded them to tell me the truth.'

'But all those people that died? There were millions at the start.'

Phillips nodded, 'And for years afterwards the State and others sent soldiers to war, to fight for a false cause. Now do you see? Do you understand why the Party and the State can no longer be allowed to get away with what they have done? Or would you still deny that this corrupt State deserves to die?'

'I only have your word for any of this. There is no evidence. Even if all this is true, what good will one small rebellion in a northern city do?'

'Every revolution has to start with a single step,' Phillips switched back to his cold self and peered through the window.

'You are insane. This is nothing,' Danny cried. 'This will be forgotten within a few days. The Party will win the election and your revolution will be trampled into the dust.'

'You're right,' Phillips conceded. 'Unless something were to happen that could finally awaken the citizens of this city.'

'Like all those protestors being killed?' Danny exclaimed in horror.

'It doesn't need to be all of those people, Danny, it just needs one memorable death, one martyr, a figurehead that would demand the people take up arms in outrage.'

Danny tried to figure out what he was getting at. Phillips took off his SmartLenses and handed them to Danny, motioning him to put them on. Then Phillips pointed down into the square, to the edge of the crowd that was being kettled by the State soldiers. With a

239

magnified view, Danny could pick out individuals in the mass. He searched for what Phillips intended him to see. He froze when his gaze landed on the young journalist from the Capital.

'With all due respect, it was between you and her,' Phillips said calmly. 'Not much of a contest in the end. No one would cry too much over the killing of an ex-State police officer wanted for treason, a middle-aged traitor with his life already in ruins, known to be on the run from prison. A young, female reporter, on the other hand, with her whole life in front of her, murdered by a vengeful State after exposing the evil within the corridors of power. That is a powerful image. Not only that, it is an attack on the freedom of the press and the freedom of speech, such as they still exist.'

'You set her up from the start. Right from when you first met her in the Capital.'

'I can't claim to be that clever. I wanted her to come here and write her story. Beyond that I had no concrete plan. Events have subsequently conspired, forced me to adapt.'

'You're a murderer, you're no better than those you seek to expose.'

'You would not sacrifice one life to bring vengeance for all the millions who have been slaughtered under false pretences? You would not take one life in order to save millions more being killed in the future?'

Danny leapt at Phillips, throwing the SmartLenses aside and tackling the taller man, pushing him backwards and down to the floor. Phillips was taken by surprise, but he soon recovered and his military experience combined with his physical advantage over Danny made it an unfair contest. He turned swiftly as they fell, so that he landed on top of Danny. Before Danny could realise what had happened, Phillips had punched him across the face, bursting his nose open. Phillips detached himself and stood over Danny, who was holding his injured face.

'Pathetic,' he spat and stamped on Danny's ribcage, breaking bones under his foot. He straightened his clothes and returned to the window.

18

It took Henrik only five minutes to drive through the empty city streets and arrive at the square. Drone tanks and soldiers blocked his entrance. He abandoned his car in the middle of the road. A soldier at the blockade raised his hand and ordered him to halt. Henrik identified himself and allowed the soldier to scan him to confirm he was the Chief Commander of the City Police Force. The soldier grudgingly allowed him to pass.

The noise was deafening, louder than during the previous days of the demonstration. The tone of the noise was different too: gone was the singing and festive, celebratory atmosphere, replaced by screaming and shouting, threatening orders from the Security Forces and the clattering of riot shields and ShockBatons. The protestors had been successfully shepherded into a quarter of the square, to the left of the parliament building. The Security Forces were now squeezing the frightened citizens into the two streets that converged there. Lying in the square behind them were dozens of injured people. No medical staff were in attendance, but some brave citizens had darted to the aid of their fallen comrades. Henrik strode through the scene, ignoring those pleading for help as he passed them. He looked around the edges of the crowd, trying to spot the familiar face he had come to find. He knew she would be there somewhere. He put on his SmartLenses and activated the facial recognition scanner. He instructed the Lenses to locate Gabriella Marino as he scanned across the sea of faces. Hundreds of people were identified and dismissed. He circled round the swirling mass of people, careful not to attract the attention of any soldiers. He reached the Parliament stairs and gained some elevation. The SmartLenses continued to identify and dismiss various faces.

Finally the lenses turned red and a message flashed up in front of his eyes: 'Helena Myers Located. Known Alias of Gabriella Marino.' Henrik strained his neck, searching in the direction the SmartLenses were pointing him. 'Magnify,' he instructed. Now he saw her. She had just emerged from the crowd, pushing another, younger woman in front of her, the journalist Maxine Aubert. A soldier in riot gear blocked their exit from the crowd, Gabriella disarmed and dropped the unfortunate soldier to the ground with one swift punch to their head. Now they were free from the rest of the citizens. Henrik watched as the two women appeared to argue. Gabriella tried to pull the journalist away with her, but Aubert stood firm, refusing to leave. Henrik began running towards them.

'There are children in there,' Max screamed at Gabriella. 'We can't just leave them.'

'There is nothing we can do for them,' Gabriella argued, 'they will have to save themselves. You are no good to them if you are arrested or injured.'

'There must be something we can do to stop this.' They were swallowed up by the jostling soldiers again, who continued their relentless push to clear the protestors.

'You can write about what you have seen. Spread the word to the rest of the State about what has happened.'

Max did not see clearly what happened next. One moment Gabriella was holding onto her hand, trying to pull her away from the riot, the next she seemed to fall over and disappear, losing her grip on Max's hand. Max thought she saw a man pulling Gabriella away from the crowd. She assumed he was helping her after she had fallen. She lost sight of them as she was swept up in the irresistible momentum of the crowd. She fought her way clear once more. She felt the blow from a ShockBaton against her stomach and doubled over. There was no electric shock to accompany the violent punch which knocked the wind out of her. She sat on her knees, trying to suck in some oxygen. Feet clattered into her, bouncing her along the tarmac surface. She felt sharp pain as her elbows, knees and hands scraped along the ground and her skin was raked away. She instinctively curled up into a ball and rolled to the side, trying to avoid being trampled. She felt a kick on the back of the head and yelled out. The noise and confusion around her reached a crescendo and then it suddenly passed. She looked up and realised she was free from the panicked crowd. She was able to stand up and felt her body, the bruises and scrapes pulsing with pain. She was relatively unscathed. As she looked towards the crowd she saw a small girl looking up at her. Tears streamed down her face as she cried out, looking for her parents. Then the face was lost in the swirl of bodies.

Max had a moment of clarity. She thought of everything that had happened over the past week. Her career was over, the State would ensure she never wrote for the media again. She had tried to use her talent as a journalist to make a difference, as Phillips had encouraged her to do. This was the result. Her words were meaningless in the face of unrivalled power, they could be dismissed just as easily as the citizens were being crushed now. She had wanted to make a difference, to expose the truth. It had been futile. Samson was right. The State would quash this rebellion before it had even taken its first breath. One person could not make a difference, especially not a journalist. She almost laughed in her emotional, delirious state at the worthless contribution she had made. Phillips had challenged her to make a difference, to take a side and make a stand. She had achieved nothing.

Then she saw the huge drone SuperTank, bigger than the numerous smaller versions that lined up alongside the soldiers. It was the size of a bus, made with grey, armour-plated steel and it was crossing the square towards the rear of the fleeing protestors. She started running. The soldiers, focussed on their primary mission to corral the demonstrators, paid no attention as she darted round to the back of the group. The soldiers had parted to let the SuperTank push along the rear of the crowd. She knew the danger in what she was doing. She hoped Phillips was right about one thing: the State would not use fatal force against its own citizens while the election polls were still open. They had pushed and harassed, they had beaten, but they had not deliberately killed. She had only one thought, to get in front of the SuperTank and finally make her stand.

There was a gap of a few metres between the front of the SuperTank and the citizens desperately trying to get out of its way as it ploughed forward. It could run over the top of her without even noticing she was there. Max stripped off her black t-shirt, pulling it over her head. She stood in the path of the oncoming SuperTank and faced it. In black vest top and trousers, armed with nothing but her t-shirt that she waved above her head, she stopped and waited. The front of the machine drew closer and closer. Ten metres away, five metres. Still she did not move. It was one metre from her. Max waited to be knocked over by the dull thud of steel, followed by the crushing sensation as tank tracks rolled over her.

It never came. The SuperTank stopped with a loud hiss from its hydraulic brakes. The controller of the drone, who would be sitting somewhere far away looking at her through the cameras mounted on the front of the vehicle, revved the engine and blasted the siren. Max's gamble had paid off. They could not be seen to deliberately murder a citizen in cold blood. Their orders were to clear the demonstration, but not with deadly force. The soldiers at the rear of the protest now took notice of the unexpected pause behind them as they realised the SuperTank was motionless. They saw the small, solitary woman standing in defiance of the armoured vehicle. The controller backed the tank up slightly and tried to steer round the unexpected obstacle. Max took a step to the side and again blocked its progress. A soldier grabbed Max and tried to pull her out of the way. She punched and scratched him, making little impact against his protective riot gear. But other citizens at the back of the group had seen what was happening. First one, then another, then another battled past the cordon to come to her aid. One of them reached the soldier grappling with Max and tore him away from her. As the soldier turned and began to beat the citizen, others arrived to help. Max staggered back in front of the SuperTank and resumed the face-off while scuffles broke out around her.

'It is a shame. In a free State, she would be an excellent journalist,' Phillips continued to watch the events unfold from the window. Danny pulled himself up from the floor, wiping the stream of blood from his face and grimacing in pain from his broken ribs. 'What she has learned is that actions speak louder than words, especially in a State where the citizens are so blinded they can no longer think for themselves. They have to be shown things in simple ways that are easy to understand. You see,' Phillips pointed out of the window as Danny got to his feet, 'that is a brave person willing to make a sacrifice in order to save others from the State.'

Danny looked down. The Security Forces had almost succeeded in moving the protestors out of the square into the street directly below them, but at the back something was happening. A small group seemed to be fighting back and a huge SuperTank had ground to a halt. Danny tried to see what had stopped the vehicle in its tracks. In front of it he could make out a female, dressed in a black vest, barring the way forward for the armoured vehicle. This single woman was resisting the military might of the State, making a defiant stand in order to protect complete strangers caught up in the riot. 'They'll kill her.' He uttered.

'She's smarter than you, Danny. She realises they cannot kill her with the surveillance cameras filming every moment of this clash. She is unarmed, she is not attacking them, she is trying to protect fellow citizens. Imagine what that would look like if they murdered her with the whole State looking on, with citizens in this city and others preparing to vote.'

247

It dawned on Danny that the woman in front of the SuperTank was Maxine. 'But then you don't get your martyr, you don't get the moment you need to start your revolution.'

Phillips sighed, 'No, which is why sometimes you have to take drastic action, force things to happen by taking the initiative.' He picked up the TouchScreen that lay on the windowsill, turning his back on Danny. 'Do it,' he said simply into the device. There was no reply from the other end of the call. Phillips tossed the TouchScreen aside. He turned back to face the room and found himself alone. The door on the far side swung shut. Phillips allowed himself a smile. 'Too late, Danny.'

Danny vaulted down the stairs three at a time, slamming into the wall on each landing as he descended as quickly as he could. He ignored the screaming pain from his ribs. He tried to take the final flight of stairs in one leap and landed awkwardly, toppling forwards and battering straight through the door that led outside. He arrived in a heap on the street, picked himself up and started sprinting towards the square. He darted past the distracted soldiers who were meant to be guarding the barricade in the street, sending one of them to the ground as he barged past. They, like others all around, had stopped doing their job to watch the unfolding stand-off between the woman and the SuperTank. The Security Forces had paused their advance while the drama unfolded. Some protestors took the opportunity to make their escape. Others joined the soldiers in watching. Danny burst onto the scene, shouting in desperation above the noise.

Max did not hear him. She stood facing the SuperTank. She felt good, she was no longer afraid, she was empowered. This was her act of defiance, this was how she stood up to the State and the Party, by confronting their power directly, by daring them to cross a line even they could not cross. By forcing them to show weakness and vulnerability in the face of an ordinary citizen. She allowed herself a smile at her small victory. She had made a difference.

Danny got to within ten metres of her when a citizen stepped into his path and knocked him over, believing he was attempting to attack Max. Danny scrambled to get free, shouting from the ground, trying to make Max hear him.

'Move,' he screamed, 'they're going to kill you.'

The single gunshot rang out from somewhere in the square. The echo bounced around the buildings making it impossible to pinpoint where the shot had come from. Danny saw the spray of blood erupt from Maxine's head as she flew to the side, thrown towards him and landing limply on the ground in front of him. Her sky-blue eyes were wide open, staring lifelessly at him. Half of her head had been blown away by the high-calibre bullet. She died instantly.

An odd moment of quiet descended over the square that had been a wall of unrelenting noise for the previous hour. Citizens and soldiers stared at the dead body lying on the ground. Both seemed equally stunned.

From within the crowd the first cry went up: 'Murderers!' It was accompanied by a whoosh through the air as a glass bottle with a lit cloth stuffed into it flew over the heads of the protestors and exploded on the ground, sending a shower of flames onto a group of unprepared soldiers. More cries followed, and a shower of bottles appeared. A wall of flames erupted all around. The crowd began to scatter in several directions. For a moment it looked like the Security Forces would be forced into a retreat, but firm orders were swiftly delivered. The drone tanks began to roll forwards once more. The SuperTank now had a clear path and resumed its forward march.

Danny crawled across the ground to reach the body of Max. As he did so he heard the artillery of the State military open up, firing against its own citizens.

Henrik James had taken her by surprise. When he had hit her across the back of her head with his gun, Gabriella had lost consciousness. When she came round she was being dragged down an alleyway leading away from the square. Only when her assailant leaned her against a wall in order to open a door did she recognise Henrik. He shoved her inside. The door swung closed behind him, plunging them into a murky darkness.

Gabriella landed on a cold, concrete floor, covered in dirt and dust. They were in some sort of disused warehouse. She looked up, trying to get her bearings. She heard a light switch click and a single bulb flickered and illuminated the centre of the room. The bright light shone in her eyes. She put up a hand to shield them.

'Why have you come back?' Henrik's disembodied voice came from the edge of the room somewhere. Gabriella tried to follow it but she couldn't make him out. He was lurking in the shadows beyond the pool of light.

'Unfinished business,' she looked into the blackness, her eyes adjusting to the glare above and the gloom beyond. Movement in her peripheral vision caught her

250

attention. She turned towards it as Henrik stepped forwards. He pointed a gun at her chest as she knelt on the floor.

'You're with Phillips?' Henrik's voice was strained.

'We want the same thing.'

'Which is?'

'An end to the Party and the way they control the State.' Gabriella didn't want to spend her time talking to Henrik, she was worried about Maxine and the fate of those outside. She searched in vain for a way to escape.

'I'm finished,' Henrik said, the gun wavering in his grip. 'I'm a dead man. The State will find me and kill me for being a traitor. My career is over, I have no family. There is nothing left. I tried to do the right thing, to be a good person, a good police officer. Now, because of him, I'm finished.'

'He didn't force you to help.'

'I just wanted to keep the city safe, to help people.'

'You still can, it's not too late.'

'It is, I killed your men, I'm a murderer. I aided the escape of a traitor. I betrayed the State.' Gabriella could see the tears running down Henrik's face. The gun shook in his hand, but he kept it pointed at her. He was unstable, one misjudgement and he would shoot. She had seen desperate people in situations like this before. Usually she was the one holding the gun.

'Killing me will make no difference.'

'If I kill you, maybe I will be forgiven.'

'We both know that won't happen. That's not how the State works.'

He was sobbing now, losing control. 'You killed my father.'

251

'You know what he had done. He was trying to kill me.' Gabriella thought back to the night she had killed Lars James. She had always known it would come back to haunt her.

They heard a loud gunshot outside. Gabriella recognised the sound from a high-calibre sniper rifle, similar to that which she used when in the State military. Henrik was startled, he looked towards the noise, his gun arm dropped a fraction. In a split second Gabriella sprang upwards and dived towards him. Henrik managed to raise the gun and fire before Gabriella flew into him. The bullet grazed Gabriella's cheek, millimetres from stopping her dead. They landed in a pile on the hard concrete. The gun spilled from Henrik's hand and clattered across the empty floor. Henrik was no match for her. Unlike his father, he did not possess the height and bulk that had made Lars James such a powerful man. Gabriella straddled him and pummelled his head with a series of blows. Henrik raised his hands to try and protect himself. When she saw that he had stopped struggling, Gabriella stopped hitting him and let his limp body fall to the ground. He whimpered, a broken man.

'Don't kill me,' he pleaded. She looked down at him as she stood.

'I don't have to. They will find you soon enough.' More gunshots came from outside. This time it was the repeated firing of automatic weapons, mixed with retaliating rifle shots and horrified screaming. She picked up the gun that Henrik had dropped. He cowered on the floor as she walked past. She left him there in the dark room, turning the light off on her way out. Entering the alleyway the door closed behind her. Henrik was left alone in the dark, crumpled on the floor.

The scene in the square had altered drastically. Gabriella left the alleyway and encountered a wall of flames spreading across the ground. The ranks of the State Security Force had scattered into disparate groups. There were running battles as soldiers charged at armed citizens. Gabriella recognised the citizens. She had seen them in the underground tunnels preparing rifles and handguns. They were the volunteers Phillips had gathered together, dressed in black, made into a motley army. Drone tanks sprayed protestors and rebels, armed and unarmed, with short volleys of bullets. It was chaos as individuals ran in all directions, some seeking shelter and escape, others charging head first towards the State Forces. Fire bottles continued to fly through the air, flames erupting as they shattered on the ground. The State military retaliated with smoke grenades and tear gas. It was open warfare. Gabriella wiped the flow of blood from her cheek and charged into the middle of the chaos, searching for Max. She headed to where they had been separated. Injured and dying bodies lay on the ground, a mix of citizens in plain clothes, soldiers in combat gear and Phillips's troops in black fatigues. She scanned the bodies and those fleeing, trying to locate Max. A SuperTank had come to a standstill in the middle of the fighting, damaged and surrounded by flames. Through the smoke and gas clouds and people running back and forth, Gabriella saw Danny. He was sitting on the ground, cradling a body in his lap. She knew who it would be before she got to him. Gabriella ran across the square as bullets and missiles continued to explode around her.

Danny saw her coming. 'Was it you?' he screamed at her as she crouched down next to him. 'Did you shoot her?'

Confused, Gabriella shouted back, 'Why would I shoot her?'

'You're an army sniper. You worked for Phillips. He killed her. Phillips. He wanted her dead. He needed a martyr to start his revolution.'

'No, the State killed her.' Gabriella refused to believe what she was hearing. She knew Phillips was trying to provoke the State, to force them to show their true colours, but he would not stoop to committing a murder and framing the State for it.

'I heard him give the order. He was planning this all along. He wanted the State to attack innocent citizens and if they didn't do it themselves, he would make it look like they did.' Danny looked at the body he held in his arms. Tears fell from his swollen red eyes, caused either by the clouds of tear gas drifting across the square, or because of the wasted life of Maxine Aubert. 'Now he has his war against the State. He has his revolution. He has his symbol of resistance.'

Gabriella understood now. It made sense. Could Phillips be that cold, that cruel? She realised the answer was yes. 'It wasn't me,' she tugged at Danny. 'Come on, we have to get out of here.' In the middle of the chaos they could not tell how the fighting was developing. The State Security Forces, having overcome their initial surprise at the armed resistance they had encountered, had regrouped on the far side of the square. They formed an organised line. The drone tanks formed up in front of them. 'They will massacre them,' Gabriella shouted. Finally, she hauled Danny to his feet. Max's body dropped from his grasp to the ground. 'We have to go if you want to survive.' She dragged him a few steps before Danny began to run with her. Bent over as grenades and bullets continued to fly over their heads, they scurried across the open square.

'There's an alleyway over here,' she called back to him. The car she had driven through the city the day before with Max was still parked at the back of the building from which they had been watching the protest unfold. If they could make it there they could get away. They barged past other citizens fleeing in every direction, fighting their way through the scrum of people. In the alleyway they joined the pack of people hurtling away from the square. Gabriella spotted the side street that would lead them to the car. She knocked over someone as she stopped, turned and managed to yank Danny in the same direction.

The side street was deserted. They slowed to a hurried jog, both exhausted. Gabriella checked behind them, but no one had followed them.

'Where are we going?' Danny asked. He didn't trust her. He knew she was a killer, he knew she was loyal to Phillips.

'I have a car.'

'To go where?'

'Anywhere.' He had no option but to follow her. They were both wanted criminals by the State, and the soldiers and police would be inclined to use deadly force now more than ever.

They turned another corner and hurried up another alleyway, emerging onto the road that ran behind the building. Gabriella saw the car parked where she had left it that morning. As they neared it, a door at the rear of the building opened. Gabriella and Danny froze as they saw Phillips exit and open the door to the car. As he prepared to get in he saw them. From the door another person emerged. Danny caught a fleeting glimpse of Casper. He carried a large sniper rifle in one hand and opened the driver door of the car with the other.

'Get in,' Phillips said to Casper.

'What about them? Are they coming with us or should I shoot them?'

'They no longer matter. Let's go.' The two men got into the car. Casper took the wheel and accelerated towards Danny and Gabriella. Gabriella raised her gun and fired, the bullets marked the windscreen but failed to make any impact. They jumped out of the way as the speeding car flew past them. Danny saw Phillips looking at them through the window as they drove away. The car taillights lit up as it braked for the corner at the end of the road and then turned, disappearing from view.

Danny and Gabriella picked themselves up and stood looking after the departed car. In the distance the gunfire could still be heard. It was sporadic now and consisted of only the distinctive automatic drone tank machine guns in short, sharp bursts. There were still shouts and screams drifting across the city sky. It was only midday, the hot sun beamed down as it had done every day for months. Election Day still had several hours to run before the polls closed across the State.

'What now?' asked Danny.

'We run,' Gabriella answered, and set off in the same direction the car had gone. Danny looked around. There was nothing he could do, there was no one else he could turn to. Cas was dead, Maxine was dead, countless citizens lay dead. Rivers of blood ran through the streets of Central City. He began running after Gabriella.

19

If the initial exit polls were right, the Central State Party had secured a huge majority in the Senate once again, as well as in the City Parliaments, and Lucinda Románes had easily defeated Johnathan Sadiq to return for another ten years as Chancellor of the State. It should have been an evening of celebration. The higher-up members of the Central Alliance Party who had been invited to The Palace were gathered downstairs, awaiting the arrival of their leader and her victory speech. They would have to keep waiting.

Lucinda Románes sat behind her desk. Teddy Davies sat opposite her. Behind him stood Field Marshall Harris Ellroy, the most senior officer in the State military. No one had spoken for five minutes as the re-elected Chancellor read through the hastily prepared report on the events in Central City. Finally, Lucinda pushed the TouchScreen away from her and sat back in her chair.

'My orders were specific and clear. The protesters were to be removed from the front of the City Parliament by approved policing methods. The idea was to establish a show of force to discourage such behaviour. I made it clear that no violence was to be used.'

'As the report states,' Teddy answered, 'the shot which killed Maxine Aubert was not fired by any State Security Force weapon. The evidence is concrete. No gun registered to the State fired a shot before that first one.'

'That hardly matters now. No one will believe the evidence, no matter how much we proclaim our innocence. What it looks like is that we murdered a young journalist because she dared to write an article criticising the State and then tried to protect citizens from being crushed by armoured vehicles.'

'The State media outlets are presenting the facts as we have them, the citizens will trust them.'

'And the Star Tribune?'

Teddy hesitated, 'Well, they are suggesting it was the State Security Forces that fired the first shot, under the orders of the State, to put down the demonstration by use of deadly force if necessary. They are suggesting their reporter was murdered by the State.'

'Do we know who was leading these rebel fighters that suddenly appeared?'

'Nothing definite, but we do have this image from a surveillance camera.' Teddy handed it over the desk for Romànes to look at. 'You recognise the man in the window, on the right.'

'Good God,' the Chancellor uttered the profanity that was banned in the State. She recognised the ex-State agent who was heavily linked to the assassinations of the Vice-Chancellor and Defence Secretary, though never publicly of course. 'Phillips.'

'It appears he slipped back into the State some weeks ago and has been organising this resistance movement.'

'And we had no idea?'

'Not until now.'

'The Central City Police, did they know he was in their city?'

'We have no confirmation. The Chief Commander Henrik James left police headquarters during the disturbance this morning and has not been seen since.'

'And this man next to Phillips?'

259

'Daniel Samson, the traitor who deserted three years ago. Escaped from police custody two days ago.'

'What a bloody mess.' She stood and looked out the window of her office. The Capital at dusk appeared normal. Drones filled the air as they caught up on deliveries delayed by the no-fly restriction of Election Day. 'Any disturbances anywhere else?'

'It appears to be confined to Central City at the moment.'

'And what is the situation there now?'

Field Marshall Ellroy spoke, 'Sporadic outbursts throughout the city, Chancellor. Further clashes between the Security Forces and this militia have continued. Protests have spread from the parliament building to other areas, though not large in scale. Casualties have reached the hundreds, but we can't be exact.'

Románes folded her arms, 'Do we have spare forces that can be deployed?'

'Two divisions are gathered. They were due to return to Laramidia at the beginning of next week.'

'Divert them to Central City. Let me make myself clear to you both. The election is over. I want these rebels crushed and crushed quickly. Understood?'

'Yes, Chancellor,' Ellroy replied.

Teddy Davies half-raised his hand in objection, 'Are you sure that is the right way to deal with this. We are talking about starting a potential civil war in one of our cities. Our military fighting against our own citizens.'

'So be it. They must be shown that they cannot defy the State in this way. They must be punished. They must pay.'

The two men were dismissed. Lucinda Románes sighed. It was not a great start to her latest term in office.

Still, she was sure this pathetic rebellion would be over soon. Things would return to normal, they always did. There were enough problems to deal with without worrying about a ragtag band of agitators in the north. A swift resolution would ensure the disturbance would not spread to the Capital. She picked up her TouchScreen and checked the speech that had been prepared for her. All the usual worries were mentioned: climate change, energy, overpopulation and the First Strike War. She assured the citizens that the Party would protect them against each problem. If only they knew the truth. If only they knew how much the Party had become entangled in its own lies and deceit. If only they knew that the war would never end because it was more beneficial for all involved to keep it going, to persist in the lie that had lasted for almost fifty years. It kept the factories open, it kept the economy running, it kept big businesses in profit, and it kept the citizens living in fear and under control.

The Press Secretary was waiting for her outside her office.

'Everything set?'

'They're waiting for you, Chancellor.'

'Very well, let's go.'

'May I say, Chancellor?'

'Yes?'

'Congratulations on winning the election.'

'Thank you, Alice. Here's to another decade in power,' Lucinda Romanes smiled and they walked towards the main hall where the faithful awaited their undisputed leader.

EPILOGUE

TWO WEEKS LATER

20

In the press conference room in the basement of The Palace, John Curran sat in the back row, preparing for the daily briefing. The temperature outside had finally begun to turn to bearable warmth after months of searing summer heat, but inside the room the air-conditioning was still out of use and the atmosphere was still and close. He mopped his brow with a handkerchief made of silk, another nod to his preference for the old style of life that was dying away with each passing generation.

In the front row the three usual suspects were lined up in their places. Frinks and Pigeon had blanked him when they had entered the room together. Curran tried not to take it personally, it was their healthy sense of self-preservation for their employment and their safety. They avoided contact with the pariah from The Star Tribune at all costs. To his credit, Mothersby, the State News television correspondent had paused beside him and offered his condolences. He didn't broach the subject of Maxine's death at the hands of the State, he only said he had always admired her as a reporter and she had seemed a talented young woman with a bright future ahead of her. The State television channel had been bold enough to not completely condemn Maxine as a traitor to the State, preferring to toe the line by describing her only as a 'controversial' journalist. Other State media had not been so reserved. In the immediate days following her death, the Senate Star and the Capitol News had smeared Maxine's posthumous memory beyond repair, labelling her a traitor and a terrorist. They had hunted down Maxine's parents at their home, questioning them as to why they had raised their daughter to hate her own country so much. Did they share their daughter's views? Did they hate the Party and the State too? François and Lauren Aubert were now in hiding somewhere else in the Capital, having been forced to flee the unwanted attention. The only respite Maxine's parents, friends and colleagues could be thankful for was the media's concentration on the fine victory for the Central Alliance Party and Chancellor Románes, which dominated the front pages for the days that followed the vote. Independent candidates had doubled their representation, thanks largely to the late backlash in Central City, but they still only amounted to a meagre five percent of Senators, with no overall control of any office, national or regional, within the State. Those independents who had been elected would soon be brought into line by the Party, as they always were during their tenure. The Party always found a way, a weakness, an indiscretion or a bribe that convinced these free-thinking idealists to fall into line on all matters of State.

The Star Tribune had trod a fine line. After the Chancellor and the State Media Compliance Department had threatened it with immediate closure unless it withdrew the initial account of Maxine Aubert's death, it had been the only media outlet to have the ongoing troubles in Central City as its lead story day after day. There had been a barrage of complaints and legal threats from The Palace and the Party, but Buzz Mayfield had stood up to some, had manoeuvred around others and had ignored the majority of them. He successfully argued that what amounted to an outbreak of civil war in a city of The State could not be dismissed. The citizens had a right to know that the State Military had been deployed on streets within their own borders. Within each story that they published, Buzz ensured that Maxine's death was mentioned. He was careful not to say that she had been murdered by State Security Forces, there was no hard evidence to confirm who had fired the fatal shot after all. They described her death only as unexplained, with supporting evidence suggesting she had become an enemy to those high up in the Party, and then left the readers to draw their own conclusion. Buzz kept her name alive and in the news. He would not let her be forgotten, or let her death be in vain.

Curran knew his old friend was hurting. They both were. They had both been fond of Maxine, they had both taken her under their wing and been father figures to her, encouraging her career, supporting her development, pushing her to try harder, to dig for the truth and never to compromise. They both knew why they had spurred her on to act in this way: it reminded them of when they had shown that same fearless desire to expose the truth. The difference with Maxine had been her ability to see it through, to carry on where others would have stopped. Curran had, Buzz had. They had eventually played the State's game and it had eaten away at their journalistic souls. With each little, insignificant detail they omitted on behalf of the Party, with each tiny white lie they participated in perpetrating, the flame of true journalism dimmed a little more within them. They had reached old age and become no better than those working at the Senate Star and Capital News: lapdogs for the Chancellor and her Party. Maxine would not reach old age but her death had awoken them from the drifting slumber they had fallen into.

But Maxine Aubert did not need the media to keep the flame of her memory alight. Her face had become a symbol. It had appeared on posters across the State, not just in Central City but to the north in the HighLand City, in the MidLands and even in some places around the Capital. She had become famous as a symbol of freedom, a masthead around which disquiet was gathering. In Central City, the group now calling themselves The Independents had adopted Maxine as the martyr for their fight against the State. Her death was used as an example of the evil that the State could commit. She was an innocent citizen, a victim, murdered by her own government for reporting on crimes that had been committed in high office. Her article, rather than disappearing, became widely available. The State censors were unable to trace and destroy every copy of it because so many flooded the cities. Her name was becoming a rallying cry that the State could not silence.

Chancellor Románes had avoided any direct media obligations in the fortnight since her election win and so had avoided any questions about Maxine Aubert. She had toured the State cities, with the exception of Central City and had been seen smiling and waving, backed by cheerful citizens applauding her victory. Her press secretary, consigned to serve for another ten years, suggested the Chancellor was too busy implementing her promised manifesto plans to be distracted answering questions from reporters. She could not avoid appearing before them in the conference room at The Palace today though. It was the anniversary of the First Strike, the beginning of the war that had defined her premiership and the world in which the State existed for almost half a century. Traditionally there should have been a military parade and remembrance service at the military memorial in the centre of the Capital. That had been cancelled. No reason was given, but it was well known that the State Military could not spare any personnel to attend the event due to the recent doubling of their involvement in Central City. There were now four divisions operating in the city, attempting to stamp out the home-grown terrorist rebels. Instead of the ceremony, Lucinda Románes had agreed to give a short speech to the media from The Palace, which would be delivered into the home of every citizen in the country.

John Curran knew that it was down to his long-nurtured and developed relationships within The Palace and the State establishment that had allowed him to retain his place within The Palace press core. The Star Tribune was *persona non gratis* among the Party and Curran was the only one of their reporters allowed to set foot inside the conference room. He had been required to smooth many ruffled feathers in order to be present that day. It would be his last day as a reporter after fifty years working consistently and diligently. He refused to be bitter about his career. He refused to ask himself what good he believed he had done? What difference did he think his words had made? He knew in the past he had done some good. He refused to believe that words were empty weapons. Words in the hands of the wrong person were dangerous and words in the hands of truth and justice still had the power and a duty to repel that danger. If anything, now more than ever, it was vital that words were used to hold those in power to account.

Following the usual routine, the press room filled up moments before the Chancellor appeared, her acolytes aimed their TouchScreens and SmartLenses towards the podium, the main camera clicked into action. Curran had left his TouchScreen at home today. He held the paper notepad and pencil in his hand, like he had once done every day as a young reporter, like Maxine Aubert had done throughout her whole career.

Once introduced it did not take Lucinda Románes long to get into her familiar flow, delivering the polished speech word perfectly as she always did, the consummate unchallenged orator. She served up the familiar platitudes to the brave men and women of the armed forces, to the factory workers who built the machinery and the operators who piloted them. Her expression of sombre grief at those lives lost in the decades of fighting was perfectly executed. This was where it had started to go wrong, all those years ago, Curran thought, as he watched her. When the Party had stopped anyone from questioning what they were doing, how they were doing it and for what reasons, they had been able to wield their power without any restraint. They had been able to get away with murder, not just in the act of going to war, but in the way they controlled the State and her citizens too. Maxine had been brave enough to stand up and ask a question in this very room that had ultimately led to her death. If only Curran and Buzz Mayfield and others before her had been brave enough to keep asking the difficult questions. It should not have been left to a young woman to make her sacrifice alone.

As Románes's speech veered into practiced manifesto pledges, without mention of the ongoing civil war within one of her own cities, Curran seized his moment. He stood up in the back row and raised his hand. Lucinda Románes saw him. He noticed the hesitation in her delivery even if no other observer did. He jumped in before she could regain her momentum.

'If I may interrupt, Chancellor,' Curran shouted. Heads swivelled round, lenses turned and focussed. Lucinda Románes tried to ignore him and carry on with her monologue. He shouted again, louder this time, forcing her to acknowledge him. He asked his question, 'Did you order the killing of the journalist Maxine Aubert in retaliation for an article she wrote criticising the actions of your government?' Others in the room tried to shout him down. Insults were thrown at him. Security officers started heading towards him. He raised his voice further to cut through the growing clamour. 'Did you order the use of lethal military action against peaceful citizens protesting against the way you are running the State?' He had time to get one last question out before he could be tackled. 'Are you responsible for murdering your own citizens?' The security guards reached him and wrenched him off his feet, hustling him out of the room. Curran did not resist. He had done what he had wanted to do.

In amongst the noise, Lucinda Románes had answered his questions. She had denied ordering the death of Maxine Aubert and any of the protestors. For once, she was telling the truth, but no one heard her answers. The cameras and microphones beaming the memorial day conference into the rooms of every citizen in the State only heard the accusations.

The beds in the dormitory were lined up along opposing walls, with a central aisle separating them. Lights out had been half an hour ago, but no child lay in their bed as the sun was setting on another fine day in Central City. Instead they sat huddled together around the windows looking out across the rooftops. From outside the boys and girls could hear the sound of gunfire and the louder explosions of grenades or missiles. It had been three weeks since the fighting had begun on Election Day. The children had heard it was now being called a civil war. They were no longer allowed beyond the walls of the hospital, but from their dormitory window they could see the freshly formed battle scars appear across the city. Each night another building seemed to be set alight or battered with heavy artillery. It was rumoured that the State Military was hunting down the rebels from one area of the city to another, destroying everything in their path in an attempt to root out the terrorists. Each morning, the children saw the aftermath of the fighting. Some familiar buildings had disappeared, collapsing into a heap of rubble. Others still stood, but were pock-marked with craters in their crumbling walls and their glass windows had shattered. Tonight, like every night, the sight of tracer rounds lighting up the night sky in bright displays entertained them. Despite warnings from the nurses not to do so, they still crowded round the windows to watch the light show once the sun had set.

One boy sat on his own, apart from the rest of the group. Lucas looked out from a separate window and listened to the distant rumble as tanks moved into position somewhere in the city. He had arrived in the dormitory a fortnight ago. It was attached to the superhospital but the children housed here had no immediate health concerns. They were cared for because they had nowhere else to go in the immediate future. Occasionally one of them would be lucky enough to be chosen to go and live with a family who were willing to foster or adopt them. Until then this would be their home and they would be looked after by the State. There was a classroom, where they attended school five days a week, they had living space, a playground and a garden. They were served food from the hospital kitchens. The nurses kept a watchful eye over them and insisted on good behaviour and high standards of hygiene.

The children in the dormitory were there for various reasons: some had been abandoned after being born with disabilities despite their parents following all the advised scientific checks and procedures; other parents had preferred to conceive without the interference of modern science but were unhappy with what nature and fate had deigned to give them; some had no disabilities at all, physical or mental, they were alone because their parents had passed away or had given them up for unknown reasons. A small group belonged to parents who had fallen victim to the State's tough immigration laws and had been deported. The children who had been born in the State were forced to remain behind while their foreign parents were shipped back to their country of birth. Whatever their differences, the children were blind to them, as children always are. Despite Lucas being the

271

only child with type-1 diabetes in the group, none batted an eyelid. Most were fascinated and interested to know more about his rare condition.

With the correct supply of insulin and a controlled diet, Lucas had recovered from the worst effects of his ordeal in the wilderness. His blood sugars were under control and he had been fitted with an artificial pancreas pump that automatically gave him the correct dosage of synthetic insulin as and when his body required it. Insulin from the State laboratory in the Capital City, the only place to still manufacture the medicine, had been ordered and a regular supply had been secured. It was hoped that the current outbreak of violence sweeping the city would not disrupt the essential supply of medicine especially if it could be brought to a swift end. No one had questioned where Lucas had come from, or how he had arrived at the hospital. If the State were concerned about his background, or how a type-1 diabetic child had been missed by the compulsory screening process, Lucas never heard anything about it. The nurses and doctors had assured the young boy that his future at the hospital was safe, his stay unlimited, until they found a family that may be willing to take him in.

From his window Lucas did not look down onto the city below him, or across at the lights that sporadically filled the sky. Instead he looked upwards. The moon shone brightly this evening, it was almost a full orb hanging in the darkness. On the surface of that silvery place there was a whole community living on a collection of bases. The bases were occupied by people from all over the world, from the African Union countries, from the European Union, from the Civil American States and the Southern Americas, from Zhonghua and from this very State. They lived together peacefully. All sides in the First Strike War had agreed that the conflict did not extend to the lunar surface. The continued success of all space exploration depended on the cooperation and trust of all involved. If only such a spirit of unity could extend to the earthly world. With his insulin dependency, Lucas knew he would be ineligible for space travel or living, unless a cure could be found for him. The bright light in the dark sky remained an unattainable dream for him.

While the others continued to chatter and take in the evening's light show outside, Lucas returned to his bed and pulled out the small cloth pouch from under his pillow. Aside from the clothes he had been given, the cloth pouch and the wooden marbles it contained were the only possessions he had. There were books and toys in the hospital which he was free to use, but they all belonged to the State. These marbles were all that he could call his own in the world. He poured the marbles onto the top of his bed cover. It was difficult to set them up to play the game Danny had taught him on his porch in the village, without the wooden circular board for them to fit into, but he tried as best he could. One of the older children came over and sat on the bed next to him and watched him move the marbles around for a while.

'What game is this?' Jenny asked. She was one of the older children in the dormitory and Lucas had learned she had lived there all her life, nearly fifteen years. On her next birthday she would leave and be given her own home and income and have to fend for herself. She had only one full arm, the other ended in a stump at her elbow. She had been born that way and disowned by her parents, who already had three perfect children, and were unwilling to pay the high taxes that the State imposed for a fourth child, particularly if that child was disabled. Jenny was given some responsibility by the nurses as one of the eldest and she liked to look after the younger children, especially when they had just arrived. She had taken Lucas under her wing in the few days that he had been with them. He had instantly warmed to her smile and kind nature. That and her long, tangled hair that she constantly played with reminded him of his mother.

'It's called marble solitaire,' Lucas said, 'it should be played on a board really but I don't have one.'

'I've never seen marbles like these before.'

'Danny made them for me.'

'Is Danny your father?'

Lucas shook his head, 'Just a friend. He saved me.' They sat in silence for a few more minutes as Lucas continued playing. Loud explosions outside caused the children at the windows to jump up with fright and then dissolve into laughter. The nurses had assured them that no one would attack the hospital, they were in the safest place in the city.

Lucas got to the end of the game, as always with a handful of marbles remaining. One day he would figure out how to complete it. Jenny helped him scoop up the wooden balls. She stopped and held one towards the moonlight coming in through the window, feeling it between her fingers.

'Do you know some of these have letters carved into them?'

Lucas nodded, 'Danny did that too.'

'What do they say?'

'I don't know,' Lucas shrugged, 'I can't spell.'

'Let me try,' Jenny offered. She took the cloth pouch and poured out all the marbles onto the bed again.

Methodically she checked each one until she had found six with letters on them. Lucas watched as Jenny laid them out and began swapping them around, trying different combinations in order to make a word. While they sat together in their own private world, the sound of the war in the city outside continued. A loud explosion shook the building, much nearer than anything previously. It was close enough to send a few of the younger children scurrying to their beds, seeking safety under their bedsheets. Jenny and Lucas paid it no heed. Eventually Jenny sat back. She read out the letters one by one.

'E-I-L-I-D-H. Eilidh.' Jenny said. 'Do you know anyone called Eilidh?'

'Yes,' Lucas said simply, 'I do.'

TO BE CONTINUED

THE STATE TRILOGY: MAIN CHARACTERS

CENTRAL CITY

Daniel Samson: ex-State police officer who fled Central City after discovering evidence of State corruption while investigating the murder of City Consul Donald Parkinson.

Franklin Samson: Daniel Samson's father (deceased).

Rosalind (Rosa) Samson: Daniel Samson's wife who took her own life after the death of their newborn children.

Isla Samson: Daniel Samson's daughter (deceased).

Hanlen Samson: Daniel Samson's son (deceased).

Henrik James: Formerly Daniel Samson's partner, now Chief Commander of Central City State Police.

Lars James: Henrik James's father, formerly also Chief Commander of the Central City police before he was killed by Gabriella Marino.

Cassandra (Cas) Ford: State Police forensic pathologist, friend of Daniel Samson.

Janette Michaels: Former Superintendent and Chief Commander of Central City Police, now Chief Commander of the Capital Police.

Archie Cancio: State Police Detective.

Gabriella Marino: ex-State soldier turned assassin, hired to kill City Consul Donald Parkinson. Aliases: **Helena Myers; Phillipa Young**

Elisabeth Sand: Nightclub owner who learned of a State trial to euthanize unborn and newborn children in order to control overpopulation in the State. She hired Gabriella Marino to kill those responsible, including City Consul Donald Parkinson. Killed by a State hit squad. Alias: **Symington**

Donald Parkinson: Respected Central City Consul with links to State high office, killed by Gabriella Marino.

Phillips: ex-State soldier and former State Security Forces agent. He helped Daniel Samson and Henrik James in their investigation into the assassination of Donald Parkinson.

Montana (Tania) Childe: Junior assistant to City Consul Parkinson, who aided Daniel Samson in his investigation. Killed by State hit squad.

Doctor Leroy: Doctor who assisted Donald Parkinson in his euthanasia trial.

CAPITAL CITY

Lucinda Románes: Chancellor of the State.

Ishmael Nelson: Former Defence Secretary of the State, murdered by Agent Phillips.

Patrick Donovan: Former Vice-Chancellor of the State, murdered by Gabriella Marino.

Johnathan Sadiq: Candidate for Chancellor of the State.

Edward (Teddy) Davies: Current Head of State Security Forces.

Field Marshall Harris Ellroy: Senior Officer in the State Military

John Curran: Veteran Journalist at The Star Tribune.

Byron (Buzz) Mayfield: Veteran Editor at The Star Tribune.

Maxine Aubert: Reporter at The Star Tribune.

Horace Frinks; Timothy Pigeon; Kelvin Mothersby: State Media Reporters

NORTHERN WILDERNESS

Rona; Bruce; Hansel; Jia Li: Village elders.

Hassan: Raiding party leader.

Matthias; Tyrell; Tia: Raiding party soldiers.

Eilidh: Member of the village who befriends Daniel Samson.

Lucas: Son of Eilidh, suffers from type-1 diabetes.

ISLAND WILDERNESS

Skylar: Cult leader.

Casper: Young member of the Cult.

For Caden Daniel and Chloe Dawn

ABOUT THE AUTHOR

Iain Kelly lives in Scotland. He works as an editor in the television industry and is married with two children.

For more information visit his website:
www.iainkellywriting.com

Follow on Social Media:

facebook.com/iainkellywriting
Instagram: @with_two_eyes
Twitter: @iainthekid
linkedin.com/in/iain-kelly-writing

ALSO AVAILABLE

A JUSTIFIED STATE
Iain Kelly

Book One of The State Trilogy

The future.

The socially reformist Central Alliance Party rules unopposed.

Poverty and homelessness have been eradicated, but overpopulation, an energy crisis and an ongoing war jeopardise the stability of the country.

When a local politician is assassinated, Detective Danny Samson finds himself at the centre of an investigation that threatens not only his life, but the entire future of The State.

Praise for 'A Justified State':

- 'the action is pacey and exciting, the characters fleshed out, nuanced and believable, the mystery…is genuinely intriguing and alarming.'

- 'the writing brought to mind Phillip Marlow, Do Androids Dream of Electric Sheep?, the world of George Smiley, and Robert Harris' Fatherland'

- 'This is a superbly well written fast paced, suspenseful mystery. A page turner as the action…makes you gasp'

ALSO AVAILABLE

STATE OF WAR
Iain Kelly

Book Three of The State Trilogy

The State is at war at home and abroad.

While the global First Strike War continues, a civil war threatens to bring down the ruling Central Alliance Party.

Daniel Samson - Citizen, Traitor, Survivor.
Gabriella Marino - Soldier, Assassin, Fighter.

Caught between the State Forces and the rebels, hunted by both sides, they must choose between their own survival and protecting the city and the citizens trapped within the war zone.

Are they willing to sacrifice their own chance of happiness to save a city from destruction?

The thrilling conclusion to The State Trilogy sees Danny and Gabriella join forces against their enemies in a fight that will determine the fate of the State, and the lives of all those who live there.